NESSIE
QUEST

ALSO BY MELISSA SAVAGE

Lemons

The Truth About Martians

Karma Moon—Ghost Hunter

NESSIE QUEST

MELISSA SAVAGE

A YEARLING BOOK

Text copyright © 2020 by Melissa Savage
Cover art copyright © 2020 by Lydia Nichols
Illustration on p. 284 used under license from Shutterstock.com

All rights reserved. Published in the United States by Yearling, an imprint of Random House Children's Books, a division of Penguin Random House LLC, New York. Originally published in hardcover in the United States by Crown Books for Young Readers, an imprint of Random House Children's Books, a division of Penguin Random House LLC, New York, in 2020.

Yearling and the jumping horse design are registered trademarks of Penguin Random House LLC.

Visit us on the Web! rhcbooks.com

Educators and librarians, for a variety of teaching tools, visit us at RHTeachersLibrarians.com

The Library of Congress has cataloged the hardcover edition of this work as follows:
Names: Savage, Melissa (Melissa D.), author.
Title: Nessie quest / Melissa Savage.
Description: First edition. | New York: Crown Books for Young Readers, [2020]
Summary: Twelve-year-old Ru reluctantly joins her parents in Scotland for the summer, where she and new friends Dax and Hammy Bean search for the Loch Ness Monster.
Identifiers: LCCN 2019009362 | ISBN 978-0-525-64567-2 (hc) |
ISBN 978-0-525-64568-9 (glb) | ISBN 978-0-525-64569-6 (epub)
Subjects: CYAC: Loch Ness monster—Fiction. | Family life—Scotland—Fiction. |
Scotland—Fiction.
Classification: LCC PZ7.1.S2713 Nes 2020 | DDC [Fic]—dc23

ISBN 978-0-525-64570-2 (pbk.)

Printed in the United States of America
10 9 8 7 6 5 4 3 2 1
First Yearling Edition 2021

For Tobin, yet again.

You are *my* wings in everything I do

and you always will be.

CONTENTS

1

BANANA FAMOUS

Words may seem innocent enough, but I'm here to tell you that they're a way bigger deal than most people know.

They are *so* powerful, in fact, that they can change you in a single, solitary second.

Words can propel you so high that you could fly straight up to the sky blue. Or can seem so heavy on your shoulders that you think you'll never stand straight again. And there's one reason for that.

Words make us *feel*.

And feelings are everything. They control who we are and how we live and every single choice we make.

My name is Adelaide Ru Fitzhugh.

Ada Ru for short.

Ru for even shorter.

I've been writing since I was born, so I know words real good. One day I plan to write words so important that lots of people are going to want to read the way I put them together. And they'll feel something while they read them too.

I'm talking about a legit, big-time writer.

And by that, of course, I mean super famous. Like go-to-the-grocery-store-for-bananas-in-a-limo kind of famous. Just like J. K. Rowling probably does. I mean, if you're as famous as her, you certainly don't go shopping in a plain old white Prius named Patty that has a SAVE THE TREES bumper sticker on it like we have.

In my Kreative Kids writing class in Denver, I learned another real important thing about words. If you want to write a really good story, I mean, a really super-good one, you should write what you know.

So I decided to think long and hard about what I know. Unfortunately, I got bubkes. And bubkes is a big problem for a serious writer. My life is actually pretty boring. Not that I'm complaining about that. I mean, I love my life on Tennyson Street just outside the city of Denver.

It's predictable.

And that's me.

But predictable isn't exactly exciting or interesting and it certainly doesn't make you *feel*. There's no *pop* to predictable, and as a writer, if you don't have pop, you've got zip. I mean, where does a girl like me find pop when I've never been kidnapped by pirates on the high seas or raised by wolves? I've never known one single animal that could talk and I've certainly never been abducted by aliens . . . at least as far as I know.

I just finished sixth grade at Skinner Middle School, I'm the president of the Tennyson Street Beyoncé Beyhive Fan

Club, and I'm a champion cupcake eater. I refuse to swim in any public pool (because of the pee) and I have an award-winning collection of ceramic kittens.

See what I mean?

That's bubkes big-time.

This year Mom even helped me start my very own podcast. It's called *Words with Ru*. The problem is, it's very hard to find something with pop in it to talk about on your very own podcast when nothing interesting has really happened to you yet. That's probably why I only have two subscribers to date.

Nan and Granddad Fitzhugh.

But if I had pop, who knows how many people I'd get.

I've been waiting all this year for something cool to happen to me.

And now, the summer after sixth grade . . . *it does.*

Dun, dun . . . *dun.*

Spoiler alert: there may or may not be an actual real live lake monster involved, but that's all I'm going to say about that.

For now, anyway.

And it all started with a Friday Family Fitzhugh Meeting.

2

WHAT'S SO WRONG WITH DISNEY WORLD?

"Hear ye, hear ye," I call out, banging my fist like a gavel on the kitchen table. "Let the Friday Fitzhugh Family Meeting come to order."

It's my job to bring the meeting to order every week. I don't wear a judge's robe or anything *that* official, but it's still a pretty big deal.

"Mom." I nod in her direction. "First order of business."

Her job is agendas and refreshments. Tonight's snack is a plastic bowl full of Jelly Belly jelly beans.

Side note: I only eat the Buttered Popcorn ones.

It's because I totally love them. It's like if I was forced to live on a desert island and could only bring two things with me for my survival, it would be Buttered Popcorn jelly beans and an endless supply of soda.

Which is the exact reason why I'm digging through the plastic bowl as Mom announces the first order of business.

"First up . . . chores and cleanliness."

I sneak a covert eye roll and keep on digging through the beans.

Other than the *hear ye* part and an occasional *order in the court*, the meetings are pretty dullsville. They *always* start exactly the same.

Who's been slacking on their chores? (Me)

Who isn't keeping their room clean enough? (Me)

Who's not making their bed in the mornings? (Yep, me again)

Who's not mowing the lawn? (That one . . . has Dad's name written all over it)

For the spring meetings we sometimes have an additional category on the agenda.

The Fitzhugh summer vacation destination.

That's also when someone inevitably brings up the subject of Disney World and asks why we can't ever go there (that's me too if you didn't already guess it).

Can someone please tell me what's so wrong with Disney World?

My best friend, Britney B, went two summers ago and said it *really is* where dreams come true. It even said so on the Disney souvenir book she brought home with her.

Me and Britney B have been best friends since first grade when her family moved two doors down from us. We like all the same movies, we both agree that adding vegetables will ruin a perfectly good pizza every time and we look just alike, with plain brown hair and skinny bodies with ugly knobby knees that we both detest. Last month, in an extremely-bad-idea best-friend pact, we both chopped our hair in bobs at the chin. I hate mine, but she loves hers. Probably because she looks way better in it than I do.

I know everything there is to know about her and she knows the same about me. That's the way real best friends are. For instance, I know that right this second, she's waiting on me to come over so we can watch *Taken Souls* on the Syfy channel. We watch it together every single Friday after the Fitzhugh Family Meetings.

When Mom is finished with her chore slacking list, she nods to me.

I pound on the table three more times. "Next on the agenda," I announce.

Mom looks at Dad. "Summer plans," she announces.

Wait . . . what? This is way earlier than usual and I haven't even planted all my Disney World hints yet.

I sit straight up and cross two sets of fingers on each hand. I close my eyes tight and wait for it.

Come on, Disney World.

Come on, Disney World.

Come on, Disney World.

"Dad's going to talk about summer plans this year," Mom says.

I peek one eye open.

Dad never leads any agenda item and he's certainly never led the summer plans one. It's unprecedented. Maybe that's a good sign.

Or maybe not.

I close my eyes tight again and wait for it.

He clears his throat.

I hold my breath. Magic Kingdom, here I come!

And then . . . he says it.

He lays a bomb on me that changes my entire life. With just one line, and believe me, it's got nothing to do with dreams coming true either.

"We are spending the entire summer in Scotland."

No warning.

No doomsday prep.

No *You had better sit down for this one.*

It has to be a joke. I give him a good long stare while I wait for the punch line.

Except there isn't one.

"Order in the court. Order in the court." I pound my fist gavel on the table, then stare at Dad. "Are you seriously kidding me right now?" I ask him. "Because it's so not funny."

He gives me his *extra-wide* grin. The one that shows all his straight white teeth and the getting-old crinkles right at the corners of his eyes, and he says, "Nope. We are going for the whole summer. We'll get to see Uncle Clive and Aunt Isla and your cousin Briony. It's been six years since we've gotten a chance to visit."

Suddenly all the Buttered Popcorns aren't sitting so well inside my belly.

"Adelaide Ru," Mom says, grabbing my wrist and pulling my hand out of the bowl of beans.

Mom's the only one who never calls me anything short. She uses my whole name every single time. She says it's because it's too beautiful a name to go short. Even though she goes short on hers all the time because her real name is Elizabeth and everyone calls her Libby.

Right this minute she's frowning hard at me. "You know I don't like it when you dig around in there with your licked-on fingers. It's gross. One more time and I'm putting the jelly beans away."

"Dad, do we really have to spend the entire summer there?" I ask him.

"We don't *have* to, my little Rutabaga," Dad says. "We *get* to."

Dad never goes short on my name and he doesn't go long either. Basically, he calls me anything with an *r* and *u* in it. *Rutabaga* is one of his favorites.

I sigh and lay my chin in my hand. This can't be happening.

Tennyson Street is my life.

My home.

My world.

I can't live somewhere else for an entire summer.

On our summer vacations, I'm usually homesick by Tuesday and already packed by Wednesday. I mean, unless we were to go to Disney World. That's a whole different story.

It's not that I don't like seeing other places. I just love our Tennyson life and get homesick real easy. The small redbrick house just outside the city is ours and always has been. It's the best house on the best street. The bright white shutters and a matching porch swing that I helped paint. Mom's rosemary shrubs lining the front walk that I helped plant. Tennyson is even where we found our three-legged orange tabby cat, Mr. Mews. He was a stray in the back alley by the garage, snacking on old leftovers from Parisi out of our garbage can. He looked up from his gnarly ravioli and actually smiled at me.

That's when I knew in my heart he was mine.

Side note: Parisi has the best spaghetti carbonara on the *planet*. And I'm not even exaggerating either.

"I'm sorry to inform you but I am unable to move to Scotland for an entire summer at this time," I tell them.

Mom raises her eyebrows at that one. "Oh?" she says.

"What about my Sunday-afternoon Bookworm Club at the BookBar? Or . . . or our Italian Wednesdays at Parisi? Or Mexican Tuesdays at El Chingon when we order our *cena y bebidas* completely in Spanish? Not to mention we just painted my room cornflower blue and put up the new curtains too. Oh, and what about my podcast? I can't let my audience down."

"I'm sure Nan and Granddad Fitzhugh won't mind missing a few episodes."

"I have more subscribers than Nan and Granddad Fitzhugh," I inform her.

"Who else?" she asks.

Silence.

"This isn't about subscribers," I tell her.

"Ru Ru Bugaboo," my dad says with that same wide smile. "We'll be back in September."

September? This is a nightmare.

"It's good news," he goes on.

"Ah, *wrong*," I inform him. "Good news would be a week at the Magic Kingdom. This is the opposite of good news. This is . . . it's . . . well, it's *bad news* is what it is."

The Buttered Popcorns are now sending a critical warning that they might want back out.

Mom chimes in. "Wait until you see where we're staying this time. It's called the Highland Club, and it's inside a Benedictine abbey. It's one of the oldest buildings in the town of

Fort Augustus and was originally built in 1876 as an abbey, but they've renovated it into modern apartments. Doesn't that sound fun?"

"Not especially," I say.

She ignores me.

"What an adventure," she goes on, popping in a green Jelly Belly.

Maybe a Sunkist Lime or Watermelon.

"I'm the number one reviewer in the Bookworm group. I need to keep up my quota because you just *know* that Emmanuelle Penney is champing at the bit to take my top spot. She's only two away." I hold up two fingers to show them both. "*Two . . . away.*"

"This is going to be wonderful," Mom goes on. "Do you remember how much fun you and your cousin Briony had last time?"

"*Remember?* How could I forget? She shaved my Malibu Barbie doll."

"Oh . . ." Mom waves a hand. "You've long outgrown Barbies, anyway."

"Barbie was bald, Mom. *Bald.*"

"I'm sure Briony's grown up just like you have," Dad chimes in.

"Did I not mention that she also still sucked her thumb at *six*? And she smelled . . . shall we say *questionable*?"

Mom isn't listening. "I think it's an amazing opportunity to get to visit family we hardly ever see," she goes on.

"Uh . . . try bizarro," I mumble. "I mean, who spends an entire summer in a whole other country? People go for a week, maybe two. Not three months. That's nuts."

Dad cocks his head to the side the exact same way that Britney B's beagle, Cheez Whiz, does when you talk to her because she only understands certain words, like *park, ball* and *pizza delivery*. For all the rest of the words she just turns her head sideways, trying real hard to figure out what you're saying. Me and Britney B call that look a Cheez Whiz. And it's Dad's Cheez Whiz that makes my heart start beating even harder because I realize that this situation is just like with Disney World.

I don't get a say.

"Dad got a position at the University of the Highlands and Islands in Inverness," Mom says. "To teach an advanced photography class for the summer term. We will be renting out our house at the end of the month to a lovely family. The Morgensterns. They have a five-year-old daughter named Delilah."

Some random girl rolling down Tennyson on *my* Razor scooter with the pink trim?

Eating *my* raspberry-filled Funfetti cupcakes at Valhalla?

Sleeping under *my* poster of Beyoncé—the *I Am . . . Sasha Fierce* album.

It's a complete and total nightmare is what it is.

"What about Mr. Mews?" I demand. "He's not going to like this one bit."

"The Morgensterns have graciously agreed to take care of him for the summer while they're here," Mom says. "They said their little Delilah loves cats."

"He's not a *cat*," I remind her. "He's part of the family, and he's not going to want to sleep with some random girl. Not to mention, he's very particular about the way his whiskers are stroked. He'll be very lonely without me here. Maybe one of us should stay home. Me and Mr. Mews could stay with Britney B. Her mom won't care."

That's when my mom's head starts with the slow nod and I know exactly what's coming.

I give her a straight pointer finger and say, "Don't even."

But she goes and does it anyway.

"How does it make you feel, honey?" she says with . . . *the voice.*

The smooth-as-silk one.

Mom's a child psychologist and teaches at the university and for her, feeling words are *huge.* It's always feelings this and feelings that, and this isn't any different.

I cross my arms tight over my chest in protest. "Frankly," I tell her, "I think it stinks."

"That's a *thinking* word, honey, not a *feeling* word," she reminds me. "Try again."

"Fine," I say. "I *feel* . . . like it stinks."

She sighs at that one and pops a red jelly bean into her mouth.

A Cinnamon or maybe a Very Cherry.

"Why can't Dad just go without us?" I ask. "Like he does when he goes to New York."

Dad's a big-time photographer. And by big-time, of course I mean famous. Not limo famous because Mom and Dad share Prius Patty, but still. His pictures have been in some of the most popular newspapers in the world, like the *New York Times*, and well-known magazines like *Smithsonian* and *National Geographic* and even in some photography museums in Los Angeles and New York. He's been asked to speak at some colleges on the East Coast, but never to teach full-time. Never for a whole entire summer.

"Because it's for a whole summer this time," Mom explains. "And you're out of school and . . . we're a family and, well, we stick together. Anyway, we'll be back by the time school starts."

"What about *your* job?" I ask her. "Who's going to teach your summer classes?"

"I'm taking a three-month sabbatical to research and write a journal article."

I don't even have to ask what her article is going to be about.

Feeling Words and the People Who Love Them

By Dr. Libby Fitzhugh, Phd (a lover of feelings)

So just like that, the Fitzhugh family summer vacation is decided and I don't get a say.

Again.

It's so unfair.

Seriously, can someone please tell me, what is so wrong with Disney World?

3

A LEGIT HAUNTED FORTRESS

It takes about a gazillion hours to make it all the way to the town of Fort Augustus.

First there's the endless airplane ride to Glasgow and then the long drive all the way up to the Highlands of Scotland, where Fort Augustus sits on some humongous lake of ominous black water that, in pictures, looks more like an ocean than just a plain old lake. Lucky for me, Mom downloaded all the Harry Potters on my Kindle for the trip. Even though me and Dad have read the series together three whole times already, we agree you can never read Harry Potter too many times.

Someone is tapping me on my leg.

"Adelaide Ru," Mom is saying. "We made it."

My eyes open.

They're both staring at me from the front seat of the backward rental car. Dad's still sitting in the driver's seat on the wrong side of the car. Which is actually the right side of the car in Scotland. But it's still wrong to me because it's opposite of the way we do things in America.

And opposite is never good.

The last thing I remember after leaving the Glasgow airport is the crazy cattle in the pastures of the green Scotland countryside. Long-haired cattle that need a serious appointment at Supercuts. I also remember Harry Potter seeing the dark and ominous Hogwarts across the vast black waters for the very first time.

I yawn without covering my mouth and stretch, wiping a small circle of fog on the window with the back of my fist, peering out past raindrops racing each other to the bottom.

Outside are gray, moody, low-hanging clouds that forgot they're supposed to be up in the sky, along with a faint drizzle that chills you all the way to the inside of your bones. I squint through the rainy haze.

"We are where . . . *exactly*?" I ask, yawning again.

"Our home away from home," Mom says. "For the summer, anyway."

I stare through the circle like it's a peephole, then close my eyes tight and open them again.

This can't *possibly* be right.

Maybe I'm still dreaming.

That's it. I'm still inside *The Sorcerer's Stone* with Harry and Ron and Hermione and Neville. I must be right because emerging out of the fog and rain is a drab, gray stone castle sitting at a point surrounded by black water and casting a shadow of evil darkness upon us all.

I stick one thumb toward the window. "We're moving to a more haunted version of the Hogwarts School of Witchcraft and Wizardry?"

Dad laughs. "Oh, my little Rhubarb." He shakes his head and opens the driver's-side door. "You're a can of corn, you know that?"

"It's stunning." Mom marvels at it through the window. "Remember I told you it's a remodeled old abbey? They call it St. Benedict's. Oh, hon, it's just beautiful," she tells Dad.

I motion to the haunted fortress that sits before us. "I mean, are you *not* seeing what I'm seeing here?"

"You mean a summer filled with adventure?" Dad pulls himself up out of the driver's seat.

"Ah, no," I say. "A haunted fortress with entities lying in wait to steal our very souls as we sleep."

Dad laughs and shuts the car door. I watch him dance a jig outside my window with complete and utter oblivion to the doom that awaits us.

"Stay a Muggle if you want to!" I call to him through the glass.

He's still dancing and still laughing.

"You know what?" Mom says then. "This would be a great time to pull out your new feelings journal."

"Just because you wrote those words on the front of it with a marker doesn't make it so," I tell her. "It's a plain old spiral notebook. And it's *blue.* You know my order of notebook colors goes red, *then* yellow, *then* purple and *then* blue."

Dad knocks on my window and makes a silly face at me.

I can't help but grin. "No one thinks you're funny!" I call through the glass.

He shrugs and heads toward the trunk of the car to unload the luggage.

"Nonetheless," Mom goes on, "I think it will be good for you to write about some of the things you're feeling this summer."

"Fine. I will," I tell her. "Do you want to know what I'm going to write on the very first page?"

"What's that?" She's already scrolling on her cell phone.

"Scarred for life."

"Mmm-hmm," she says, her eyes still on the tiny screen.

"Mom, I'm being serious here. There's no way I can spend an entire summer in *this* place."

She's moved from her screen now to focusing on reapplying her lipstick in the mirror of the passenger-side visor. It's the Sun Kissed Mauve one that she bought special for the trip. She let me get a Dr Pepper Lip Smacker but I forgot it in the bathroom at the Denver airport on our way here. Now I'm cursed with dry, Dr Pepper–free lips for an entire summer while some random girl is smacking sweet, balmy, peppery lips all over Colorado.

"Mom, are you even listening to me right now?"

"Oh, Adelaide Ru, you're so dramatic," she tells the mirror.

"You can't see it because you're a Muggle. Just like Dad."

"What's that again?" She rubs the top Sun Kissed lip with the bottom Sun Kissed lip and then turns her head right and then left to examine whether it's just the right amount of mauviness for her liking.

"A person void of magical powers."

"Ahhh, right," she says, snapping the visor back into place.

"Lucky for you . . . you have me," I go on. "Because I can see

17

what you can't. And I see a haunted fortress where our souls are vulnerable to extraction."

"Adelaide Ru, it's an abbey. Monks used to live here before they made it into condos. It's *definitely* not haunted." She eyes it through the window. "It's . . . you know . . . *religious*. Or at least it used to be."

"I think the words you're searching for here are *diabolical phantasms*," I mutter. "It's probably filled to the gills with them."

"And those are?"

"Ghosts," I explain. "Dead monk ghosts wandering lost, shaking their chains in the attic above while the occupiers of the rooms sleep, completely unaware of their impending doom."

She's staring at me.

"You know, your garden-variety soul invasion . . . body snatching . . . or demon possession. That kind of thing," I go on.

She just blinks at me before finally saying, "*Where* do you get this stuff?"

"The Syfy channel."

She rolls her eyes at that one and grabs the door handle. "Come on, let's help Dad with the luggage."

But before she pulls herself out of the seat, she puts her arm around the headrest and turns her whole body to face me again.

"I'm going to challenge you to make the best of this," she says. "I'm sure you can do that for Dad. He's so excited to teach at the university here. I want you to look at this like an *adventure*. When will we ever get this chance again?"

I look her straight in the eye and cross my arms over my chest. "Hopefully . . . *never*."

"Well, I have complete and utter confidence that you can rise to this challenge," she tells me.

"I don't know where you get *that*," I say.

"Please try to remember that this is a wonderful opportunity for us to visit with family we don't get to see very often and maybe even learn more about the Fitzhugh heritage."

"I'm from Denver," I remind her.

"*You* may have lived your whole life on Tennyson," she says. "But Dad's story starts here. Now, let's go and help him."

"Mom." I put a palm on her shoulder. "I'm begging you. There's still time. Let's just get on a plane to Orlando and chalk this all up to one big mistake."

She smiles. "We'll be fine, I promise you. Now, come on," she says, pushing her door open and slipping out into the fog.

I stare at the haunted hulk before us one more time and sigh before opening my door. Dad parked the car in the circular drive, right in front of the ancient double wooden doors, which are so tall, you almost can't see the top of them because of the fat, low clouds swirling around us. Those doors remind me of the Wicked Witch of the West's castle.

"Zuma?" I hear Mom call to Dad while she goes back to scrolling on her phone. "What's the name of the caretaker again?"

"I can't remember . . . Schnebly, maybe?" Dad calls with his head in the trunk.

Everyone calls my dad Zuma. He goes short on his name too. Real short. It started with something having to do with the zoom lens and just morphed into Zuma Hugh for an artist name because it's way shorter and easier to remember than his actual name. His given name is Marmaduke Siles Fitzhugh and I'm not even joking either. Only Nan and Granddad Fitzhugh and Uncle Clive still call him Marmaduke Siles. Which I laugh at every time I hear it and then Dad pretends to be mad about it even though he really isn't.

It's kind of our thing.

Actually, Dad doesn't get mad. At least I've never seen him mad. If he had his own feelings journal, I bet it would never, ever say *mad*. I mean, I've seen him serious, *real* serious, like the time when I was five and drew a Crayola family portrait on the living room wall while he was out mowing the lawn and Mom was busy in the downstairs office working on another journal article. That time he got real serious . . . but never mad.

He's also the funniest person I know. But don't tell him I said so. It'll go straight to his head.

He's still stacking the suitcases on the ground from the trunk of the car while Mom is scrolling through the contacts on her phone.

"*Schnebly?* Are you sure?" she says.

Mom keeps searching, and Dad keeps stacking.

I grab a blue duffel bag and pull the strap over my shoulder. "You believe in the undead, Dad?" I ask.

Dad pops his head up from the trunk. "The undead?" he asks.

"Yes," I say.

He bends down until he's eye to eye with me, and all serious-like he says, "Do you really want to know what I think of vampires?"

My eyes get wider. "Yes."

He leans in even closer, a heavy palm placed on each of my shoulders, his jaw clenched. He looks to the left and then the right and says, "They're a real pain in the neck," followed by a loud *HA* and a slap on his knee.

I try my hardest this time not to smile, but I fail miserably. "No one thinks you're funny," I tell him with a big grin.

"Are you kidding? I'm *hiiiiilarious*," he tells me, setting another suitcase on the ground.

And then before I even have the chance to say anything more . . . it happens.

All my fears are realized in a single, solitary moment.

The tall, ancient wooden doors belch out a horrid *creeeeeeeeeak.*

The door opens and it steps forward. An actual apparition, just like I warned them about.

A ghostly image of a woman in an ugly black dress and hideous man shoes stands before us behind a curtain of gray fog.

The undead coming to feast on our very souls and use our bodies as hosts.

I knew it.

Mom and Dad are going to get a big, fat, hairy I-told-you-so for this one.

4

DO *NOT* MESS WITH THE UNDEAD

The Prince of Darkness has risen and lives in Fort Augustus, with lips the same color as the orange sauce in a can of SpaghettiOs and skin the color of Elmer's glue. Well, not the white slop out of the bottle Elmer's, more like the kind that's dried and more translucent and is squeezed out between uncooked macaroni pieces on a kindergarten pasta masterpiece.

And if I've learned anything from the Syfy channel, it's this . . . steer clear of boogeymen, poltergeists, giant spiders and circus clowns at all costs. And the most important thing to remember, above all else . . . do *not* mess with the undead.

"Cheers," the disembodied spirit calls out to us in a voice that is anything but cheery.

I grab Mom's hand and weave her fingers with mine, not once taking my eyes off the figure standing before us.

"My name is Euna Begbie," the apparition says. "I am the

caretaker for the university-owned flats here at St. Benedict's Club at the abbey."

The apparition's accent is thick just like Uncle Clive's and Aunt Isla's when they call us on the holidays. Dad has lost his mostly, more so than Nan and Granddad Fitzhugh, who moved to Boca ten years ago. Dad's only comes out now on the words with *r*s that require a tongue roll and also the *hork*ing words, which are words with a *hork* from the back of your throat that sounds suspiciously similar to Mr. Mews coughing up a hairball.

The ghostly figure is at least two heads taller than Mom and one taller than Dad and about ten over me. I can tell she's skeleton skinny even though her black dress goes all the way down to her bony white ankles. And her sleek black hair is pulled into a slicked bun that is so tight, I'll bet you any money her eyes can't even close all the way when she blinks.

Which I haven't seen her do yet.

"Hello, Ms. Begbie," Mom says. "We are the Fitzhugh family."

Euna Begbie nods once, eyeing each of us and then staring hard at me. And I just know it's because she's scoping out a nice juicy neck vein to feast on when I'm sleeping.

That's how the undead are.

"Welcome," Ms. Begbie says. "The university-owned flats are all located on the fourth floor. Ye have been assigned to flat 402." She pulls a skinny old iron key out of the pocket of her dusty dress and hands it to Mom.

"I'm Libby, and this is my husband, Zuma," Mom says. "He will be starting next week as a visiting professor of photography at the University of the Highlands and Islands in Inverness."

"Just for the summer," I add. "We aren't staying. And . . . people are expecting us . . . you know, *to return*."

Euna Begbie looks down her nose at me.

"Cheers, Ms. Begbie!" Dad calls out with a hearty wave from the trunk, completely oblivious that this woman most likely possesses a membership card for Club Undead.

I shake my head and roll my eyes.

Such a Muggle.

"We're so excited to be here!" he goes on. "I'm from the Highlands originally. My brother, Clive, and his wife, Isla, own Leakey's Bookshop in Inverness."

"Lovely." Euna Begbie gives Dad another slow nod.

I've learned from Dad and from Nan and Granddad Fitzhugh that *cheers* has a lot of meanings all at once. It can mean hello or thanks or enjoy your food or even goodbye sometimes. Kind of like *Aloha* in Hawaii. We went there three years ago and we didn't stay in any haunted fortress either.

It was the Hilton Waikoloa.

When we checked in there, we got flower necklaces called leis and fancy blended drinks in tall, curvy glasses with long straws and a pineapple flower on top.

"Please." Euna Begbie motions toward the open door. "Follow me and I will show ye to yer quarters."

I peek inside the double arched doors and then stare up at Mom with Mickey Mouse in my eyes and a desperate and silent final plea for Epcot in my soul. But right this minute, she doesn't give two hoots about what feeling word I'm thinking of.

And then in a flash a small boy with white-blond hair under a gigantic captain's hat comes flying out from the abbey so fast, the wooden doors don't even have time to belch another creak. He taps a glossy, twisted wooden cane in one hand and holds the leash of a curly red dog in the other as he darts past us. He's wearing a traditional Scottish plaid kilt, knee-high socks, and a dark green Windbreaker with two words written in white letters down one sleeve.

NESSIE QUEST.

"Ms. Begbie. That sticky toffee pudding was brilliant. It was well tidy scran indeed," he calls with a wave.

The woman's orange lips crack a smile for the very first time. "Cheers, Hammy Bean," she says, waving after the boy.

"Tatty bye," the boy calls, hustling off toward the drive.

I lean in close to Mom. "Did he say *tater fries*?" I ask. "Because I'm starving."

Euna Begbie snorts. "He said *tatty bye*," she informs me. "It's a less-formal way of sayin' goodbye in Scotland."

"Oh," I mumble.

"You'll learn more Scottish verbiage soon enough, lass," she informs me.

I want to tell her big, fat, hairy chance of that one.

My plans include staying holed up in my room watching funny animal videos on YouTube and texting with Britney B for Tennyson updates until September.

If . . . we make it out of Scotland alive. And that's a big *if*.

"Please follow me," Euna Begbie says, turning back toward the abbey.

Mom heads in after her, yakking it up about what

ingredients go in sticky toffee pudding, while my eyes stay fixed on the curious boy as he scrambles off.

His feet skip instead of step and his arms swing wide while he talks and laughs back and forth with the red dog, which barks back at the boy as if they're having a real conversation.

"Excuse me, Ms. Begbie," I call after them. "What's a Nessie Quest?"

She chortles a laugh at the back of her throat and calls over her shoulder at me without even stopping. "Nessie Quest is one o' the Loch Ness tours at the pier run by the Tibby family," she says. "And Nessie, o' course, refers to our resident lake monster."

I stop dead in my tracks and clutch the duffel bag to my chest.

"I'm sorry, y-your resident *what*?" I stutter.

This time she turns back to look at me over her shoulder. "Lake monster," she says again. "Nessie, the Loch Ness Monster."

I knew we should have gone to Disney World.

5

~~~~~~~~~~

DEVIL'S FOOD AND A SKELETON KEY

Inside the conjuror's castle, the Elmer's glue–skinned Euna Begbie leads us down a long stone corridor.

Her in front, then me, and then Mom.

Leading us deeper and deeper into the belly of the beast.

"Do you live on the fourth floor too?" I call to the woman, crossing all four sets of fingers in hopes that she doesn't.

"I live in the west tower," she tells us. "Flat one six six."

I swallow and turn to give Mom a look. "Did you say . . . *six six six?*"

"One sixty-six," she corrects me.

"Mmm," I say, eyeing her from behind.

I *know* I heard her right the first time. And everyone who's anyone knows what 666 stands for.

It's only the call sign of pure evil.

And if Scooby-Doo taught us anything, it's that the care-taker is always the villain.

"If ye need anything, that's where ye can find me," she calls back to us. "I'm available until five o'clock each day."

It's hard to keep up with Ms. Begbie because her legs are so long that for every one of her steps, Mom has to take three and I have to practically run. Lucky for me I wore my Nikes with the pink swoosh, but Mom chose her knee-high boots. The ones with the solid wood heels. She clacks with each step, the sound of those dumb heels echoing all the way up to the tall ceilings, which are striped with thick, ancient wooden beams. The tall, arched stained-glass windows are filled with see-through staring faces within multicolored panes . . . *watching.*

Their eyes following us with each step we take.

Ghostly eyes with evil intent.

The cold, drafty halls are silent except for faint sounds of guitar music coming from somewhere and Mom's stupid heels against the hard stone floor.

Clack. Clack. Clack.

Past a door marked POOL AND SPA.

Clack. Clack. Clack.

Past a door marked BILLIARDS.

Clack. Clack. Clack.

Even past a door that has the word TOILET on it.

I hide a giggle behind my hand at that one. Britney B is going to die when I tell her this. Who puts TOILET on a sign instead of RESTROOM?

Gross.

Euna Begbie hangs a louie at the TOILET, finally stopping at the bottom of a wide, squared-off spiral staircase that looks like it goes on forever. She probably doesn't want to hear Mom clack all the way up to our apartment.

I don't blame her.

"I'll leave you to it," she tells Mom. "If you have any questions, please ring or come and find me in the west tower. Good day."

She turns to leave.

"Excuse me, Ms. Begbie," I call after her.

She stops and faces me.

"So yeah . . . um, so you were saying something about a monster in that lake out there? You were kidding, right?"

"Nae," she says. "The story of our monster is quite real. It's a legend rooted in the past, when the great explorer St. Columba sighted it in the waters of Loch Ness in AD 565. Do ye know that our Loch Ness is so deep, it can fit the whole world's population many times over?"

Loch is one of those horking words, and when she says it, she sounds just like Mr. Mews with his hairballs.

"Have you actually seen the thing? I mean, with your own eyes?" I ask Ms. Begbie.

Ms. Begbie nods slowly. "Only once," she tells me. "When I was just a wee lass about your age. If ye listen verra closely, ye might *hear* her coming."

I swallow. *"Hear her?"*

"That's right," she says, and then bends down until she's eye to eye with me. "Ye always hear her coming first. The bubbles. The bubbles always come first."

She turns then and we watch her slide her man shoes down the hall until she turns another corner and is gone.

"Great," I say to Mom. "A haunted fortress and a monster that resides in the waters that surround it? We may be bordering on questionable parenting at this point."

"I think you'll be just fine," Mom says, hoisting her luggage and starting up the steps. "Come on, let's tackle this staircase."

I point toward the top of the squared-off spiral. "That's probably the portal," I tell her.

"The what?"

"Where the poltergeist gets in."

She just blows air out of her mouth, shakes her head and keeps on clacking.

Right above the second landing, on about the fourth or fifth step, is some kid strumming on a guitar. He seems older than me, but not by much. He's legit cute. Like so cute, I suddenly can't feel my legs.

I stare at the boy while he plays, oblivious to our presence. He has longish, dark, wavy hair with long bangs that hang in his eyes. He's wearing a short-sleeved T-shirt over a long-sleeved one, with a beaded necklace around his neck and rope bracelets on his wrists.

"Hey there," I say to him.

He ignores me.

I try again. "That's real nice," I say as we step past.

His flat palm hits the strings with a slap, bringing the music to an abrupt halt. He swings his hair to the side and looks up at me with seaweed-colored eyes.

"Yeah?" he says.

I only nod this time because suddenly I can't feel my tongue either.

He goes back to strumming and I go back to climbing.

Mom is already five steps ahead of me, and after making it to the third landing, I'm breathing heavy and have to stop and change hands.

I sigh and keep on. With each step, I name all the things I'm missing right this second.

Riding my bike down Tennyson.

Playing flashlight tag with neighborhood kids at César Chávez Park on the corner of Utica.

Mr. Gomez's homemade *papas fritas y guacamole* at El Chingon.

The warm feel of Mr. Mews's belly when I stick my face in his fur while he naps in the sun.

And last, but certainly not least, a monster-free neighborhood where I can sleep without worrying about something coming to eat me in the dead of night.

I miss *home*.

The smells. The feels. The places. The people.

This isn't home and it never will be.

Not even for a summer.

"Mom?"

"Yeah?"

"Scotland bites."

She's already clacked ahead ten steps. "Sounds like a good thing to write in your journal."

"Oh, I plan to," I call from behind. "Along with *homesick*."

"Are you sure you've been here long enough to be homesick?" she asks me.

"I don't think there's an official time assigned to measure

the volume of homesickness," I tell her. "You either are or you aren't and I *am*. I definitely *am*."

"Well, then I guess that would be a good word to add to your journal too."

I follow her all the way up to the fourth floor, which is so high that I bet you any money if there were a fifth floor, we'd be knocking on actual pearly gates.

"Here it is," she says, putting down the suitcase in her hand and slipping the key into the lock.

I lean my cheek on the arm of her tan raincoat. "That's a weird-looking key," I tell her. "It's so long and skinny."

"These are called skeleton keys," she explains.

I raise my eyebrows at her. "*Skeleton* keys?" I say. "Want to guess my feeling word for that?"

"Nope," she says, turning the key until the lock clicks.

She steps over the threshold of doom. "Ooooh. It's nice and toasty warm in here. This is adorable," she coos, making her way down the hall to check out the bedrooms.

I sigh, set my duffel bag down and step into the living room. It doesn't look anything like ours. There are two long red velvet couches that face each other, with an extra-wide square wooden table in the middle.

On one wall are floor-to-ceiling arched windows, and on the other is a fireplace with a fire burning inside it. Dad said that even though it's summertime, the mountains in the Highlands have moody weather and it's cold and rainy a lot of days. Which is also why Mom made me take all my flip-flops out of the suitcase and put in my tall rain boots instead. The hearth is stacked with extra firewood and the mantel is full of photographs of the town.

Storefronts and boats and festivals and people.

I zoom in on one particular boat that has the same words painted on it as the kid with the red dog had on his Windbreaker. I pick it up and examine it.

Nessie Quest.

On the breakfast bar that borders the kitchen is a plate of plain square cookies with a handwritten note.

Welcome to Fort Augustus

I take a whiff of one and place it back on the plate.

"Adelaide Ru," Mom says. "Either eat one or don't. Don't sniff it and put it back."

"Yeah, but there's nothing in them," I say. "How can you eat a cookie with no chips or nuts or M&M's or anything?"

"Can't you think of one nice thing to say about Euna Begbie leaving us a plate of homemade cookies?"

I think it over. "Yep," I say. "At least they're not *devil's food.*"

Mom rolls her eyes at that one and pops a cookie into her mouth. "I wonder what's taking your dad so long. Why don't you go and meet Dad on the stairs and help him with the rest of the bags?"

I sigh. "Fine."

Dad is already on the third-floor landing when I make it out to the staircase. I look down the squared-off spiral and see him working his way up to our floor.

"Where have you been?" I ask him.

"Oh," he calls up when he sees me. "I was talking to a nice couple who are here on vacation for the summer. The, uh, the Cadys, I think they said, from Manhattan. So, how is it? Pretty nice?"

I shrug. "If you call an actual lake monster that feeds off the flesh and bones of small children in the waters just feet from where your daughter lays her very head . . . *nice.*"

Dad stops for a minute and pretends to think hard about my question with his nose in the air. "Nope," he finally says, stepping up to meet me. "That doesn't sound nice. Libby? Sound nice to you?" he asks Mom, who's heading out the doorway of the flat.

She stops in her tracks and puts her nose in the air too, pretending to think hard about his question. "Nope," she says. "I don't think it does."

"You guys are hilarious," I tell them. "But you'll be sorry when you find me on the shore of this lake with a big, fat monster bite out of me."

"Ru Ru, Nessie has never eaten a single child that I'm aware of," Dad tells me. "But you're quite an overachiever. Maybe you'll be the first."

I throw my palms up to the sky. "You knew about that thing and you *still* brought us to this place?"

Dad puts a heavy palm on my head and strokes my hair. "Nessie is just a story, Rubbaboo," he says. "A legend. It's not *real.* I grew up on this loch; don't you think I would know if there were a monster in it?"

"Yeah, well," I say. "I remain unconvinced."

Mom grabs a duffel bag from Dad's shoulder and a suitcase from his hand.

"You heard Dad, it's a legend, honey," she says. "We took you to Pikes Peak too—did we see a real *Bigfoot*?"

"That's totally different," I tell her.

"And why's that?"

"Ah, *hello* . . . Bigfoot are *nocturnal*," I inform her. "Night dwellers. The chances of a sighting in the daytime are slim to none."

Dad's still smiling. "Where did you get that one?"

"It's common sense."

"Zuma," Mom says, grabbing another suitcase and heading back through the doorway of the flat. "Please stop encouraging this."

He winks at me and turns on his heel to head back down the stairs for more bags.

"Dad." I grab his arm. "I have a real bad feeling about this place," I whisper. "I mean, *real* bad."

He wipes the heavenly staircase sweat beads off his forehead. "Oh, Rumorbug," he says. "You're a can of corn. There are more bags . . . want to help me?"

"No," I say. "I think I'll go and get the monster 4-1-1 from that boy playing guitar on the second floor."

Dad's eyebrows crinkle together all serious. "What boy?" he asks.

My mouth falls open. "Wh-what do you mean, *what boy?* The boy on the stairs with the guitar . . ." I trail off when I see his Cheez Whiz look of confusion.

"Rudy Tudy," he says. "There *is* no boy on the stairs."

I cover my mouth with my hand and whisper between my fingers. "You mean . . . you can't *hear* that?"

His face cracks then and I get another one of his *HA*s.

I put angry fists on my hips and watch him laugh his stupid head off while he bounds down the steps. As he hits the third-floor landing, I grab the carved wooden rail that runs along the fourth-floor hallway with both hands and hurl my words down after him through the center of the staircase.

"No one thinks you're funny," I holler.

"Oh, I bring the party," he calls back over his shoulder. "And it's a doozy."

"Laugh it up now!" I call down after him. "But you won't be laughing when our bodies are ravished by soulless entities looking for a host!"

The music stops and the boy with the guitar stretches his neck to look up at me through the heavenly spiral.

"Oh, uh . . ." I laugh, waving. "Sorry," I say.

He sits there considering me for another minute and then says, "You got a brother?"

"Who? Me?" I point to myself. "Ah . . . no, it's just us. Me and my mom and dad."

"Mmm" is all he says, considering me for a few more seconds.

Then he stands up and puts his worn leather guitar strap over his head and swings the guitar onto his back, before disappearing down the second-floor hall without saying anything else.

I stand at the rail a few minutes more, thinking hard about all the feeling words that would best describe the guitar boy for my journal, and I make one very important decision.

That kid is getting a page all to himself.

6

~~~~~~~~~~

EVIL SPIRIT PATROL

That night the Muggles are in bed by nine-thirty.

Since I slept on the plane and also in the backseat of the backward rental car, I stay up to ward off the evil spirits and keep our souls safe from extraction. Not to mention there has yet to be confirmation of whether this Loch Ness Monster of theirs is solely aquatic or makes an appearance on land now and again. As far as I'm concerned, best not to take any chances.

I take first watch in my yellow flowered nightgown and Hello Kitty slippers after they say good night. Dad with a salute to wish me luck on my mission and Mom with a warning to be in bed by ten-thirty and no later.

"But, Mom," I say. "Everyone who's anyone knows the evil spirits don't show their faces or start their undead shenanigans until the stroke of midnight."

"*Ten-thirty,*" she says again, this time with bigger eyes and a voice that really means it.

I guard our haunted flat to the tune of the ticking grandfather clock in the hall and the stomps of my Hello Kittys on the wooden floor planks. Up and down the hall with dedicated fervor. Since Mom didn't pack any garlic for the trip and I can't find anything even closely resembling a stake that could go through a heart, I'm left with a single defense.

The feather pillow from the bed in my room.

Okay, so a pillow wallop to the face may not sound like a very lethal option when it comes to the undead, but I didn't finish. The pillow on my new bed has one very stinging *zipper* on the end of it. And while it may not pierce a heart like a stake or cause a melting sensation like a clove of garlic, it can cause a good red mark that smarts like nobody's business. I found this out myself during the Pillow Fight Incident of 2018 at Emmanuelle Penney's birthday slumber party.

Whether or not it was an *accidental* pillow wallop to the face is still a matter of raging Tennyson Street debate.

Tick. Tick. Tick.

March. March. March.

Like a carefully created musical ensemble, my Hello Kittys stomp to the beat.

Up the hall. Turn. Down the hall. Turn.

At every fifteen-minute interval the grandfather clock chimes like cymbals, adding to the melody. For every hour, the clock chimes in a cymbals solo.

Ten cymbals for ten o'clock.

Eleven cymbals for eleven o'clock.

And then . . . *the stroke of midnight.*

Twelve cymbals.

Let the ghostly mayhem begin. And it does too. The evil

spirits are awakened on the very last chime to begin their evil taunts. The first sound comes from the attic above the ceiling.

Pound. Pound. Pound.

The next from the hallway outside the front door.

Stomp. Stomp. Stomp.

And then in an orchestrated concert of spookiness, Mother Nature kicks in with her thunder cracks, tapping rain and wicked wind that rattles the windowpanes.

I get my feather pillow in the ready position.

Attic *pounding.*

Hallway *stomping.*

Thunder *cracking.*

Rain *tapping.*

Clock *ticking.*

Hello Kitty *marching.*

And my own heart beating.

"I'm ready for you, undead," I whisper. "You're not taking us."

And then it happens . . . *a moan.*

It stops my Hello Kittys in their tracks.

I know it's the moan of *the undead.*

And I know exactly what that means too. *Taken Souls* says it's exactly what happens right before they strike. It's when I hear the second moan that I have no choice but to do the unthinkable.

Wake the Muggles.

I throw the pillow and run. I run as fast as my Hello Kittys will take me, flinging open their bedroom door and lunging like an Olympic long jumper with all my might on top of their bed. A very loud *ugh* is what comes out of Dad because it's him that I land on.

He sits bolt upright. "Rumorbug?" he whispers. "Is that you? What . . . what time is it? What are you doing?"

My heart is thumping so fast, I can feel it in my ears and I can't keep the breath in my lungs long enough to get the words out.

"Ah, only guarding our souls from extraction," I huff out at him.

"Uh-huh . . . right, yeah, how's all that going?" He rubs his left eye and grabs his glasses to see the blue numbers on the digital clock next to the bed. "Wait. You were supposed to clock out from your shift by ten-thirty."

"Yeah, well, lucky for you I didn't!" I exclaim. "Because I *heard* them."

"Who?"

"*Them,*" I say. "The *undead.* They're here to steal our very souls. We need to evacuate the premises immediately."

He blows a burst of air out of his mouth and then flops back down on the pillow.

"Dad." I shake his leg. "I heard them myself. All I can say is I told you so. At this point we'll be lucky if we escape with our very lives."

"Libby." Dad pats the lump that is Mom and then pulls the thick comforter over his head. "Your daughter has some feelings to discuss."

Mom sits up still half asleep. "Huh?" she asks. "What is it? Adelaide Ru? What are you doing up? Do you need something?"

"You bet I do," I tell her. "Holy water and a priest."

She shakes her head at me. "I'm getting rid of the cable," she tells me. "The minute we get home. Gone."

"But, Mom, you don't understand. I heard the moans," I go on. "The *Taken Souls* paranormal investigators say it's the first indication the evil spirits are about to strike."

She takes in a long, deep breath and then blows air just like Dad did.

"What?" I throw my palms to the ceiling. "Google it if you don't believe me."

She flips her side of the comforter over Dad. "Come on, let's go back to bed. I'll go with you." She puts her feet on the plush forest-green rug and holds out her hand.

In my room, Mom tucks the heavy feather comforter all around me, turns the light off and slips into the other side of the canopy bed.

I snuggle up next to her, tucked tight under her protective arm.

"Try to get some sleep," she whispers, kissing me in the middle of my forehead.

The smooth sound of her breathing and her predictable smell make me feel a lot safer.

She smells like home.

And while predictable doesn't tell a story that pops, tonight it makes me feel a whole lot better.

I sigh. "Mom?"

"Hmmm?"

"I'm pretty sure I won't be able to make the best of Scotland. I don't know how. And you want to know what else? Britney B hasn't returned even *one* of my texts. Not a single one. And I've sent her like five. I bet that sneaky Emmanuelle

Penney is going to steal her away from me and I will be best-friendless when I get home. They're probably eating *our* veggieless pizzas and watching *our* Beyoncé YouTube videos together as we speak. They'll oust me from the Beyhive."

"Honey, it's only been one day." Mom kisses my forehead again. "I'm sure Britney B will get back with you by tomorrow or the next day. And I still have faith that you can make the best of things here for the summer."

"I'm trying," I tell her. "But monsters *plus* evil spirits is a little more challenging than I'm capable of."

Mom pushes my bangs off my forehead. "Euna Begbie said this abbey was over a hundred years old. Just think of all those happy families. The family picnics and the holiday celebrations spent in front of the fireplace. The monks who worshiped here and did wonderful things for all kinds of people in this world. There's goodness in this place. I can feel it."

"And what if you're wrong and the undead take me when you're asleep?"

"Well, then I'll miss you," she says.

I sit up. "That's all you have to say?"

She laughs and pulls me back down so we're nose to nose. "You know what I think?" she says. "I think . . . maybe you've got a story starting here."

A *story*?

"Weren't you looking for an adventure to write about?" She gives the air a big sniff. "I smell something interesting happening in this place."

"You do?"

She sniffs again. "Yes, and I think it smells . . ." She sniffs one more time. "*Very* interesting."

And then I sniff. "All I smell is haunted abbey."

"Hmmm" is all she says.

"But wait," I say. "I could write about the haunted abbey and how the people disappear one by one. Or a story about that creepy Euna Begbie and how she possesses the souls of the people who come through the wooden doors of St. Benedict's. *Wait*," I say, sitting up with my finger in the air. "I've got it . . . *the lake monster*. I can write a story about a lake monster."

She smiles. "I think you're onto something."

I snuggle back in, wrap my arms around her and give her a tight hug. "Thanks, Mom."

"Now, please, will you go to sleep?" she says.

"Yes," I say. "Good night."

"Good night, my little author," she says, and turns over on her pillow.

I lie there looking up at the ceiling, thinking about my new story. A lake monster . . . it's *perfect*. I've never read one single book about a real live lake monster. I mean, Harry Potter may have battled a lot of magical villains, but he never, ever went toe to toe with a wild beast that swims the deep, dark waters of Loch Ness. All I need now is to find some interesting characters to share in the adventure.

Harry Potter wouldn't be who he is without Hermione and Ron.

My eyes are wide open.

My heart is racing.

My insides are fluttering.

This time for a whole different reason. I stare at the ceiling, my fingers itching for the clicking of the keyboard. Tomorrow is the day I begin the search for my story.

I can't wait.

My lids refuse to close.

Something inside me feels like it's going to burst.

"Mom," I whisper.

Sigh.

"What now?" she asks.

"My eyeballs are too excited to sleep."

7

A DAPPER QUIGLEY

The next morning my mission begins.

Not warding off evil spirits this time, because we actually survived the night with our souls intact. So there's a very slim possibility that I may be wrong about the whole haunted thing. But I'm not letting go of the idea completely just yet. The undead can be sneaky, so it's best to keep your guard up.

My mission today has nothing to do with apparitions or zombies. Today I'm on my way to town to find some supporting characters for my story.

And somehow the morning sun makes the town feel a whole lot less scary than it did with clouds that refused to stay in the sky where they're supposed to be, fogging and glooming the whole place up. Today the sky is a bright blue, the clouds are white and fluffy and the sun is rising bright above the tiny town.

First things first: characters.

At least my Ron and Hermione.

After breakfast, I bound down the heavenly spiral to the lobby with one of Dad's old cameras around my neck, secretly hoping to see the guitar boy again. I even snuck some of Mom's Sun Kissed Mauve just in case. But the halls of St. Benedict's are quiet except for laughter, fun-time screams and splashing coming from behind the door marked POOL AND SPA.

It's still early and the small town is just waking up. Shops haven't opened yet and the rising sun is making it rain orange and pink and purple instead of drab gray. The waves of Loch Ness shine like diamonds, making it hard to believe that the deep, inky-black water is hiding a beastly lake monster somewhere underneath.

And there's all the green too. It's the very first thing I noticed when we landed in Glasgow yesterday. The green.

Velvety rolling hills.

Ivy-covered stone fences.

Leafy trees.

Cushy moss between the cracks in the sidewalks.

In Jelly Belly terms, it'd be like: Green Apple, Kiwi, Lime, Watermelon, and Juicy Pear all at the same time.

I make my way through the grounds of St. Benedict's, past the life-sized chess set, through the trees and on to the pier. A canal runs through the center of town and into the loch, with sidewalks on either side of it and walking bridges that go across.

I examine all that is Fort Augustus through the tiny, square window of Dad's camera. I love when he lets me use it. It's way better than my iPhone to take pictures. And not to brag or anything, but Dad's not the only photographer in the family.

The camera has a long lens and a button on top that you push when you find just the right shot. And then the shutter inside the lens makes this glorious clicking sound that tells you that you've captured something . . . something very special. A moment in time that will never, ever be reproduced.

That *click* is the best part of it. It's like an exclamation point at the end of an exciting sentence that makes you feel something real important. And there is nothing better than that.

Dad says his photos are so good because he captures the soul of every shot. I haven't learned how to catch any souls yet, but I keep trying.

"Good mornin'!" a voice calls out from behind me in a thick Scottish accent. I squint through my lens to see a very old and very tiny man with a mop of white hair coming out from under a tan flat cap. If I could come up with one word to describe him, I would call him *dapper*. Mostly because of his slick, shiny leather shoes, crisp blue-and-white polka-dot bow tie and red sweater vest over a navy button-down shirt.

I aim my lens at him.

Click.

"Good morning," I say back.

"I've not seen the likes of ye in this town before." He smiles at me from under his cap.

"We're just visiting for the summer," I tell him.

He holds out a hand and I take it in mine for a proper handshake.

"Nice to meet ye." He smiles again. "Yer name, lass?"

"I'm Ada Ru," I say.

This time I see how green his eyes are and they remind me

of the green of the velvety Scotland grasses lining the hills and the curly mosses covering the stone fences.

"Quigley is the name," he says. "I do cashier work here a few days a week." He points up at the store sign above us.

"Ness for Less Market," I read aloud, shielding my eyes to see the specials of the week carefully written with bright yellow paint in the window.

5p off haggis
£1 off salmon

"We haven't made it to the market yet," I tell him. "We just moved into St. Benedict's Abbey yesterday."

"Working here gets me oot o' the house now that I'm retired so I can meet all sorts o' interestin' people from all over the world." He tips his cap at me this time. "Like ye, lassie."

"I'm sorry to have to tell you this, but I'm not very interesting," I say. "Not yet, anyway, but I'm working on it. Today, in fact."

"And how's that, lass?"

"Because," I say, "I'm a writer and I'm writing a story about your lake monster and today I'm looking for my supporting characters."

"Och, a writer!" he exclaims. "Braw! That's lovely."

"I'll be my own protagonist, of course, but I need to find more characters. Besides the monster, that is. Maybe you'd like to be one of them? You have a very interesting name for a character."

He clasps his hands together in front of him. "How wonderful! To be included in someone's story? Now, that is somethin' I didn't expect when I started my day. Maybe ye could make me, ah . . . taller in yer book?" He stands on his tiptoes.

I laugh.

"I could do that," I assure him.

Then he pulls off his cap to show me his shiny bald head.

"Wi' a full heid o' hair, if ye please."

I laugh again. "Sure," I tell him.

"Well, it's been most wonderful meetin' ye, lassie," he says, peeking at a shiny silver watch on his wrist. "Now I'd best be on my way."

"Oh, okay," I say. "Goodbye, Mr. Quigley."

"It's just Quigley, love." He waves a hand over his shoulder on his way down the sidewalk. "Quigley Dunbar the Third. Tatty bye."

I squint and aim, watching him whistle a happy tune on his way.

Click.

"Excuse me, Mr. Quig . . . I mean, Mr. Dunbar . . . the Third," I call after him. "But you passed the store."

He stops whistling and turns back to face me. "I canna properly start my day without a sack o' biscuits from a Wee Spot o' Tea an' Biscuits to have with my tea this mornin'."

"Oh," I say. "Goodbye, then."

He waves again and starts back on his way while I head down the pier in the opposite direction.

Next to Ness for Less Market is Farquhar's Famous Fish House, where a large man with a round middle and an extra chin is coming out the front door with a broom.

"Good morning, lassie," he calls.

"Good morning," I call back with a wave.

I watch him as he sweeps up a cloud of Fort Augustus sidewalk dust. The front windows have cardboard signs taped to them with customer quotes, making sure that anyone who walks by knows that this shop has the best fish and chips in Scotland. Anders from England says they are *brilliant* and Lynn from New York City *thought she died and went to heaven* when she tasted them. But I wonder what makes them famous.

Click.

I can still smell the sweetness of a Wee Spot of Tea and Biscuits baking all their treats when I make it to the pier near the loch. It makes my stomach rumble even though I already had cinnamon toast for breakfast.

I focus my lens way out on a point where the Boathouse Restaurant sits at the edge of the shore. Round red wooden picnic tables in the grass out in front are ready for hungry tourists after a day of sightseeing, already set with napkin holders and salt and pepper shakers.

Click.

At the very end of the pier sits a beach made of smooth stones, where canoe trips and other water activities are advertised with a sign that reads FANCY A PADDLE?

Click.

Near the beach, at the very end of the pier, I see three very old men sitting in a line on an old wooden bench. All three of them are wearing those same type of flat caps as Quigley Dunbar III, except theirs are black, not tan tweed, and the wool sweaters they're wearing are bow-tieless and definitely more nubby than dapper. Each man is holding black binoculars tight against his eyes, aimed straight out at the waters of Loch Ness.

Click.

Then I notice a tall white booth right on the dock next to a large white boat bobbing in the canal. Green letters painted on both the booth and the sign read:

NESSIE QUEST
Loch Ness Tours Daily

Click.

Another boat bobs in the water farther down the dock. Except this one is a sleek and sparkly green speedboat with letters that read:

MONSTER CHASER
Tours every hour
8:00–5:00

Click.

That's when something darts in front of my viewfinder and I pull the camera away from my eye to see a boy and his dog. The exact same boy from the abbey. The one in the plaid kilt and dark green Windbreaker with the white letters down the sleeve. He skips on by me with his glossy, twisted wooden cane and his barking dog.

I watch him through the lens as he and the dog slip in the side door of the *Nessie Quest* booth. The booth hatch opens and the boy takes off his green Windbreaker, hangs it on a hook and leans two elbows on the counters and his cheeks in his hands. When I zoom in on his T-shirt I can see a dinosaur-like green monster on the front with just two words scrawled across the bottom.

NESSIE LIVES.

Click.

8

TIDBITS APLENTY

I lean against the iron fence lining the yard of a stone house along the canal and watch the curious boy while I pretend I'm not.

He's still leaning on the counter of the *Nessie Quest* booth. But he's looking right at me. I mean, I think he is. That's what it seemed like, anyway, from what I can see of his face underneath that stupid, gigantic captain's hat that looks three sizes too big for his head and hangs way down below his eyebrows.

I pretend to ignore him and busy myself by rubbing at a scuff mark on the pink swoosh of my right Nike. But when I peek again, he's *still* staring. So I lick my hand and rub the swoosh some more, then give him a sneaky side-eye glance.

He's *still* staring.

"Hey," I finally call out to him. "Why don't you take a picture? It lasts longer."

The boy's chin pops off his hand while the red dog

scrambles up off the floor behind him, putting two curly red paws on the counter.

"Pardon?" the boy says properly in that same Scottish accent as Ms. Begbie and Quigley Dunbar III.

The dog gives me a *woof* and sniffs the air in my direction.

"You're staring at me," I call out to the boy. "And it's rude."

He's definitely younger than me, maybe eight or something, but still, that's no excuse.

"Hasn't anyone ever told you that it's not nice to stare?"

The little weirdo just grins real big at me with these super-deep dimples on each cheek. "I *wasna* starin' at ye."

I stomp up the dock and toward his dumb booth with my hands stuck firmly to my hips and Dad's camera bouncing against my chest. "Ah, yeah you were. I saw you."

"Well, if you are quite sure ye saw me starin' in yer direction, then it must mean that you were starin' at me as well."

The kid's got me there.

"*No*," I snap. "I actually sensed it *before* I saw it."

His laugh comes out in a burst this time, which I also don't appreciate.

And I tell him so. "Stop that laughing," I command.

He stops the laughing but not the grinning.

"Is that all ye came over here to say?" he asks.

"Well . . . no," I say. "Originally I came over here to tell you that I don't appreciate you staring at me, but now I'd also like to add that I don't appreciate you laughing at me either."

He tilts his head to the right and considers me for a moment. "You're quite bossy, arna ye?" he asks.

"Did you just rip on me and then ask me to agree with you?" I say.

The boy shrugs. "Just an observation. Is there anything else ye'd like to say while you're here?"

I think about it. "I guess not," I say.

"Well, then you've said what you've come to say," he tells me. "Ye can be on your way. Unless . . ." He stops.

"Unless what?" I ask.

"Unless you fancy a tour." He holds up a ticket.

I swallow.

"A ticket?" I ask, pointing to a boat bobbing in the water. "For that?"

"A tour o' Loch Ness," he tells me.

He rolls his *r* just like Euna Begbie and horks the word *loch* just like Mr. Mews horks his hairballs.

I glance toward the water and see people handing tickets to a round, red-haired woman in the same captain's hat and the same dark green Windbreaker with white lettering on the sleeve.

Except her hat fits her fine.

"You mean . . . go on the *water*?" I ask.

"That *is* where the tour o' the loch takes place."

"Uh-huh . . . and it's a tour of what . . . *exactly*?"

"The history o' the Highlands, includin' the famous Urquhart Castle and, o' course . . . what truly *lies within the deep, dark waters o' the loch*."

The way he says the last part makes me think he'd be a real good announcer on the Syfy channel.

Except for the hairball horks.

"Well, I can see the lake perfectly fine from here," I tell him. "Why would I need to get in a boat to look at it?"

He laughs again. "Indeed," he says. "Some people are too feart."

"*Feart?*" I ask. "What is that?"

"Afraid," he says. "Sorry, we use a lot o' Scottish slang wi' each other that we tone down for tourists. I forget sometimes."

"Yeah, well, I didn't say I was afraid," I inform him.

"Many people are feart of our Nessie."

I laugh at that one a little bit harder than I mean to. "That Loch Ness Monster thing?" I ask. "I'm sorry to rain on your parade here, but my dad says that thing's not real."

He scoffs at me. "Do ye live under a rock?"

"*No,*" I snap. "*Denver.*"

"Right. That explains it then, doesna it?" he says.

I put my hands on my hips again. "Explains what?"

"It explains why ye dinna ken anythin'."

"I do too know something. In fact, I know plenty of things," I tell him. "Probably way more than you."

"Like what?"

"L-like, I know that thing out there is just a story," I say. "My dad told me so. And he's from here and way older than you. Like *decades.*"

He motions for me to come closer with a curled-finger wiggle.

"I'll let you in on a wee secret," he whispers.

I lean in. "What?"

"There is always some truth to every story. The nonbelievers are only nonbelievers because they dinna really ken anythin', so they just say it's not true. It's a lot easier to do that than to actually open yer mind to learn facts about new possibilities. The thing is . . . you're here and that tells me ye want to ken the truth. Here's yer chance." He waves the ticket in the air. "O' course, it's not everyone's cuppa tea."

"You can say that again," I mumble.

"And o' course, not everyone has the tidbits for it," he goes on.

I give him my very best Cheez Whiz. "The what?" I ask him.

"Tidbits."

"Is that some kind of Scottish thing too?"

"Nae, it's Hamish."

"Huh?" I ask.

He grins two deep dimples at me again. "Hamish Bean Tibby at yer service." He tips his gigantic hat at me, just like Quigley Dunbar III did. "But ye can call me Hammy Bean for short. Bean for even shorter."

"*Hammy Bean?*" I say. "Your parents named you after a casserole?"

"Nae, after my great-grandfather."

"I was kidding," I tell him.

"I'm not. My great-grandfather was the Earl of Scott, Hamish Bean Tibby the First," he tells me, and then leans in close and whispers again. "We're royalty, if ye must ken. But dinna tell anyone, it's a secret. For security reasons, ye ken."

"*Royalty* royalty? Like Kate and William and Harry and Meghan?"

"Haud yer wheesht," he tells me with a finger over his lips.

"Haud my *what*?"

"Wheesht," he repeats. "It means *shush*. Remember . . . it's a secret."

"Right, sorry," I say.

"Anyway, it's okay if ye dinnat have them is all I'm sayin'," he goes on.

"Don't have what?"

"Tidbits, guts, bravery, and the like."

"Listen here." I stand a little taller. "I have tidbits *aplenty*. Tons of them, in fact. I'm loaded to the brim with tidbits, if you must know."

He waves the slip of paper again.

"Tickets are ten pounds," he informs me. "That's includin' the tidbit discount."

Nessie Quest Tours
Admit One
£10

"Wait, what kind of discount is that?" I ask him. "The ticket says ten pounds right on it."

"Right. The discount is applied in advance, considerin' that only people wi' tidbits buy the tickets anyway." He pushes a button on the cash register and it beeps out a total. "Will that be cash or credit?"

"Yeah, well, the thing is . . . ah . . . I . . . I mean . . . I'm supposed to be back in one hour. My mom told me so."

"Brilliant." He sets the ticket on the counter and pushes it toward me. "The tour is exactly fifty-five minutes. Will that be cash or credit?"

"Okay . . . yeah, um . . . but . . . so the thing is that I don't have any money with me," I tell him.

"Mmm," he says. "No money?"

"Right." I pull the insides of my jeans pockets all the way out to show him. "No money, see? Nothing."

He juts a chin in the direction of the boat. "Is the lady with the curly red hair lookin'?" he asks.

I bite my bottom lip, stretch my neck and give a quick peek around the booth. The red-haired lady is talking and laughing with the people already boarded for the tour.

"No," I say. "She's busy."

He pushes the ticket even closer to me. "You can owe me."

I put a single finger on it and push it back. "Yeah, but the thing is that . . . um . . . the thing is . . . you know what it is? Here's what it is—" But he doesn't even let me finish.

"As I thought," he says. "No tidbits."

I stomp a single Nike on the dock. "Stop saying that stupid word," I snap.

A gray camouflage walkie-talkie radio sitting on the counter beeps and a woman's voice calls out from the speaker. "Mamo Honey to Captain Green Bean. Come in, Captain Green Bean. Over."

Beep.

The ham-and-bean-casserole kid picks up the radio and presses the black button and it beeps again.

"Captain Green Bean here, over," he says into the tiny speaker.

"Rendezvous at the *Nessie Quest* straightaway," the woman's voice says. "We are ready to crack on with it."

"That's a roger, Mamo Honey," the kid says. "Over and out."

"Who was that?" I ask.

59

"I have to go," he tells me. "My Mamo Honey is the captain on the boat. She's my grandmother. *Mamó* is *granny* in Gaelic. I'm the official announcer for the *Nessie Quest* boat tours. I tell the tourists all aboot the history o' Loch Ness and Scotland and, o' course . . . the history of the monster. Not to brag, but I ken everythin' there is to ken aboot everythin' when it comes to this loch. Ye dinna ken what you'll be missin'. Please excuse me now; I've got to close up shop."

He hangs a new sign on the hatch before slamming it closed.

GONE TO FIND A MONSTER

The red dog emerges from the side door first, followed by the kid holding his leash.

As the boy locks the door, the dog stops in front of me to give me a good sniff and taste my hand with his tongue.

"Hi, boy." I bend down, reaching a hand to pat his head. He licks my hand again and then a wet tongue crosses my nose.

"She's a girl," Hammy Bean tells me. "Mac-Talla Tibby."

"That's a real cool name for a dog," I say. "Is it Scottish?"

"It's Gaelic for *echo*," he tells me.

"I like it," I say, giving her a scratch under her chin.

Mac-Talla holds up a paw for me to shake.

I shake it. "Nice to meet you, girl," I tell her.

"Lead the way, Mac-Talla," the boy calls to her.

Mac-Talla barks three times and runs out in front of Hammy Bean and his twisted wooden cane, pulling him toward the *Nessie Quest* tour boat.

Mamo Honey starts up the engine, and the smell of gasoline swirls through the air.

I follow Hammy Bean to the end of the dock. "So . . . you're saying without a doubt, you believe that thing's out there?"

"O' course it is," he calls over his shoulder.

"Yeah, but, I mean, have you ever actually seen it with your very own eyes?"

"If ye really want to learn more aboot it but dinna want to pop into the water to do it, ye can always meet me at my hoose on Wednesday mornin'. That's when I work on my Nessie newsletter."

"Why would I want to do that?"

"Because you're interested in learnin' the facts," he calls back to me. "I can tell. My hoose is the one wi' the red door on Bunioch Brae. *Tibby Manor* is etched above the door."

"You still didn't answer my question," I call after him. "I asked you if you've seen the thing with your own eyes."

He stops and turns to face me again. "Not exactly."

"Well, right there, then, I can't accept your testimony. You can't say something truly exists if you haven't seen it with your own eyes."

He laughs again.

"What are you laughing at *now*?" I demand.

"You."

"And why is that?"

"Because ye dinna ken anythin'," he tells me.

I point to myself. "*I* don't? Me? That's some talk coming from some eight-year-old."

"I'm ten . . . *and* three-quarters."

"That doesn't help your case any," I inform him.

"If ye rely on only one of yer senses, ye can miss oot on some really important things," he tells me.

I consider this. "What is that supposed to mean? Seeing it is everything."

He smiles. "Not everythin'," he says, placing a hand on top of Mac-Talla's head. "I canna see it, but I ken it's there."

"You can't see it because it's not real."

He cocks his head to the side. "I canna see it because . . . I'm *blind*."

That's when the world stops like someone pushed the Fort Augustus Pause button.

I stand frozen, staring at him.

"Y-you're . . . *what?*"

"Blind," he says, reaching for a silver handle stuck to the side of the boat.

I watch him pull himself into the boat and then Mac-Talla takes a giant leap, landing next to him. "Remember, it's the hoose wi' the red door." He waves from the water. "Tatty bye, Denver!"

My mouth falls open, but nothing comes out of it.

9

A WICKED MARE

Another rainy day in the Scottish Highlands.

And also a greener day.

So far, I haven't been able to capture the *soul* of the green in any of my photographs the way Dad captures it in his. We downloaded all the shots on the computer last night and I didn't catch souls in any of them. Dad said it can be a hard thing to learn. But the thing is, he does it *every time*.

So today, with Dad's camera hanging from my neck, I'm hunting for souls to capture.

"Where is this place?" I call up to Dad in the backward rental car.

We're on our way to the city of Inverness to visit Uncle Clive, Aunt Isla and Cousin Briony, aka Malibu Barbie Hater.

"Leakey's Bookshop is in downtown Inverness." His eyes meet mine in the rearview mirror.

"Is it like the BookBar at home?"

"Don't you remember it?" he asks.

"No," I tell him.

"I think you were there at least once. Right, Lib?" he asks Mom.

"Yeah," she agrees, turning to face me. "We had hot chocolates in the coffee bar with Briony and Isla. You don't remember?"

I shake my head.

"Well, maybe it'll come back to you when we get there," she says.

"I was probably so traumatized from the Malibu Barbie incident that I blocked it out."

Mom snorts at that one. "I seriously doubt it."

"She was bald, Mom," I tell her. *"Bald."*

"Oh, I remember," she assures me.

"By the way," I tell them, "I met this kid yesterday who went on and on about that monster of yours."

"Did you now?" Dad says in the mirror.

"Yep," I say. "And he said it's real and those who don't believe it just don't know the facts of it."

"Uh-huh," he says, coming to a stop at a red light. "And where did you meet this lad?"

"In town," I say.

"In town where?"

I shrug. "He runs the *Nessie Quest* booth."

Dad laughs. "Ahhh, *a tour boat company on Loch Ness?* I'm sure they don't have financial motives to keep that ridiculous story alive."

Mom turns to face me again. "Honey, it's not true."

"Yeah, well, he sure seemed to think it was real."

Dad grins at me in the mirror. "Did he try to sell you a ticket?"

I shrug. "Maybe."

"Mmm-hmmm," he says, eyeing me in the mirror with a smile. "That's a yes."

Inverness ends up looking a lot like Tennyson, with shops and restaurants lining the streets.

Leakey's Bookshop is on Church Street. It's a redbrick building with five tall windows and a glass door with a gold bell that dings when you open it. *Click.*

But the inside of Leakey's looks more like something out of an epic Disney movie than just a plain old store in the town of Inverness.

There are books everywhere.

And I mean everywhere.

Not just neatly lined on shelves but stacked in haphazard piles everywhere you look. Beautiful old books with leather covers and aging pages in between them and new books with brightly colored jackets. And right in the middle of the shop is a huge potbellied stove burning a bright orange fire inside. There's an iron spiral staircase up to a second open level that wraps around the edge of the walls so that you can see all the way down to the bottom.

The shop is filled with people quietly browsing in the stacks, sipping on hot drinks in dark green paper cups with LEAKEY'S printed on them.

"Whoa," I say. "This is crazy."

Mom puts her arm around my shoulder. "This is one of my very favorite places on earth," she tells me.

"I totally get that," I say, aiming my camera.

Click.

"It's epic," I tell her. "Can I get a book today?"

"Absolutely," she says. "Let's get a few to take back with us."

A shiny bald head with wild gray-haired wings on each side pops up from behind the stacks of books piled high on a wooden desk near the stove.

Uncle Clive.

I'd recognize him anywhere from the holiday pictures they send every year.

"Marmaduke Siles!" he hollers.

I hide a giggle behind my hand at that one and Dad gives me a poke while I watch a squatter, wider, balder version of him make his way over to greet us. Uncle Clive wraps his arms around Dad's waist because the gray wings on his bald head only come up to Dad's chin. Then when he's finished squeezing Dad like a grizzly bear, he squeezes me and Mom too. When he's all done, he takes a step back to get a good look at us.

Uncle Clive looks like the type of bookseller who gets so caught up in all his stacks and stacks of books that he forgets the simple things. Things like whether or not the buttonholes match the buttons correctly on his checkered blue shirt, which they don't, or whether his gray wings need combing down, which they do.

"It's so good to see ye all!" Uncle Clive exclaims with his hands on his hips. "Cor! Lass, have ye grown," he tells me. "I think you're even taller than my Briony. Briony, Isla!" he calls out. "Come here, my darlins, an' say hello to Uncle Marmaduke Siles, Aunt Libby an' Adelaide Ru."

Aunt Isla darts through a door behind the wooden desk and clasps her hands in front of her.

"Oh my giddy aunt!" she gushes. "It's about time we saw ye in person."

Aunt Isla is a very tiny woman, dressed in a smart black turtleneck and matching pants, with graying hair braided and then rolled in a neat bun at the back of her neck.

She rushes over with open arms and big hugs for all of us. "It's brilliant to see ye all. Briony!" she calls toward the back room. "Come an' say hello!"

"You have a lot of books," I tell Uncle Clive. "Don't they all fit in the shelves or something?"

He chuckles.

"You sound just like my Isla." He clasps her hand and gives it a squeeze.

"Aye," she says, nodding. "I've told him a million times."

Uncle Clive glances around the room. "It is a wee bit o' a mess in here, inna it?" he says. "She's always tellin' me I need to organize this place. But I quite like bein' surrounded by books everywhere I look. Like I'm swimmin' in a sea of them. I dinna mind if it's a bit higgledy-piggledy a'times."

Even though he's the very opposite of Dad in many ways, when he smiles, he does it the exact same way as Dad, showing all his straight white teeth.

"I like it this way too," I tell him. "It reminds me of a Disney movie. I think if Belle had her very own bookshop in that French provincial town, it would look exactly like this, and you actually look a lot like her father, Maurice."

His bushy gray eyebrows stand at attention straight up

toward his shiny bald head. "Brilliant!" he exclaims. "Shall I keep it this way, then?"

"Absolutely," I say.

That's when I see my cousin Briony pop her head out of the back room.

"It's aboot time ye made it here," she calls out to us.

She looks just like her pictures. She's skinny like me, but a few inches shorter. Her dark brown hair is like mine, except she didn't cut it in a bob in a bad-idea best-friend pact. Hers is long and in a ponytail that hangs on her back.

"I'm just buzzin' to have ye visit!" she exclaims, curling her arm around mine.

At first glance, she doesn't look like your typical maimer of Barbie dolls. She has a nice smile just like Uncle Clive and Dad have, with straight white teeth. I wonder if I look like Dad when I smile.

"Come on." She pulls me toward the door. "I have to take ye to So Coco for a treat. Ye will absolutely love it; everythin' there is well tidy scran. I promise ye. Mam and Da," she calls to them as we make our way down the stairs. "We're going to So Coco for biscuits."

"Braw!" Uncle Clive says. "Sounds wonderful, my darlin'."

"Is it okay?" I ask Mom.

"Of course," she says. "You two have fun."

After we zip up, we head to whatever So Coco is, and as we scurry down the sidewalk between raindrops, Briony links her arm with mine, chattering on about all the fun we're going to have together this summer. Past yummy-looking cafés and bistros, past colorful gift shops filled with thick, authentic Scottish wool sweaters, touristy T-shirts, red-and-green-plaid towels, socks and even Scottish plaid boxer shorts. The sidewalks are filled with people, even in the rain.

Briony blabs on while I peek in each store window lining Church Street and then High Street when we turn the corner.

"I'm just buzzin' to know you'll be here to spend the entire summer," she is saying. "Just gobsmacked."

"Uh-huh," I say.

"My verra best friend, Evangeline, is travelin' wi' her family so much this summer. That's why it's even more brill to have ye here. Otherwise, I'd be stuck. Havin' no one to hang wi' all summer is a mare indeed."

"A mare?" I ask her.

"Ye know . . . a nightmare. A mare."

"Oh, right," I say.

She still has her arm linked with mine as she chats on.

Then something in the window of the next shop, called Highland Souvenirs and Gifts, catches my eye and I stop dead in my tracks.

"What's all that?" I ask.

The window is filled with green stuffed animals that have long necks and flippers instead of feet. All of them have wide, innocent monster grins.

"Och, that's the *famous* Loch Ness Monster."

"That"—I point to the glass—"is what the thing looks like?"

She rolls her eyes to the sky. "Certainly not," she says, pulling on my arm again. "It's a rubbish story really, just a tourist thing."

The rain is falling harder now, the drops tapping on my hood.

"You mean, you don't believe in it?" I ask her as we hurry on.

She shakes her head. "I'd have to be dafty to think it's true."

"Dafty?"

"Like silly . . . ye know, an idjit or a dunderheid," she tells me. "Most locals know it's not true."

"Most isn't all," I say.

"Well, o' course there are some who are daft enough to believe it. There are groups who scan the loch every year with their high-tech sonar scannin' devices to look for somethin' livin' deep in the waters. It's called the Nessie Race, but no one ever finds anythin' other than a distant photo or blurry image. Truly, if there were somethin' deep in the loch o' the monstrous sort, someone would ha' found it by now. Anyway, there are much more important things to think aboot," she says. "Like do ye have a boyfriend?"

I think about the guitar boy on the heavenly steps.

"Me? No," I say.

"Me either," she tells me. "But I'm quite open to it."

I laugh at that one.

"Have ye ever had a French macaron?" she asks. "So Coco is a scrummy wee café to warm our cold bones wi' tea and a French macaron—chocolate-an'-chili is my absolute favorite. They're well tidy scran. Or there are chocolate truffles that are pure magic if ye like. Just wait until ye taste them."

I stop and turn to face her head-on. "Okay, Briony," I say. "I have another very important question to ask you."

She stops then too and turns to face me.

"Aye?" she asks.

"I get that you don't believe in lake monsters, but do you

believe in one or more of the following?" I tap each on a finger as I list them. "Haunted houses, ghosts, zombies and/or the undead?"

I wait, watching her eyes squint and her lips pinch together in a tight line before she says, "That's quite a different story then, inna it? If ye find yourself in that sort o' company, it's just one wicked mare."

I bob my head up and down inside my hood in a slow nod. "A legit, big-time mare."

10

ORANGE POSSIBILITIES

Okay . . . fine, I'm willing to admit that there's a slim chance that I'm wrong about Euna Begbie being the *actual* spawn of Satan. Annnnd . . . I'm not too proud to admit that she may not be a card-carrying member of the undead either. In fact, it's very possible there's nothing paranormal about her. At least that's where the evidence leads at this point.

Especially in the light of day.

The fact is, it's very possible that she's just a regular woman. *With* two very odd exceptions, which include but are not limited to the following:

Her fashion sense.

And an excessive fondness for the color orange.

Not just on her lips either.

I find this out the very next morning when Mom sends me out to a Wee Spot of Tea and Biscuits for fresh scones and bread and also makes me stop in at Euna Begbie's flat to thank her for the chocolate cookies, which turned out to be way more tasty than devilish.

After I knock on the door marked 166, the towering woman appears in the doorway in her black dress, holding an orange ball of yarn, two knitting needles and one-third of what looks like a blanket.

"Cheers," she says in a voice that's anything but cheery.

"Cheers, Ms. Begbie," I tell her. "Thank you for the yummy cookies that you made for us. They were actually really good."

Euna Begbie smiles an orange SpaghettiOs smile at me.

An actual smile, which makes her way less scary. Not completely, because you never know with the undead.

But the smile definitely helps.

"I'm quite delighted to hear that," she tells me, stepping aside and waving a hand toward the flat. "Please come in."

"Oh, ahhhh . . . *inside?*" I say.

So I know I said that in the light and with the orange smile she was much less scary, but that was from the safety of the hallway.

"Aye," she says, pushing open the flat door a little bit wider.

I picture the headline. WITHOUT A TRACE is how the paper will describe my unfortunate disappearance.

AMERICAN GIRL VANISHES IN SCOTLAND

PARENTS EXPRESS REMORSE FOR NOT
CHOOSING DISNEY WORLD WHEN THEY
HAD THE CHANCE

73

"Please," she says, motioning me in.

I laugh nervously and move a heavy foot forward and then the other, stepping slowly through the doorway. And that's when I see it.

A legit orange obsession.

There is orange everywhere.

No . . . I mean *everywhere*. And in every shade imaginable.

In Jelly Belly terms it'd be like: Sunkist Tangerine, Peach, Cantaloupe, Orange Sherbet, and Chili Mango all at once.

To be honest, Jelly Belly could get some new orange ideas from all the different shades in flat 166. Maybe like: Fort Augustus Sunrise, Buffalo Wing, Nemo Fish, President Trump Cheeks or even Jar of Cheez Whiz.

"Whoa," I tell her. "That's . . . uh, well . . . that's a whole lot of orange is what it is."

She smiles a bit bigger. Not so big that you can see actual teeth, but big enough that it makes her look way less evil. And I wonder why she doesn't do it more often because she'd scare far fewer children if she did.

I watch her sit down on an apricot sofa near a large, arched picture window overlooking the loch. Outside, I can see velvety green hills circling the loch waters. The loch is bustling with activity, with both small and large boats zipping back and forth across.

"Please have a seat." Ms. Begbie motions to an apricot-colored chair.

"Oh, ah . . . thanks," I say, sliding a hesitant cheek onto the very edge.

"Orange reminds me o' the sun risin'," she says, sitting on the couch across the room and going back to her knitting.

"My verra favorite part o' the day. It's the time when I have my orange spiced tea and my orange scones from a Wee Spot o' Tea an' Biscuits and I write in my mornin' journal aboot all the possibilities that day can bring. *Orange possibilities.*"

"Orange ones?" I ask. "Are they different from the regular kind?"

"Och aye," she tells me. "They are a verra special kind and only come up with the sun."

I point to myself. "I have a journal too, Ms. Begbie, but it's more about feelings than possibilities."

"Is that right?"

"Yes," I say. "Maybe I should be adding the orange kind of possibilities too."

She nods and I watch her knitting needles wiggle back and forth as she ties tiny knots together with the sharp ends.

"Wait," I say then. "Like what kinds of possibilities?"

"Like *anythin'*," she says. "Anythin' can happen. That's what makes each day so full. The *possibilities*. Who we will meet. What we will learn. How we will see somethin' in a new way we never even guessed could be."

I nod then. "I think I might know what you mean, Ms. Begbie," I say. "I'm a writer, you know, and I'm searching for my story now. My story and all the supporting characters in it."

"Brilliant!" she exclaims. "Have ye met Hamish Bean Tibby yet?"

"Oh, yeah," I say. "I met him yesterday."

"He's quite a canny wee lad."

"If you mean a *know-it-all*, I agree," I tell her.

She laughs. "He has a lot goin' on in that heid of his," she says. "I think he'd be an excellent addition to your adventure."

"How do you know him?"

"I'm his teacher," she says.

"You teach school *and* manage the university flats at St. Benedict's Abbey at the same time?"

"Nae," she says. "I homeschool him here."

"Oh," I say. "Why doesn't he go to a real school?"

She pauses for a moment and then says, "This has proved to work best for his needs."

I'm not exactly sure what that means, but I don't ask any more.

"Why does he wear that plaid kilt?"

"He's quite proud o' his Gaelic heritage," she says. "And it's also used as the official uniform for many schools in the Highlands."

"He has to wear it while he's being homeschooled?"

"Nae," she says. "It's not required, he just wants to dress like the others. The thing is, he never takes his kilt off, while other children change into street clothes when school is over."

"I'm planning on going to visit him today at his house," I tell her. "He invited me. I guess he knows all about the Loch Ness Monster. And he believes the thing is real too."

She nods. "Did you know that his grandmother, Mamo Honey, is a famous Nessie hunter from the sixties and seventies? She once worked with the esteemed Loch Ness Project."

"She did?" I say.

She nods again.

"Hmm," I say. "In my research, I'm finding that some people believe in that thing down there and some people think it's a silly story. My cousin Briony told me there's some race about it but no one has won it yet."

"Aye." Ms. Begbie nods. "The Nessie Race."

"Is Mamo Honey in the race?"

"Mamo Honey officially quit her search for evidence to prove the existence o' the monster on September sixth, 2011."

"Why? What happened on September sixth, 2011, to make her want to quit?"

Ms. Begbie pauses again and then says, "That's her story to tell, lass. However, I will tell ye this. She never, ever speaks of it, so best not to ask."

"Oh," I say. "But Hammy Bean *is* in the race?"

"Aye, Hammy Bean and Cornelius Barrington, who lives in his camper van lochside past the Fort Augustus beach. He helps on the *Nessie Quest* and is a mate o' Mamo Honey. Corny an' Hammy Bean make a good team."

"How . . . how does he search for Nessie when he can't . . . well, when he doesn't . . . I mean—"

"He can't see," she says.

"Well . . . yeah."

"That would be a wonderful question to ask him on your visit today, lass," she says. "I'm sure he'd love to talk to ye aboot it."

"It's okay to ask? I mean, it won't be rude to ask him about that?"

"If you're curious, it's better to ask him questions than to avoid him because ye dinna understand him," she says.

"Okay," I say. "I'll ask him."

I watch her work her needles. I'm seeing Euna Begbie in a whole new light today. A kind of Fort Augustus Sunrise Orange one.

With lots of possibilities inside it.

And that's exactly how I come to the realization that Euna Begbie isn't the evil villain I first thought she was.

Not even close.

But I sure wish she'd wear something brighter than that black dress of hers and ugly man shoes. Except, I don't know exactly how to tell her without hurting her feelings that she'd look a whole lot better in a pair of orange Nikes and a sweatshirt. So I decide to tell her what I like instead.

"Ms. Begbie," I say.

She looks up from her needles. "Aye, lass?"

"I like it when you smile," I tell her. "It's very . . . very . . . orange."

That's when I see the corners of her lips reach all the way up to her cheekbones, until actual teeth are showing. More than I've ever seen on her before.

See what I mean about words and how important they can be? With just a handful of them, I made that smile. And seeing it now makes me wonder what it was that I thought was so scary about her in the first place.

11

MAKING TRAX WITH DAX

After lunch with Mom in our flat, I head out to find Tibby
Manor.

On my way down the heavenly spiral, I name more of the
things I miss about home with each step.

Mr. Mews's fish breath and sandpaper kisses.

Veggieless pizzas from Parry's.

Watching for cute boys on the sidewalk out front of the
house with Britney B.

"Hey!" a voice snaps. "Watch where you're going, why
don't you!"

I stop dead in my tracks, surprised to see the guitar boy
sitting in the same spot.

"You almost stepped on Ole Roy," he informs me, picking
up the guitar lying next to him on the stairs.

Other than me and him, there isn't a single, solitary person around.

"Ah . . . *who?*" I ask. "Because I only see you." I point to him. "And me." I point to myself.

"Ole Roy," he tells me, putting the guitar in his lap and adjusting the tiny knobs at the end of the handle while picking at the strings. "It's this guy here."

"You . . . *named* your guitar? *Thaaaat's* pretty weird."

"This guitar just happens to be a Gibson Roy Smeck. One of the best guitars money can buy. It took me three whole years to save up my allowance for this thing. It's named after the famous musician Leroy Smeck. One of the best guitarists to ever live on this planet. His nickname was Wizard of the Strings, and you don't get that for nothing."

And then he starts to play. I sit down on the step above him, wrap my arms around my knees and listen. It's the same music from the other day and it seems to float all the way up to the beams lining the tall ceiling of St. Benedict's and maybe all the way to heaven. I bet even the stained-glass faces are listening.

"I'm from America too," I finally say. "I notice you don't have an accent."

He just keeps on playing.

"Your mom or dad teaching at the University of the Highlands and Islands in Inverness like mine?" I ask.

"No," he says. "We rent the same flat in St. Benedict's each summer. We've been coming for the past three years. My mom took this mail-in DNA test and found out she's one-eighth Scottish, so we've been coming here in the summers so she can learn more about our family ancestry."

"We're from Denver," I tell him.

"Manhattan," he says without looking up.

"Oh," I say. "What is it that you're playing? I really like it."

"You probably won't know it," he says.

"Yeah, well, you don't know that," I say. "I know lots of music. I'm the president of the Beyoncé Beyhive Fan Club on Tennyson."

He places a palm flat down on the strings, bringing the music to a quick halt, and looks up at me. "Beyoncé?"

"Yeah," I say. "Have you heard of her?"

He starts strumming again. "Everyone has heard of her," he says. "But that's not the kind of music I'm into."

"Hmm," I say. "Not even 'Single Ladies'? That's my favorite one."

He laughs. "Nope."

"So what kind of music do you like?"

"Have you heard of Taylor?" he asks.

"You mean Swift? Sure, everyone knows her."

He shakes his head at me. "No," he says. "*James* Taylor."

"Mmm . . . maybe," I say. "Does he do that video with the backup dancers who shimmy under the waterfalls?"

"Ah . . . *no*. He would *never* do anything like that."

"Oh."

"Have you heard of Jim Croce? Cat Stevens? Otis Redding? Carole King? Bread?" he lists. "Any of those sound familiar?"

"Bread," I say. "Sure, I've heard of bread. I had mine toasted with cinnamon and sugar this morning," and I let out a loud *HA* just like Dad does.

He just stares at me, unamused.

"Bread . . . is a band," he explains. "The singer/songwriter musicians of the seventies were simple, like with no equipment at all. Just a guy and his guitar. You know, pure."

81

"Or a girl, right?" is all I can think of to say.

"Of course," he says, and then goes back to strumming. "My grandpa Larry played for Carly Simon and toured most of his life with her and her band. He taught me everything he knows."

"That's cool." Maybe he could be one of my supporting characters. Not my Ron or anything, but he's got a brooding hippie vibe going that might work for a minor character. Not to mention the kid is legit cute. I mean, seriously.

He keeps on playing and I keep on listening.

"Do you write and sing your own music too? Like the singers and the songwriters did?" I ask him.

"Just write it and play it," he says. "I don't sing it. Not in front of people, anyway."

"How come?" I ask. "How will people know what you have to say if you don't share it?"

He stops playing again and stares at me with those seaweed eyes. At least that's how I described them in my feelings journal.

"If you don't share it," I ask him, "how do you expect anyone to know what was so important about the songs' words? I mean, the musicians chose specific words to put together and you like the ones they chose, right? You should probably share yours too."

He keeps staring like maybe he's really thinking hard about what I said.

"So . . . ah, y-yeah," I stutter, getting up from the step. "I'd like to hear more about what your words mean and all, but I have to get going. I'm meeting someone."

"Who?" he asks.

"This kid I met up at the dock."

"What kid?"

"Well, honestly, I can't remember his real name, but it's something like Ham and Bean Casserole, and also . . . he has this red dog . . . and he works the *Nessie Quest* booth and is kind of a know-it-all, if you ask me."

"Oh, yeah, I know that kid. But I'm pretty sure his name isn't *Casserole*," he mocks me.

"You want to make a bet? It's the closest name to a casserole of anything I've ever heard before. Did you ever think that maybe his parents were just fond of casseroles?"

He blinks his seaweeds at me and says, "No."

"It's possible," I say.

"I really don't think so."

"But you know him, though, right? I mean, you've talked to him?" I ask.

"Not exactly."

"You come here every summer and you've never talked to the kid?"

He shrugs. "Nope."

"Haven't you ever gone on one of those *Nessie Quest* tours?"

He starts strumming again. "N.I.," he says.

I give him a Cheez Whiz. "What?"

"Not interested," he tells me.

"So you don't believe in the monster?"

He shrugs again.

"So what *do* you do when you come here?"

"You're looking at it."

"You just strum your guitar all summer long?"

He stops again and looks up at me. "I go to a private school in New York City and my parents made me a deal that I can have my summers off for my music if I get straight As in school during the year. So all I do in the summer is write music, play guitar and record. I have my own YouTube channel with almost five thousand followers. It's called Making Trax with Dax."

"That's really cool," I say. "Five thousand is a lot. That sort of makes you famous."

He shrugs.

"I don't have a YouTube channel, but I have my very own podcast."

"Really? How many subscribers you got?"

"Oh, ah . . . you know, I'm not really sure of the latest numbers. I can't even remember the last time I looked, but yeah . . . it's a lot, you know, I mean, people are listening."

"Right on," he says, nodding and giving me a one-lipped smile that is definitely going to make it into my feelings journal.

"So do you happen to know where Bunioch Brae is?" I ask him. "That's where this kid's house is. On Bunioch Brae."

He juts his chin toward the window. "It's up on that side of the mountain. I can show you if you want."

"Oh, ah . . . yeah, I mean, that'd be okay," I say.

"Groovy," he says. He slides the worn leather guitar strap over his head and twists the guitar around so that it lies flat across his back, and starts down the hallway.

I scurry after him, catching up at the TOILET door and pointing to the guitar bouncing against his back. "You're bringing that thing?"

His legs are much longer than mine, so for every one of his steps I have to take three, which means I'm basically jogging next to him.

"Everywhere I go, Ole Roy goes," he informs me.

"Well, I suppose Ham and Bean won't mind if Ole Roy visits too," I say.

He looks at me funny then. "I may not know the kid, but I can tell you for a fact that Ham and Bean is not his name."

"Wanna bet?" I challenge.

"Yeah," he says.

"Fine by me. I'll bet you a million dollars there's a casserole in there somewhere."

On our way to find the house with the red door, I learn that Dax is one year older than me. He's thirteen and going into eighth grade at some fancy private school in Manhattan where he wears a blue suit jacket with an eagle's crest every single day and never has gym because they don't have a gymnasium.

It makes me wish I could go to a fancy private school in Manhattan.

I loathe gym and everything it stands for.

He also tells me that he lives in a penthouse apartment off Central Park, which is like a regular apartment only way bigger. He's an only child like me and lives with his mom, Lucy, and his stepdad, Gary, but spends more time with his live-in nanny named Luna Santa-Maria than his parents, who are always working or at a cocktail party. He has a golden retriever named Taco who is keeping his grandma Betty company in Queens while he's in Fort Augustus for the summer.

I also find out Mr. and Mrs. Cady drive a fancy BMW, because Dax waves to them when we see them pulling out of the abbey drive on our way to find the house on Bunioch Brae.

"It's right there." Dax juts his chin in the air. "Red door, right?"

I look up at a gray stone house with a small rectangular window above a bright red door with TIBBY MANOR etched in curly letters.

"That's it," I say.

To the side of the house is a matching stone shed, the size of a garage, with two ancient wooden doors shut tight, their ancient iron handles wrapped with a heavy chain and padlock.

"What do you think they need to keep locked up so tight?" Dax just shrugs.

"Go and peek," I tell him.

"I'm not going to peek in their garage," he informs me, and then points to a tiny brass knob next to the red door. "Ring the bell."

I push it and nothing happens.

I stare at him. "It's broken."

"It's an old-fashioned doorbell. You pull it," he instructs me.

I grab the knob between my pointer finger and thumb and pull. Somewhere inside, a bell rings and a dog barks.

I pull it again.

Ring.

Bark. Bark. Bark.

And then again.

Ring.

Bark. Bark. Bark.

"That's the weirdest doorbell I've ever seen," I tell him.

"Maybe you should pull it again," he tells me.

So I do.

Ring.

Bark. Bark. Bark.

"I was kidding," he says.

"Oh," I say. "It's just so weird. Who knew they had door-bells like this in the olden days?"

Flat, barefoot-sounding footsteps slap the floorboards inside and the red door flings open.

It's Ham and Bean in the same outfit he wore the other day—plaid kilt, Nessie T-shirt and knee-high socks—minus one too-big captain's hat and slick, shiny cane. With his curly-haired dog.

"Who keeps ringin' that bell?" he demands while Mac-Talla gives us the once-over. "Have ye no doorbell etiquette at all? Possibly you're from a doorbell-less planet such as Mars?"

"*No,*" I snap. "Denver."

A slow, deep-dimpled smile spreads across his face. "Ahhh, right. *Denver,*" he says. "It appears that ye have found some tidbits after all. Brilliant."

"I told you they were never lost, didn't I?"

Dax looks at me, scratching Mac-Talla on both ears. "You found some *what?*"

I wave my hand as if to erase the word from the air between us. "Never mind," I tell him.

He just raises his eyebrows and says nothing.

"It's her courage," the boy informs him. "Unfortunately, she's missing a good-sized helpin' o' it."

Dax's head starts bobbing up and down. "Yep, I can see that."

"Hey," I say, putting my hands on my hips.

"I told her to stop pulling on that bell, but she insisted," Dax tells him, turning to me with a wide smile, his teeth clenched together.

I watch Ham and Bean scanning the space in between us, searching for the exact location of Dax's voice. "Who are ye?" he asks.

"I'm . . . um, Dax," he says. "Dax Cady. Our family rents a flat at St. Benedict's Abbey in the summers."

"Hamish Bean Tibby," Hammy Bean says. "But all my mates call me Hammy Bean."

"I told you!" I say to Dax. "I said Ham and Bean and I was right. That'll be one million dollars, please."

Dax just rolls his eyes and holds out a hand to shake Hammy Bean's, but Hammy Bean doesn't shake it.

"Ah . . . he's holding out his, ah, hand there," I tell Hammy Bean. "To shake yours."

"Oh." Hammy Bean holds out his hand, and Dax grabs it.

"Are ye Denver's brother?" Hammy Bean asks, excitedly pumping Dax's hand like it's his first time.

"No," Dax says. "We just met three days ago."

"He wanted to come along and meet you," I tell Hammy Bean. "He plays the guitar—and he brings it everywhere."

"Brilliant," Hammy Bean says. "I love music. Both of ye,

please come in." He opens the door even wider. "Do ye play the bagpipes too?"

"Ah, no," Dax says. "Just the strings."

Me and Dax step inside the front hall of the ancient house. Above us a grand chandelier hangs with a million tiny bulbs. Dark floral wallpaper and etched wood paneling cover the walls around us, and wide wooden boards creak and groan under our feet.

"Hammy Bean," someone calls from the depths of the manor.

"Aye," the boy replies.

"Who's at the door, love?"

"My new mates." Hammy Bean smiles.

Then from around the corner the woman with the wild red curls appears. Hanging from around her neck and tied tight around her middle is a long apron with a giant cartoon Nessie on the front.

"Oh, michty me!" she exclaims, clasping her hands and marveling at us like she's never seen children before.

"I'm Mamo Honey," she booms with excitement. "Welcome to Tibby Manor. Come on in for a bosie," she says, pulling us in for a warm hug and squishing me and Dax together.

She smells like a mix of peppermint and flowery perfume.

"She's here to learn more about Nessie and she brought a friend with a guitar," Hammy Bean announces.

"Brilliant!" Mamo Honey says. "I just put a batch of tea-cakes in the oven."

"Mrs. Tibby?" I say. "Euna Begbie told me that you were once one of Scotland's most famous Nessie investigators."

"Please call me Mamo Honey, and aye, I was a foundin' partner o' the Loch Ness Project in 1972," she informs us. "We were pioneers in gatherin' some o' the very first documented evidence."

"But you don't do it anymore?" I ask.

"Nae" is all she says.

"Mrs. T, is this you?" Dax asks, squinting at one of the large black-and-white framed photographs lining the hall.

"Och, aye," she says. "'Tis."

I stand next to Dax and gaze at the picture. It's of a much younger and way thinner Mamo Honey on top of a VW van, posing next to a long telescope pointed right at the water.

A bell tings in the kitchen.

"Gads." Mamo Honey jumps and scurries off down the hall. "I have to check on my teacakes. Tatty bye for now," she calls over her shoulder.

I stare up at the next photograph.

Mamo Honey is posing with the other members of the group at the edge of the water, all of them dressed in the same gray sweatshirts with THE LOCH NESS PROJECT INVESTIGATION TEAM on the fronts in large black letters.

"So do your mom and dad live here too?" I ask Hammy Bean.

He hesitates. "Nae, they don't live wi' us," he says. "They're both doctors an' work for Doctors Without Borders. They're too busy savin' lives around the world to live in this small town. But they visit when they miss me. Which is a lot o' the time."

Doctors?

I want to ask him how actual royalty has the time to do

all that and still be royal, but I don't. "Hurry now," he calls, rolling his double *r* and running down the hall. "I'll show ye some stuff."

We watch Hammy Bean find his way to the staircase by running one hand along the wall and keeping the other outstretched in front of him. I follow him and Dax follows me, but I stop when the very last framed picture catches my eye. It's a dark figure with a very long neck sticking out of the water and an even longer body clearly seen just under the waves.

"Wait. What is that?" I ask.

Hammy Bean turns back to me at the bottom of the long wooden staircase. The centers of the steps are covered with a red-flowered runner. He reaches a hand out, feeling for the banister, and grabs it. "Which one?" he asks.

"The very last one," I tell him.

"That's . . . Nessie," he says.

I gasp. "The *monster*?"

"That is so super groovy," Dax says under his breath.

"Mamo Honey took that picture in 1974 oot at the village o' Dores Beach."

"Man," I say, examining the picture. "She must be super famous for that, huh?"

"If famous means everyone who's anyone kens who she is, then aye, she's famous," Hammy Bean tells me. "But ye need more than just a picture for definitive proof."

"Like go-to-the-store-in-a-limo-to-buy-her-bananas famous?"

He gives me a funny look. "She walks to the store wi' her shopping cart."

"Hmm," I say. "I guess it's only J. K. Rowling who does that."

"J. K. Rowling goes to the store in a limo?" he asks.

"I'm pretty sure," I tell him.

"Well, come on," he calls over his shoulder, starting up the steps. "You came to learn some facts, didn't ye? After today, I bet ye will never, ever doubt the existence of our monster again."

12

A FORCE TO BE RECKONED WITH

In the attic of Tibby Manor is a small room with a large tri-angular window looking out on Loch Ness. In the window is a long telescope, which looks like the very same one Mamo Honey posed with in the photo in the hall.

The room is filled with more old photographs of Mamo Honey's investigations and one gigantic and very ancient wooden desk. Hammy Bean sits down on a tall leather office chair behind it.

"This is my official office," he says with his chin in the air, spinning the chair in a circle.

"It's *yours* yours?" I ask. "I mean, all of it? Just for you?"

"Well, it used to be my Mamo Honey's, but it's mine now."

"What do you need an office for?" I ask him.

He stops the spinning and places his fingers on the keys of a laptop on the desk in front of him. "So good o' ye to ask, mate," he says. "You are talkin' to the editor in chief of the *Nessie Juggernaut*, thank ye very much."

I blink at him for a few more seconds and then say, "Is it okay if I ask you some things about not being able to see? I mean, Euna Begbie said if I have questions—"

"O' course," he says. "Ask away."

"Okay," I say. "Sooooo . . . how do you use a computer? I mean, how do you know what's on the screen?"

"Great question!" he exclaims. "Let me show ye."

I watch him tap on the keyboard. While he does, the computer shouts every single thing that's on the screen. Hammy Bean goes so fast that the voice can hardly keep up with him.

"That's so cool," Dax says.

"My computer can say *words* for when I'm readin' and letters for when I'm typin'. I have an online computer teacher from Glasgow named Jonjo who taught me everythin' I know. There's actually a lot o' technology oot there that helps people who are blind to do lots o' different things." He pulls out a flat electronic thing that's about the length of a ruler and only a little bit wider.

"I can load books onto this wee computer an' read them in Braille."

"But there's no screen on it," I tell him.

"Watch this," he says, pushing some buttons.

I watch as a Braille sentence miraculously pops up on the part that runs along the bottom of the computer while he runs his pointer finger over it.

"I brush over the sentence wi' my finger to read it, an' when I'm done wi' that one, the next sentence pops up an' then the next one an' the next one. This allows me to read my books completely in Braille if I don't want to listen to the audio version. I've read every one of the Harry Potters on this."

"I love Harry Potter," I tell him. "So then you know Braille too?"

"Absolutely."

"Maybe you could teach me sometime?"

He smiles with the deepest dimples I've ever seen on the kid. "I would love to teach ye!" he exclaims.

"Cool. So what the heck is a *juggernaut*?" I ask, squinting through the tarnished gold telescope.

Down below I can see the same three old men still lined up on the bench with binoculars aimed at the black chopping waters of the loch.

Hammy Bean stands up behind the desk and clears his throat like he's getting ready to give a speech. "The true definition o' *juggernaut* is *a force to be reckoned wi'*," he says. "It's like the *Inverness Courier* or the *Daily Record*. Except it's a juggernaut, not a courier or a record. It's a force to be reckoned with. Understand?"

"Yeah, but what is it . . . *exactly*?"

"The official Nessie newsletter of the Highlands," he announces proudly, feeling on top of the desk for a pile of papers, grabbing the first two, then holding them out for me.

I take them from his hand. "What's this?"

"My newsletter," he says proudly.

THE NESSIE JUGGERNAUT

Created By: Hamish Bean Tibby, Editor in Chief

"Why a newsletter?" I ask.

"What do ye mean?"

"I mean if you're so good at technology, why don't you do

95

something electronic like a blog or a zine or a podcast to get your message out there? You can reach way more people that way. Even Dax has his own YouTube channel, and he's got like a billion followers."

Hammy Bean sits down again, puts his chin in his hand and sighs. "A billion? Really?"

"Five thousand," Dax says.

"Same difference," I say. "I mean, how many followers could you possibly have for a newsletter?"

Hammy Bean shakes his head and throws out his hands. "I'm missin' oot on my billions," he agrees. "But there's a lot o' people who read my newsletter too. Maybe I could do both."

"Yeah." I shrug. "But just think of how many more you could reach with a podcast."

"What *is* a podcast?" he asks. "How does it work?"

"It's like your very own radio program, but not on the air-waves, they're on . . . you know, podcast waves. My mom set up mine and I bet you she'd do it for you too. She did most of the work to get it up and running, but now I do almost every-thing myself, even the editing. I can show you that part once she creates it. Plus, I could help with writing because . . . I'm a writer, you know."

Hammy Bean sits straight up in his chair. "Ye are?"

"I've only been writing since I was *born*," I tell him.

"I'm hirin' a new *Juggernaut* employee to help me. Well, more like a reporter/secret agent type."

I blink at him. "Are you kidding me right now?"

"I need someone to interview the other members o' the Nessie Race to get some good intel from their teams to include in my newsletter."

"And I could also write the copy for the podcast shows?" I ask.

He nods in agreement. "But I'm the on-air talent," he says.

"Deal!" I tell him.

"Brilliant!" he says. "Oh, and one more thing."

I watch his fingers feeling for the drawer handle on the right side of the desk and then digging through a messy drawer.

"So who would be your ultimate-of-ultimate interviewees for, like, your very first official podcast?" I ask him while he digs. "I mean if you could ask anyone. Living or dead."

He stops digging and faces me again. "Anyone?"

"Yep."

"I dinna have to think aboot that," he says. "It would be the one an' only Tobin Sky, PhD."

"Never heard of him," I say. "Dax?"

Dax has found a worn leather chair in the corner and is plucking the strings on Ole Roy. "Professor Sky is only the greatest cryptozoologist of our time."

"The greatest *what*?" I ask.

"Cryptozoologist. It's a scientist who studies hidden animals that have yet to be discovered."

"Oh, right, like the Loch Ness Monster."

"Right," he says. "Although his specialty is Gigantopithecus, the giant ape—"

"Oh, you mean Bigfoot? I know all about him."

Hammy Bean sits straight up in his chair. "You've had a Bigfoot experience?"

"Well, not exactly, but the elusive Bigfoot is quite a popular legend in Denver because of all the mountains."

"Tobin Sky has seen one, an' he got it on film too. He an' his partner, Dr. Lemonade Liberty Witt. Tobin Sky came to the university in Inverness to speak once and Mamo Honey and I went to see him. He's amazin'. I want to be just like him when I grow up."

"If he's someone you want for your podcast, then we should make it happen," I say.

"Why would someone like that want to be interviewed by me?" he asks.

"Are you kidding? Once you have a podcast and some followers and you're famous, it will be a whole other ball game. And get this, maybe Dax could write and play an intro for you."

Dax's head pops up that time. "I would totally do that," he says.

I knew he was listening.

"I could make you a totally groovy intro on Ole Roy here," Dax tells Hammy Bean.

"Ye *named* yer guitar?" Hammy Bean asks.

I point to myself. "That's what *I* said."

"Here, check this out," Dax says.

We listen as he starts to strum, bobbing his head as he's searching for the words.

"*Nessie Jug ie bah, dah, tah. With Hammy Bean as your host. Come with us as we explore. The Loch Ness Monster off the shore.* . . . Hmmm," he says, looking up at us with an unsure one-lipped smile and . . . those eyes.

The seaweed-green ones that do something very strange to both my insides *and* my outsides.

"That's actually just off the top of my head," Dax says. "I'll . . . keep working on it."

"You want me to come up with the word part?" I ask him. "I can do it if you want me to."

"*No,*" he snaps. "I told you I write my own songs."

"Yeah, but I'm really good with words too. Check this out. *Hammy Bean's phat, with his Crypto Chat—*"

"I said *no,*" Dax says again. "I can do it."

"Fine," I say. "But I still get to be a reporter, right?" I ask Hammy Bean.

"Reporter/secret agent," he corrects me.

"Yeah, right," I say.

"To work for the *Jug,* ye have to be a force to be reckoned with. Are ye sure ye can be a force?"

"I can totally be a force," I assure him.

"You're hired!" he announces, grinning so big it shows his deep dimples again. "First things first. All *Nessie Juggernaut* reporters need a radio."

"How many reporters/secret agents have you had?"

"Technically . . . you're the first," he says, digging through the desk drawer again and then handing me a gray camou-flage walkie-talkie that's so small, it fits right in the palm of my hand.

"Whoa," I say. "This is cool."

"It's not *cool,*" he informs me. "It's a high-tech device used for the purposes o' any and all top-secret *Jug* communica-tions."

"It looks like a toy."

"Well, it's not," he insists. "I told ye, it's a high-tech device."

I look it over. "Where did you get it?"

"They were two for one at Smyth's Toy Superstore in Inverness," he says. "But it's still high-tech. Now listen carefully because this is imperative. Are ye listenin'?"

"I'm listening."

"Whatever ye do . . . never . . . *ever* . . . I mean, *absolutely* never . . . use any channel other than five. Do ye understand?"

I wave it in Dax's direction. "Only official reporters/secret agents get this," I say with a wide grin.

He doesn't even care because he's already trying to find just the right tune for Hammy Bean's intro.

"Denver, this is important," Hammy Bean says.

"Yeah, I got it," I say. "Channel five. Why?"

He leans in close this time and whispers three words: "*Nessie Race spies.*"

I blink at him. "Did you say . . . *Nessie Race spies?*"

"Aye," he says. "The Nessie Race is highly competitive in the Scottish Highlands. *Highly* competitive. Includin' us, there are three other groups determined to be the first to make a major discovery in Fort Augustus alone. And they will do anythin' to make it happen . . . even *spy.* That's the real reason I havena hired anyone local. I dinna need any double agents at the *Jug.*"

"Right," I say. "So five and only five. Got it. What else?"

"On air, we only talk in code. Never, ever reveal top-secret intel over the airwaves unless it's in code. Understand?"

"Like what kind of code?"

"It's specially designed code that you'll need to learn. I'll email a chart for ye to memorize. That's verra important."

"Got it," I say.

"I mean, super-duper important."

"I heard you. I'll memorize them."

"And never, I mean never . . . *ever* turn the radio off," he instructs me. "This is critical. The radio must be monitored day and night for any and all official *Nessie Juggernaut* business. Do ye understand?"

"Yep." I nod.

"Also, we must only use handles on the radio, kind o' like nicknames, so people dinna ken it's really us. Never, ever call me by my real name."

"Okay," I say. "What do I call you?"

"My handle is Captain Green Bean," he informs me. "And yours will be Denver."

"Got it," I say. "So what's my first assignment, boss?"

"I'm glad ye asked." He scooches his official office chair closer to the desk. "The town clishmaclaver is that the Loch Watchers had a sightin' three days ago," he tells me. "I would like ye to interview them an' find out what they saw an' get as much information as ye possibly can."

"Who are they?"

"One o' the competin' teams in the Nessie Race."

"Where do I find them?"

"They sit at the edge o' the loch every day, watchin' for the monster."

I glance out the window toward the water. "You mean those three old guys with the binoculars on the bench next to the beach?"

"That's right."

"Why don't *you* just do it?"

"Are ye gonna accept yer first assignment or aren't ye?"

"I'm on it," I say. "What are their names?"

"Right, ye need to find that oot too," he tells me, pulling a small yellow pad and a ballpoint pen out of the desk drawer and handing them to me. "All I have is their aliases."

"You mean their handles? Like on the radio?" I say.

He smirks. "Not exactly—these are names Cornelius and I have come up wi' on our own, based on their, ye know . . . *individual traits.*"

"Oh, I've heard of Cornelius," I say. "Euna Begbie said he lives out past the beach in his camper van."

"He's one o' ours," Hammy Bean says. "He gave up his whole life in London twenty years ago just to move to the Highlands and find the monster. Ye'll meet him soon enough."

"Okay, so what are the aliases of the old guys?"

"Cornelius says they always sit in the same exact order, so it goes like this, in order of appearance." He counts them on his fingers, thumb first. "Number one is Lord Grunter."

I scribble the name on my pad.

"Second in line is the Duke of Buttcrack," he says. "For obvious reasons."

I snicker at that one and scribble it down.

"And the last one?" he says. "Ready for it?"

My pen is poised.

"Ready," I say.

"Sir Farts-When-He-Laughs."

13

FAMOUS FISH AND FURRY TUNA

I *detest* tuna casserole.

It's vile on all levels.

Especially when Mom forgets to crumble the potato chips on top of it, because the potato chip pieces are its only redeeming quality.

But don't tell her I said so.

What I never would have guessed in a million years when Mom takes me to lunch the next day at Farquhar's Famous Fish House in town is that Tuna Tetrazzini would become one of my new favorite things about Scotland. That's because the Scotland kind of Tuna Tetrazzini doesn't come from a can with a mermaid on it. And there isn't a single pea in sight.

This Tuna Tetrazzini is a *cat*.

I meet her for the very first time at Farquhar's Famous Fish House. She's curled up on the counter next to the cash register and purrs when I scratch her on top of her head. I find out from Mr. Farquhar that Tuna Tetrazzini doesn't belong to the Farquhar family, or anyone else in Fort Augustus, for that matter. Technically she belongs to the whole town and it's everyone's job to love and care for her.

And they do too.

Next to Mr. Mews, she's the sweetest cat ever, with a white-and-black mustache, and she purrs when you pet her on her belly as well as when you scratch her head. She also seems to take a special liking to me, because when she wakes up from her counter nap, she jumps down and rubs her side along my leg over and over. She probably senses that I'm a cat person and maybe even how much I miss Mr. Mews.

Cats are sensitive that way.

"Take a look at the menu," Mr. Farquhar says, standing in front of the register and waving a hand at the large blackboard stuck to the wall behind him.

On the board is a long list of fish basket choices neatly printed in white chalk. Mr. Farquhar is about as tall as Dad, with a whole lot more in the middle. Mr. Farquhar has a scraggly beard with more gray than black, and he's wearing a white grease-spotted apron that's more grease than white.

"Ooh, can I have pudding for dessert?" I ask Mom, pointing to the board, where there is a list of different flavors. "It looks like they have three different kinds. Red, black, and white. That's probably Scottish for chocolate, vanilla, and . . . maybe red velvet or strawberry."

Mr. Farquhar chuckles and when he does it, his belly dances up and down under the apron.

"Lass, that type o' puddin' refers to a Scottish meat dish. Black puddin' is blood sausage wi'—"

I don't get all of what he's saying because I'm too busy swallowing down a gag from the first part to hear the second.

"No thank you on the bloody pudding, Mr. Farquhar. In Denver, we don't put bloody meat in our pudding."

Mr. Farquhar chuckles and his belly bobs. "Nae?"

"Never," I say. "Just sweet things like chocolate or vanilla or butterscotch. Never meat. Never, *never* meat. So if you don't have the sweet kind of pudding, I'll just stick with your famous fish. Wait . . . you don't make your fish with bloody meat stuffed inside it, do you?"

He chuckles again. "Nae, lass, it's nothin' but a fish wi' a battered topping."

Mom holds up two fingers. "We'll take two orders of fish and chips, please," she tells him. "Extra tartar sauce."

After Mom pays, we find a tall table with red stools right by the front window. I get busy telling Mom all about my new position while she makes out a grocery list for our next stop at Ness for Less.

"He even made me an actual reporter," I tell her, rubbing Tuna Tetrazzini's belly while she purrs in a ball on my lap. "Well, reporter/secret agent, whatever that means. His newsletter is called the *Nessie Juggernaut*. I told him he needed to update his whole operation if he wants to be relevant. You know, like adding a podcast. Do you think you could help him set up his own podcast the way you did for me?"

"Of course," she says, writing the word *mayo* on her list.

"And . . . Dax is busy making a musical intro for the podcast. He's the boy who was playing guitar on the steps when we first moved into the abbey. I'm thinking I'll ask him to do one for *Words with Ru* too," I go on. "I'll wait and see what he comes up with for Hammy Bean first. But it'd be cool to add a musical intro. Don't you think, Mom?"

She smiles. "Sounds good. By the way, I saw Euna Begbie on my way out today and she was telling me about these Brie and bacon sandwiches that are popular here. How does that sound for lunches this week?"

I shrug. "Fine," I say. "But I'll have mine with the crust cut off, Velveeta instead of Brie, hold the bacon."

Mom blinks at me. "That's just a plain old cheese sandwich."

"Brill." I give her a thumbs-up.

"*Brill?*"

"That's what Briony says for *brilliant*," I inform her. "Brill." She smiles and goes back to her list.

"And you want to know what else?" I go on. "Today, for my first assignment, Hammy Bean told me to interview the Loch Watchers. They're another team that's part of this thing called the Nessie Race. That's the unofficial contest to be the first to get the best evidence to prove the existence of the monster."

Mom looks up again. "What about some more scones from a Wee Spot of Tea for breakfasts?"

"Sure," I say. "I like the orange ones, and look at this too." I take my new walkie-talkie off my belt loop to show her. "It has a four-and-a-half-mile radius and we can only talk in code because of"—I look to the right and then the left—"*Nessie Race spies.*" I whisper the last three words.

She smiles at me and then exclaims, "Oh!" as she scribbles down *3 onions* on the list.

The radio beeps in my hand and Hammy Bean's voice comes out of the speaker.

"Captain Green Bean to Denver? Come in, Denver? Do ye read me? Over."

"See?" I say, pointing to the radio. "That's my official handle. I have to get this. You know, official *Jug* business and all."

She nods and grins. "I completely understand," she says, going back to her list.

I push the button on the side just like Hammy Bean showed me. "Denver here," I say.

Silence.

I push it again. "*Hello?* Is anyone there?"

Hammy Bean's voice comes out of the speaker. "Ye have to say *over* when you're done talkin' or I willna ken you're done. Get it? Over."

"Oh, right," I say. "*Over.*"

"I'm just checking in to make sure you're listenin' in case some real important Nessie business happens that I need ye to report on. Over."

"Well, I am," I assure him. "Over."

"I just emailed you the official walkie-talkie spy-prevention codes for any and all communication starting immediately," he informs me. "Learn them. Live them. Be them. Over."

I look at Mom. "The kid's a little intense about all this Nessie Race business," I tell her.

"Clearly," she says.

"That's a ten-four," I call into the radio.

"Ye forgot to say *over.* Over."

"Sorry," I say. *"Over."*

"I will be expectin' a debriefin' on the Three Bears once ye've obtained the intel. Captain Green Bean is over and out," he says.

"Ah . . . okay, Denver is over and out."

I clip the radio carefully back onto my belt.

Mom's just grinning at me and flicking her pencil in the air back and forth between her thumb and pointer finger.

"What?" I say.

"I knew you would rise to my challenge," she tells me.

"Don't get crazy or anything," I tell her. "I'm still homesick as all get-out. And Britney B texted me that she saw Delilah Morgenstern trying to walk Mr. Mews down Tennyson on a leash."

"I still love seeing you're enjoying yourself here, making friends and learning something new about the area."

"Mr. Mews was on a *leash*, Mom. A *leash*."

"I'm sure Mr. Mews will rise to his challenge too," she tells me.

"Here we are, ladies," Mr. Farquhar says, carrying two plastic baskets lined with red-checkered paper and filled to the brim with fish sticks and thick potato fries. "Two orders o' Farquhar's famous fish an' chips. Cheers."

"Mr. Farquhar?" I ask him, taking a giant bite of a chip, which is really just a flat French fry. "What makes your fish so famous?"

"Ahhh." He places his pointer finger against his nose. "There's a secret seasonin' combination in the batter, and o' course the top-secret homemade tartar sauce," he tells me, winking at Mom. "A family recipe handed down from my great-great-great-granddad Colonel Ian Stewart, a fisherman in the North Sea for a right many years."

"That's a lot of *greats*," I say, taking a bite of famous fish.

"It certainly is," he agrees, watching me chew my first bite, covered in a generous helping of homemade tartar sauce. "How is it?"

I swallow. "I can *definitely* see why you're famous."

I take another bite of famous fish slathered in tartar sauce. "Mr. Farquhar," I say. "Do you believe in the Loch Ness Monster?"

"Aye, of course, lassie."

I look at Mom. "See?" I say.

She just smiles and nods.

"As you may or may not already know, I've just been named official reporter for the *Nessie Juggernaut*, which will be expanded into an upcoming podcast, available for download where you get your podcasts. It is now my job to do interviews on eyewitness accounts and other relevant Nessie things. Would you be interested in being interviewed for the program? On the record, of course."

"Nae, I wasna aware o' your new position." He pulls out a red stool from under the table and slides himself onto it. "But I would be delighted to oblige. The name is Fergus Farquhar. F-E-R-G-U-S."

"Okay, hold on," I tell him, pulling my iPhone out of the back pocket of my jeans. "Please speak clearly into the speaker."

He starts again. "The name is Fergus Farquhar," he says.

"Thank you, sir. And just so we know your level of knowledge on the subject, could you answer some questions for us?"

"Aye."

"Have you seen the monster with your own eyes?"

"Back in 2012 I was out sweepin' the front walk near the canal side." He juts a chin toward the front of the store. "In the water, oot front here, somethin' caught my eye."

"There?" I point. "Right in front of the shop past the sidewalk?"

"Aye," he says. "I canna say wi' certainty what it was. But when I got closer an' took a keek at it, I saw somethin' under the water that was longer than the Tibbys' *Nessie Quest* boat an' Jasper Price's *Monster Chaser* put together. The thing splashed about and stirred up the loch just under the surface. Like it was stuck in the canal an' tryin' to get back oot to the main part o' the loch."

I swallow. "And you think it was one of . . . *them*?"

"I dinna ken what it was, lass, but that's the mystery then, isn't it? Everyone is seekin' an answer to determine what people ha' been seein' all these years. And that's no wee feat. This loch contains more fresh water than *all* the lochs in England an' Wales combined. The monster could be anythin', and there are certainly a lot o' differin' opinions aboot it."

"Like what?" I ask.

"No one kens for sure," he says. "And all those who participate in the Nessie Race believe somethin' different."

"You mean, like if someone spotted a Bigfoot or a Kraken or even an extraterrestrial, we know exactly what they *are*, but this thing could be a lot of different possibilities?"

"Aye. Take that bloke there, Jasper Price?" He points to a man polishing the brass rails on the green speedboat bobbing in the water. "He runs the *Monster Chaser* daily tours, an' he dinna ha' a doubt it's an actual plesiosaur."

"Is Jasper Price a part of the Nessie Race too?"

"Aye, he is," Mr. Farquhar says. "An' see those blokes there?"

He points to the three old men with binoculars lined up on the bench by the beach.

"The Loch Watchers," I say. "They're my very first assignment."

"Those right numpties each have a different theory o' what is in the deep waters of the loch. They sit by the water all day every day wi' their binoculars and argue about who's right."

"What do they believe it is?" I ask.

"I'm sure they'll blether on to ye all aboot it in yer interview."

"It sure sounds like the Nessie Race is some serious business around here," I say.

He nods. "Aye, indeed. And those are just our local competitors. There are many others from different countries, even scientists who have come here all the way from America. There's one chap, a French artist, Dureau Bouvier, who wraps his boat in black plastic an' sails through the waters o' Loch Ness once a year, beatin' on a large drum on the highest deck o' his ship, callin' out to Nessie to come to the surface for a blessin'."

I chew on the end of one of my fish sticks and then swallow. "So, Mr. Farquhar, what do *you* think is living in these waters?" I ask him.

"It's not the most interestin' opinion, I'm afraid."

"That's okay," I tell him.

"I think it's nothing but a sturgeon," he tells me.

"Is that another kind of whale?" I ask.

"Nae, lass. It's a fish."

"A *fish*?" I say. "Just a plain old fish?"

"Aye, it's one that can grow to many meters in length, and in a loch this size, hidden in deep waters for all these years, that sturgeon could be the largest in history if someone ever caught it."

"Are sturgeons supposed to be extinct, like dinosaurs?"

"Nae."

"So . . . really just a regular old boring fish?" I ask.

He nods. "I told ye it wasna the most interestin' opinion."

"You're right about that," I mumble. I consider this and take another bite of famous fish.

PAGE ONE

It all started with just a regular old boring fish.

Dullsville supreme.

"What does Hammy Bean's team think it is?" I ask Mr. Farquhar.

He gives me a full-on Cheez Whiz. "What do you mean, lass?"

"Hammy Bean," I say again.

"Honey Tibby's lad?"

"That's right."

"Well, that wee lad is not exactly considered part o' the Nessie Race for discovery," he tells me.

I look at Mom, then back at Mr. Farquhar. "Why not?"

"This is a serious race wi' serious scientists and investigators, and I reckon a few dunderheids to make it interestin'." He gives me a wink. "But nevertheless, dinna ye doubt that there is a serious search for real evidence happenin' in this loch."

"But Hammy Bean is as serious as you get," I tell him. "*Believe me.* To the point of being fairly obnoxious about it, if you ask me. He probably knows more about what's living in this loch than anybody besides maybe Mamo Honey, and that's only because she was a famous investigator at one time."

"Well . . ." Mr. Farquhar pauses. "Honey Tibby gave up her investigations long ago, so no one really considers her a part of the race either. She spends her time runnin' the *Nessie Quest* tours now and tendin' to the lad. You ladies enjoy yer lunch. Please let me know if there's anythin' else I can get for ye." Then he stands and heads back toward the kitchen.

I press Stop on my iPhone and call after him.

"Mr. Farquhar," I say. "Does anyone in Scotland believe that people are just seeing things or even pulling practical jokes just to fake people out?"

"Aye, there have historically been hoaxes, even datin' way back. Google the *1934 surgeon's photo.* That was the longest-running hoax. But dinna let that dunderheid fool ye, lass. There is somethin' *verra* big swimmin' in those waters. The question is . . . *what is it?* And who will be the first to find it?"

I give Mom a big grin. "See?" I say.

14

LOCH WATCHERS ON THE RECORD

"Mom," I call from her closet after lunch the next day. "Where's your tan hat? The one with the black band around it?"

"Why?" she calls back from the living room.

I pop my head around the corner and see her sitting cross-legged next to the coffee table, typing on her laptop.

"I need it," I tell her.

"Ahh . . . one of the bottom drawers of the dresser, maybe?"

I pull open one drawer.

Mom's sweaters.

Then another.

Dad's polo shirts.

Then another.

Bingo.

I find the hat I'm looking for next to Dad's baseball hats and extra spiral notebooks. All blue.

I set the hat on top of my head. Last night, I spent hours

Googling *fashion choices for reporters* and found that most old-time reporters used to wear this kind of hat, which is called a fedora. On the brim they attached a small sign that said PRESS. But most importantly, each reporter always, *always* stuck a yellow pencil behind one ear.

I straighten out the brim of Mom's hat and tuck my freshly designed PRESS sign into the brim. Then I slip a newly sharpened pencil from Dad's backpack behind one ear and examine myself in the mirror.

Perfect.

"Check me out," I say, darting into the living room and turning in a circle to model my new look.

She stops clicking the keys of her computer and takes her glasses off.

"Well, well." She beams. "What's all this?"

"If I'm going to be a real reporter, I have to look the part, right? I'm interviewing the Loch Watchers today. I'm going to record the interview on my iPhone so you can upload it when Hammy Bean gets his podcast going."

"Sounds great. You look *fabulous.*" She smiles. "Very official. I love it. Can't wait to hear the interview. Do you have your questions ready?"

"No," I say. "I'm just going to wing it, but it's going to be epic orange."

"Epic *what?*"

"It's an inside thing between me and Ms. Begbie," I tell her.

She grins big at me. "Well, good luck," she calls. "Can't wait to hear about it."

❧

The Loch Watchers are sitting in a line on the same bench just like they were that morning I took their picture. In the exact same order too. Just like Hammy Bean said.

Lord Grunter.

The Duke of Buttcrack.

And Sir Farts-When-He-Laughs.

Each one of them holding binoculars focused directly on the loch.

I stand tall and official-like right in front of the Loch Watchers and clear my throat.

"Excuse me, please," I announce in a very official kind of way. "My name is Adelaide Ru Fitzhugh, and I'm a reporter for the *Nessie Juggernaut*." I point to the brim of my hat. "I'm here to ask you a few questions about your Nessie-spotting experiences and see if you will go on the record with your responses." I grab my iPhone from my pocket.

One by one each man lowers his binoculars and blinks at me.

Lord Grunter gives me a grumpy once-over. "Eh?" he grunts at me, cupping the back of his ear with one hand.

"Lass says she's a reporter," the Duke of Buttcrack shouts in his direction.

"A reporter?" Lord Grunter scoffs with a phlegm rattle, and goes back to his binoculars while the other two men stare up at me.

"That's right," I say. "If you would, please, take turns stating your name clearly, speaking directly into this." I hold the iPhone up. "And any identifying features or relevant details about yourselves that you'd like us to share in our podcast."

The Duke of Buttcrack and Sir Farts-When-He-Laughs look at each other and then back up at me.

"Your *what*?" Buttcrack asks.

"Our podcast," I say again, slower this time.

"What's a bloody podcast, lass?" Sir Farts-When-He-Laughs wants to know.

"It's like radio stations, except instead of music there are shows and interviews and stuff like that. And instead of it being on the radio, it's an app."

"Who'd ye say ye are, lass?" Buttcrack asks.

"My name is Adelaide Ru Fitzhugh," I say again. "I'm an official reporter for the *Nessie Juggernaut* and I'm writing a story on the Nessie Race. I'm hoping your team wouldn't mind commenting from your perspective." I show them my iPhone again. "On the record."

The man on the end, Sir Farts-When-He-Laughs, lets his binoculars swing against his sweater and stands up first.

"Sterling Jack is the name." He holds out a hand with five crooked fingers.

I shake his hand and then push the red button on my iPhone.

"You said your name is Sterling Jack, is that correct?" I say, into the speaker this time.

He nods.

I motion to him to say more.

"Aye," he says. "That's correct, lass."

"Thank you, Mr. Jack," I say. "Please, will you comment on your position regarding your beliefs and/or findings when it comes to the lake monster known as Nessie?" I hold the phone out in his direction.

He clears his throat and leans in closer toward the speaker. "I am a member of Team Loch Watchers, established in 1984. I've lived lochside since I was a wee lad," he says. "I've had a total o' five Nessie sightings in my lifetime."

I can feel my eyes get wider. *"Five whole times?"*

"Aye," he says. "And I will tell ye this wi' all certainty. I know, beyond a doubt, that the thing swimmin' out there in those waters is a sirenian."

"A what?" I ask.

"It's considered a sea cow, like a manatee, except the sirenian swim in cold water, an' even though it looks like a whale, it's closer to an elephant. The largest one ever found was over ten meters."

Lord Grunter lowers his binoculars again. "Poppycock, Jack," he grumbles. "Lass, don't ye listen to his crackpot ideas for one more minute. I'll tell ye exactly what's down in that loch," he adds, making sure to give a Mr. Mews hork to the word *loch*.

"Please state your name for the record, sir?" I hold the phone in his direction.

"Cappy McGee," he says, leaning forward with one hand holding solid on his knee.

"Thank you, Mr. McGee. You don't think it's a sirenian, is that correct?"

"It's a kraken, lass," he tells me. "I ken that's what it is because I've seen it *six* times and that's more than five, as you well know. And I'm sure it's a cephalopod-type creature and not a sirenian."

Mr. Jack scoffs at him and waves a dismissive hand.

"Six times *is* a lot of times," I agree.

"Will ye quit bloody fillin' that lass's head with such nonsense?" the Duke of Buttcrack grumbles.

I hold the phone toward him. "Do you have a comment as well?"

He stands up then and gives his baggy khakis a good yank up over his big, round middle. But even with the worn leather belt, they don't seem to want to stay there.

"I'm Norval Watt," he says. "I've seen the monster only once, but it's not a kraken or a sirenian."

"And your thoughts about what it might be are . . . ?"

"It's an undiscovered mammal o' some sort, not yet catalogued. My best guess is a cross between a seal an' something else. Or an otter an' something else. Here, let me show you where we saw it last."

We all watch as he heads to the edge of the pier, and when he takes his hand off his belt to point toward the water, we all see exactly why Hammy Bean calls him the Duke of Buttcrack.

"Ew," I mumble, slapping a palm over my eyes. "Mr. Watt, I really think you should sit back down, sir."

"Norval!" Cappy McGee calls out with a snort of laughter. "Pull up them bloody trousers!"

Norval Watt gives his pants another good yank, and a concert of laughter hits me.

A trio of hoots ending with a phlegm rattle and one solo toot.

15

A HAGGIS HUNGER STRIKE

As it turns out, Briony is no longer a Malibu Barbie shaver or a closeted thumb-sucker and she actually smells just fine. Not to mention she was right on about the chocolate-and-chili macarons.

They were scrummy big-time.

It's her house that's the problem.

Which I find out when we're invited to a traditional Scottish dinner on Friday night after Uncle Clive closes up shop. Dad drives the backward car to a place just past Inverness called Dores, a village even tinier than Fort Augustus. It's directly across the loch from Fort Augustus but it still takes over an hour to get there on the winding A82 highway.

Their house is kind of in the countryside and looks normal enough as far as I can see through the window of the backward car. It's a stone house, covered in ivy, sitting on the very top of a hill, with two chimneys puffing ghostly shapes out into the night.

But once inside?

It smells even worse than when Mom boils Brussels sprouts for dinner, and that is a stink that lasts for days.

This odor is more like a combination of boiled turkey gizzard and vile vegetables.

"Hurry on now!" Briony calls to me, grabbing my arm. "I'll show ye my room."

She darts up a long staircase while the grown-ups clink glasses, talking over each other in loud, happy voices. I follow Briony up the stairs, running my hand along a polished wooden banister, down the hall and into the room at the very end on the right. It looks nothing like mine on Tennyson. Instead of cornflower walls, hers are pink, and instead of ceramic kitties, she has strangely decorated glass eggs that she calls Fabergés lined neatly on the shelves of a glass cabinet.

I sit down on her bed and take it all in.

"What do ye think?"

"It's pretty," I say. "But honestly? Your house smells funny."

She laughs. "That's the haggis."

"I've heard of it, but what is it . . . *exactly*?"

She laughs again. "You'll find oot soon enough. It's actually quite good, if ye don't think aboot where it comes from. An' even better if ye put ketchup on it."

"Where does it come from?" I ask her.

"Believe me, ye dinna want to ken," she says. "Hey, want me to show ye a game?"

I shrug. "Sure."

"It's called Cat's Cradle," she tells me, grabbing a string of purple yarn tied in one big loop.

I watch her wrap the yarn around her fingers until she's created a fancy design.

"Now pinch the yarn where it comes together in an x," she tells me. "That's right. An' wrap them back under and take the yarn onto yer fingers."

I make a mess of it three times until I catch on and then we pass the fancy yarn knots we create back and forth on our fingers until Aunt Isla calls us for dinner.

Uncle Clive and Aunt Isla sit at either end of a giant table in the dining room with Dad and Briony on one side and me and Mom on the other.

I scan the table for recognizables.

Mashed potatoes. Check.

Vegetable medley. Gross, but check.

A gravy boat. Check.

Then I eye the platter in the center of the table, stacked high with gray meat patties.

Briony opens her eyes wide in my direction, giving the meat platter a nod, and then mouths the word *haggis* at me.

For a very brief moment I consider becoming a vegetarian and wonder if it's against the rules to make pepperoni exceptions. Without the occasional pepperoni pizza, I might actually die a little inside. Plus, I hate all vegetables . . . so there's that.

Maybe just a hunger strike would do the trick.

This one time, Ariana Shoesmith said she couldn't eat hot dogs for hot lunch and no one believed her until she blew chunks all over the cafeteria. After that, they never made her eat hot lunch hot dogs again.

Blowing chunks may be the way to go here.

Leave it to Dad to find a positive spin on something as disgusting as stinky meat.

"Please pass the haggis," Dad says, rubbing his hands together. "Mmm-mmm . . . I haven't had this in years. It smells scrumptious, Isla."

We pass the dishes around the table, filling our plates. I take an extra heaping mound of mashed potatoes and drown it in gravy in hopes there's no room left for vegetable medley or haggis.

But lucky me, Mom finds room to slide a patty next to my mashed potatoes.

"It's fabulous, Rutabaga," Dad says. "My grandmother and grandfather used to make this dish for me and your uncle Clive every Sunday. It's Scotland's most famous food."

"Don't you want a better life for your daughter?" I ask him.

He smiles that smile. The one with all the teeth.

"You're going to love it," he says.

"That's highly doubtful," I grumble.

Uncle Clive and Briony laugh bellowing chuckles while Isla waves a hand at us.

"Hey, Rudy Tudy," Dad says. "Did you end up finding any supporting characters in town today for your new story?" He turns to Uncle Clive. "She's a writer, that one," and he points a fork at me.

"Jings!" Uncle Clive beams over at me while he chews his gray meat.

"I certainly met some interesting people," I say. "And just so you know, you all seem to be in the minority when it comes

123

to believing in the Loch Ness Monster. There are a lot of people searching for that thing down in the water. Have you heard of the Nessie Race?"

"Oh, it's rubbish," Aunt Isla says. "They've never found anythin' worthy of our time to even consider it."

"This one kid I met says that everyone who's anyone believes it's true and that people who don't believe it just don't know the facts of it," I say.

Dad takes another mound of meat from the pile at the center of the table and places it on his plate.

"That kid said *every* story has some fact to it," I go on.

I watch Uncle Clive, Aunt Isla, Mom and Dad all exchange amused looks.

"Rutabaga," Dad says to me. "I told you, Uncle Clive and I grew up on this loch. Your aunt Isla too. It's nothing but a story."

"Well, there's nothin' wrong with tellin' stories and gatherin' some good research, but just make sure ye dinna get caught up in the hype o' it all. There's nothin' to it," Aunt Isla tells me.

Dad puts his elbows on the table and leans in my direction.

"It's already been proven that the loch doesn't have the ecosystem to support a species of animal that large," he tells me. "The loch only contains approximately twenty tons of fish, and a species of animal that large would need far more to sustain itself and continue to reproduce. Also, the bottom of the loch is flat and perfect for discovering fossils and they've never found anything. Not to mention, the water is too cold, and historically we know that plesiosaurs are tropical animals and couldn't survive the temperature of Loch Ness."

I eye him suspiciously. "You sure seem to know a lot of facts about it," I accuse him.

"We grew up here," he says. "You don't think we did our own investigating?"

I sit up in my seat. "You did?"

"Of course," he says. "And we're saving you the heartbreak of getting your hopes up."

I look at Uncle Clive and he nods.

I sigh and slump in my chair, poking at the meat mound on my plate.

"So is this like some kind of a stinkier, more crumbly hamburger patty or something?"

"Just try it," Dad says

"Ada Ru." Aunt Isla leans in my direction. "Ye dinna have to eat it, darlin'. I won't be offended in the least."

"Thanks, Aunt Isla. No offense, but . . . it kind of stinks like gizzards," I tell her. "Like the kind that come with the turkey at Thanksgiving. Except it'd be like if Nan Fitzhugh forgot to cook all the rest of the good turkey parts like the legs or the wings or even her yummy almond-orange stuffing packed on the inside. It'd be like all she did was boil the gizzard, grind it up and serve it in gray meat patties without any sweet potatoes with toasted marshmallows on top or pumpkin pie either."

"I love her orange stuffin'," Briony pipes up. "When they were here last year for Thanksgiving she made her famous stuffin' and it was pure deid scrummy. Her tatties too. She makes the smoothest tatties, withoot a single lump."

I look at Dad.

"Mashed potatoes," he tells me.

"Oh," I say.

I eye the meat again and cut into it with my fork. "I mean, like, what's it *made* of . . . exactly?" I ask again.

Dad takes a big breath and lets it all out. "A meaty pudding made with chopped heart, blended with lungs and encased in the stomach of a lamb and thickened with savory blood—"

I hold up a hand and swallow down a gag.

"Are you kidding me right now?"

"*Wa-ah-ah.*" Dad laughs his evil laugh.

And it's at this moment in time that my official haggis hunger strike begins.

Lucky for me, after dinner, Dad stops at the McDonald's in Inverness for a six-piece chicken nuggets with BBQ sauce.

And that night before bed, I make good and sure to thank God for chicken nuggets, but I leave out the haggis. There's nothing about bloody meat encased in a lamb's anything that I'm even remotely thankful for.

16

A TOP-SECRET BOBBLE

Hammy Bean wasn't kidding about manning that stupid radio day and night.

He beeps in the very next morning before the crack of possibilities even has the chance to show its orange face.

Beep.

"Captain Green Bean to Denver. Come in, Denver. Over."

I one-eye the antique alarm clock sitting on the night table.

The big hand is on the twelve and the little hand is on the . . . I squint . . . *five.*

I pull the pillow over my head.

Beep.

"Hello? Come in, Denver. Do you read me? Over."

I squeeze the pillow even tighter against my ear.

Beep.

"I sure hope ye can hear me because you're supposed to be mannin' this radio at all times. Denver, do you read me? Over."

I grab it from the table and push the button. "I'm here," I say.

Silence.

"Hello?"

"You forgot to say *over*. Over."

"Fine," I say. "Do you happen to know what time it is? Over."

"Five o'clock. Over."

"Right. Five o'clock . . . *in the morning*. People are still sleeping at five o'clock in the morning. Like me—*I* was sleeping. Over."

"*Thaaat's* a roger, Denver," he says, completely unfazed. "But Nessie news never sleeps, so get yourself oot of your scratcher an' put on your baffies an' get ready for the day. Over."

"Is that code or something? Over."

"Nae, it means get oot of bed and get your slippers on because this is a counterespionage Nessie emergency. Over."

I yawn. "Uh-huh."

"This is what we call a preemptive strike in the news business," he tells me, and then his voice comes over the radio in a whisper. "*I have a top-drawer bobble*. Over."

I stare at the speaker. "*Excuse* me? Over?"

"Didn't you memorize your codes yet? It's a top-drawer bobble. *Real* top drawer too. Over."

I stare at the speaker. "I have no idea what you're even talking about right now."

"Are ye tellin' me that ye didna memorize any of your codes yet? It's a top-drawer bobble. *Real* top drawer too. Over."

"I've been busy," I tell him. "I interviewed Mr. Farquhar

and the Loch Watchers and I have it all recorded so we can edit it for the podcast. Just wait until you hear it. I got some really good information. Over."

But he's way too focused on his top-drawer business to care about my Loch Watcher findings.

"Top-drawer bobble equals *top-secret intel.*" He's back to whispering again. "Over."

"So what's so top-secret that you couldn't wait until sunup? Over?"

"A price cut on salami is on the horizon but the sale is null an' void," he tells me. "He needs to be neutralized. Over."

"Huh?"

He breathes an exasperated sigh into the radio speaker. "Reporters/secret agents at the *Jug* need to know the codes to prevent information interception. Over."

"Yeah, yeah, live them, be them, da, da, da," I say. "But can't you just tell me in regular English *this* one time? Over."

"And compromise our lead in the Nessie Race? Never. Over."

"Just this once and I promise I'll learn the codes," I say. "And I mean, is there really a lead in this thing? Plus I will guarantee you there is no one listening at five in the morning. Over."

"That's negative. I was on channel three this morning and overheard Jasper Price on his CB radio. He's plannin' a media event based on a photo taken from yesterday. Over."

"Who's Jasper Price? Over?"

"A rival Nessie tour. Over."

"So what do you want me to do about it?"

"From what I heard his methods are highly suspect," he

tells me. "And you're not to be the one to neutralize the hoax before it gets too far. Over."

"Uh-huh, and how do you know all this?" I ask.

Silence.

"By spying, right?" I ask.

"Sometimes you're forced to infiltrate the enemy camp," he informs me.

"So, *you* spied."

"I'm telling ye, he's settin' up a hoax an' that's the important thing to focus on. Over."

"How do you know all this for certain? Over?" I ask.

"In 1967, this bloke by the name o' Dick Raynor got a good bit o' footage that captured the most famous movin' images of the monster to date. It was taken near the village o' Dores an' many people believed it was Nessie, except fourteen years later, he realized he hadna shot the monster a'tall. In the film, it looked like a silver line across the black water, but it was really a group o' birds called mergansers," he explains.

"The mother bird flits across the top o' the water, kickin' up spray in spurts, and then stops and waits for the bairns to catch up. From a distance, it appeared to be a long creature with a large wake. For fourteen years, many thought this to be real footage. Jasper Price is plannin' to use the same type of video an' pass if off as a monster sightin'. Over."

"How do you know so much about all this? Over?"

"Mamo Honey kens. She kens everythin' there is to know aboot the race an' the monster an' everythin' in between. Over."

"So then why did she quit? Over."

"Will ye focus?" he says. "I'm tellin' you that the clishmaclaver is that Jasper Price plans to present this same footage as evidence to get ahead in the race. Over."

"So basically . . . you're saying he's lying about the whole deal. Over," I say.

"Right," Hammy Bean says. "Can ye infiltrate the *Monster Chaser* and try to see what you can get from Jasper Price this mornin'? He's usually gettin' the boat ready by seven o'clock. It can be a totally different story for the autumn newsletter, another angle. He's goin' to ruin the integrity of the race with a hoax like that. Over."

"I'm on it," I say.

"Roger that. Meet me at the *Nessie Quest* booth at ten so I can hear that interview and the one with the Three Bears an' Price Cut on Salami? Over."

"Who? Over?"

Another sigh. "Jasper Price, *Monster Chaser.* Over."

"Oh, right," I say. "Ten, um, ten—"

"Gads! It's four, ye dunderheid, it's ten-four. Study your codes! And remember to say *over*, will you?"

"Okay, okay, geez," I say. "Denver is over and out."

17

ONE SALAMI . . . *NEUTRALIZED*

I can't go back to sleep after Hammy Bean's wake-up call, so I decide to start my story, seeing as I have so many interesting supporting characters.

Not to mention one elusive lake monster.

Whatever the thing is supposed to be.

I open up my laptop and rest my fingers on the keys.

Horror

PAGE ONE

No one thought a summer in Scotland would turn into a nightmare vacation with a terrorizing prehistorical dinosaur stalking the small town of Fort Augustus and taking its children in the dead of night.

Hmm. Maybe.

Realistic Fiction

PAGE ONE

It all started with a plain old fish.

Booooring.

Fantasy

PAGE ONE

It was a nocturnal fire-blowing dragon that flew over the small town of Fort Augustus, searching for children to take back to its nest. Dinner for later.

A possible contender.

"Adelaide Ru?" Mom calls from the kitchen.

I look at the clock on the side table and realize I'm already late for my Salami assignment.

Mom cracks the door and pokes her messy bedhead through it. "Want an orange scone and some tea?" she asks.

"Can't," I tell her, pushing the comforter aside. "I've got to get out to Jasper Price's boat before his first tour."

She nods, yawns and then slides her slippers toward the kitchen.

Sci-Fi

PAGE ONE

Everyone knows two things about Fort Augustus, Scotland. An alien ship has landed at the bottom of Loch Ness and townspeople have gone missing ever since. But it's twelve-year-old Adelaide Ru who learns the real truth, that aliens now walk the streets of the small town in human form, surviving solely on orange-flavored pastries.

Definitely a possibility.

❧

On my way down the heavenly steps in St. Benedict's Abbey, I cross my fingers that Dax is on the stairs with Ole Roy.

But he isn't, so I head straight to the dock to find the *Monster Chaser.*

Romance

PAGE ONE

Dax pulled his jean jacket off and wrapped it around Ada Ru's shoulders. His seaweed eyes met hers. He was smitten at the very first sight of her that first day at St. Benedict's Abbey.

And she was smitten with him too.

❧

Jasper Price is already at the dock, polishing the shiny brass rails that circle the whole outside of the *Monster Chaser.* He's a tall, skinny man with a sunburned forehead and mirrored sunglasses.

"Excuse me, please. I'm Ada Ru Fitzhugh, a reporter with the *Nessie Juggernaut.*" I point to my Press hat. "Can I have a word with you on your latest findings?"

He shades his glasses with the back of his hand and looks up at me.

"Pardon me, lassie?" Jasper Price says.

"I said that I'm Ada Ru Fitzhugh, a reporter for the *Nessie Juggernaut*. Do you mind going on the record about your latest . . . *findings*?" I hold up my iPhone and push the red button.

He just stares at me. "How did *ye* know aboot it?" he finally asks.

"That's a very good question," I say. "We have what you call a nose for Nessie news, Mr. Price. And at the *Jug* we're good at . . . ah, shall we say *undercover* work. Do you care to comment, sir, on the pictures you plan to present to the media later today?" I hold the phone closer.

He keeps staring, until he finally pulls himself up out of the boat and stands directly in front of me on the dock.

"Who are your sources?" he demands with his hands on his hips.

"A reporter never reveals her sources," I inform him. "But I will tell you this: our investigative work has concluded that you have taken pictures of the merganser birds and plan to pass this off as official evidence. Like Dick Raynor, except as we all now know, Dick Raynor discovered his error fourteen years later and told the truth. Because real scientists are out for the truth, Mr. Price. Not to win a race at all costs. So my question is, care to comment on your false findings?"

He breaks out in a slow smile. "That's rubbish."

"Far from it," I say. "And we would like to give you the opportunity to comment on the story we're planning for our new podcast, available for download wherever you get your podcasts."

His smile slips off his lips into a scowl that seems stuck for good. "A podcast?"

"That's right, and we have lots and lots of subscribers, thousands the last I looked, and I'm sure they would all be very interested in knowing that you've turned the Nessie Race into something it is not," I inform him. "Now, would you like to go on the record or not?"

He takes his mirrored sunglasses off and bends down to meet my eyes, peering at me with a dark scowl under bushy eyebrows. "Nae," he sneers. "An' tell yer wee friend to stay off channel three."

I swallow and push Stop on the phone. "I'm sure I don't know what you mean."

"Uh-huh," he grumbles.

"Well, my business is done here," I tell him with a salute. "You have yourself an orange day."

Then I turn and head down the dock without ever once looking back until I make it to the canal side. I pull my walkie-talkie off my belt and push the button.

"Denver to Captain Green Bean," I call into it. "Come in, Captain Green Bean. Over."

"Captain Green Bean here. Over," Hammy Bean says.

"One Salami . . . *neutralized*," I tell him.

"Well done, Denver. Over."

"I can't wait for you to hear this. I definitely think I got him to reconsider his . . . evidence," I tell him. "I don't expect to be hearing anything about any merganser birds now that

136

I'm through with him. And you want to know what he said? He said to tell you to stay off channel three. Over."

"He kens who I am?"

"Of course he does. He said it, didn't he? Over."

"I guess so. Well done, Denver! Top-notch reportin'!" Hammy Bean sings out. "Rendezvous at Nessie's home base in fifteen acorns. Over."

I stare at the radio.

"Ye dinna have any clue what I just said, do ye? Over."

"*Thaaaat's a roger*, Captain Green Bean."

"Meet me at the booth in fifteen minutes. Over and out."

18

A POOPING GOOSE AND A BLUE SUBARU

My Nikes are so excited about the whole Jasper Price thing, they feel like sprinting to the *Nessie Quest* booth, but Hammy Bean won't be there yet, so they sprint to Ness for Less for a can of Coke and a Kit Kat bar first.

When I push open the front door, the bell on the top dings. There is a mom with a little boy on her hip squeezing melons in produce, an older lady smelling loaves of bagged bread in the bakery and two teenagers reading car magazines in the corner. Quigley Dunbar III stands behind the register and Dax is sitting on the counter strumming on Ole Roy. And I think, I mean, it's possible I actually caught him singing too. But if he was really and truly doing it, he stopped as soon as he saw me.

"Hi, Mr. Dunbar the Third," I call.

"Hello, Ada Ru." He waves a hand in the air. "I hear you're acquainted wi' young Dax here?"

"Yep," I tell him. "Hammy Bean hired us both for the *Nessie Juggernaut.*"

"So I've heard," he says. "Dax is playin' some o' the jingles he's workin' on for his new radio show. Has he played them for ye yet?"

"Ah . . . no," Dax mumbles. "Not yet."

"Why do you share your words with Mr. Dunbar the Third and not with anyone else?" I ask him.

"QDT is a professional musician," Dax informs me. "*And a music teacher.*"

"You are?"

"Aye, I was a music teacher for forty-two years an' I've played in many folk bands around town as well, lass. An', well, young Dax here is pure deid brilliant at playin' that guitar."

"So you're his teacher?" I ask.

"Not officially."

The bell on the door dings and an old woman in a shawl and pushing a shopping cart walks in.

"Good morning, Mrs. Beliani," Quigley Dunbar III calls out to her.

"Good mornin'," Mrs. Beliani calls back.

I take a Coke from the cooler near the register and a Kit Kat bar from the candy section and set them on the counter. "I'll take these, please," I tell Quigley Dunbar III.

He grabs the glasses hanging by a chain on his chest and slips them across his nose while he slowly pushes buttons on the register.

"That will be one pound an' thirty-one pence, please."

I pull coins from my jeans pocket, put all of them on the counter and push them in his direction.

Dax slides the coins off the counter. "Haven't you figured out the money yet?" he asks, going through them, taking a few from the pile and giving the rest back to me.

"Oh, big whoop," I say. "Mr. Dunbar the Third doesn't mind."

"Not in the least, lass," he tells me with a smile, dropping the right coins in the right compartments and closing the drawer.

"I heard you haven't even memorized your codes yet," Dax says, shaking his head at me.

"For your information, I've interviewed five people already on Nessie sightings—what have *you* done?"

"Me?" He smiles smugly. "You mean besides almost being done with the intro for the podcast? I've started your precious Harry Potter series. I'm already on book two. Annnnd . . . what else? Oh, I learned *all* the *Nessie Juggernaut* codes."

I blink at him.

"The codes? Since when do you need to know them?"

"Since yesterday, when Hammy Bean decided to assign me a radio too." He takes it from his belt loop to show me the same gray camouflage walkie-talkie.

I put my hands on my hips. "Why do you get one?" I demand.

"Because the music man flies south when it's time to milk the cow even though the raccoon walks alone."

"What's that supposed to mean?"

"Memorize your codes," he tells me.

"Well, I bet you don't know who Price Cut on Salami is."

"Jasper Price," he says.

"What about the Three Bears?"

"The Loch Watchers." He smiles.

"Oh, so what," I snap.

He just grins even bigger and goes back to messing with the strings on Ole Roy.

"Well, I better get going," I tell Quigley Dunbar III. "I have a very important meeting with Hammy Bean to discuss"—I turn to Dax—"*very* important business."

Dax slips off the counter and slides Ole Roy across his back. "Me too," he says.

"What do *you* have to meet him for?"

"I'm going on my first *Nessie Quest* tour with him and Mamo Honey." He smirks. "Have a groovy day, QDT." He waves as he heads out the door.

I follow on his heels.

"I would go too," I tell him. "If I wanted to, I would."

"Uh-huh," he says, taking those same long strides.

I scramble to keep up with him. "Did he tell you I didn't have the tidbits to go on that boat? Because I have them. I have plenty of them. I'm filled to the brim with tidbits."

"So you say," Dax says flatly. "*Excessively.*"

That's when an idea for the perfect first page comes to me.

Murder Mystery

PAGE ONE

The lake monster eats the boy whole. And the boy's name was Dax Cady.

Just when Dax and I end up at the *Nessie Quest* booth, I hear Hammy Bean talking to a dad buying tickets for his whole brood of kids to take the first scheduled tour.

"My Mamo Honey is the captain o' the *Nessie Quest*," I hear Hammy Bean saying. "I stay with her while my parents are busy bein' missionaries overseas. They bring food and water and other resources to the lads and lassies in Uganda and the Congo. That's why they arna here helpin' us run the business. They're changin' the world."

"How wonderful," the man says, handing over his credit card.

"Aye, it is." Hammy Bean pushes the buttons on the cash register.

I pull on Dax's arm and lead him around the side of the booth. "Wait. *Missionaries?*" I whisper. "He said they were royalty when I first met him and then he told us they worked for Doctors Without Borders."

"So?"

"So?" I scoff. "Clearly he's lying."

"No duh," Dax says. "Please tell me you didn't really believe the whole deal about royalty, did you?"

I blink at him. "Why wouldn't I?"

"Because Scotland hasn't had royalty since 1745," he tells me. "Google it."

"Fine, but that's not the point—the point is why is he lying?" I say.

"Who cares?" Dax pulls his sleeve out of my grasp and heads toward the front of the booth.

"Hey, HB, what's up?"

Mac-Talla barks and puts her pink paws on the counter to get a pat on the head.

"Howzitgoan, mate," Hammy Bean says to Dax.

"I'm here too, Hammy Bean," I say.

"Denver! Cheers!"

Mac-Talla licks my fingertips, and I give her pink nose a kiss.

"Hammy Bean, how do you know it's us without our telling you so?" I ask him, scratching Mac-Talla on her head.

"Yer voice," he says. "Your eyes remember faces, and my ears remember voices. An' my nose remembers too. Ada Ru, ye always smell like coconuts."

"I do?" I say.

"Mmm-hmm," Dax agrees, his eyes glued to the pages of one of Hammy Bean's *Nessie Quest* brochures.

"Oh," I say. "But I mean, like how can you remember *everyone's* voice?"

"Well, not everyone's." He grins with the deep dimples. "Just important ones."

Suddenly the whole lying-about-his-parents thing seems less of a big deal than it was before.

"*Important?*" I ask, pointing to myself, even though I know perfectly well he can't see me. "You think I'm *important*?"

"Of course," he says. "Both of ye are the verra first employees o' the *Jug* and you're . . . my mates."

"Yeah, but I'm like your *first* mate, right?" I ask him. "Because I'm your first reporter/secret agent and all."

"Well, to be an official first mate by definition ye'd actually have to go on the water," he tells me.

Dax's laugh comes out in a burst. "Yeah," he says. "You'd have to find your tidbits for that first."

My fists find my hips again. "I told you before. They aren't lost."

"Well, that's brilliant news," Hammy Bean announces. "Because the tour leaves in five minutes. Since you are both official employees o' the *Nessie Juggernaut*, yer fees are waived."

"The eagle will take flight when the sun rises west and the goose poops on the blue Subaru," Dax says to me with a wide smile.

Hammy Bean giggles behind his hand.

I scowl at them both. "What's that supposed to mean?"

"Memorize your codes," Dax tells me.

"Since when is official *Nessie Juggernaut* business so important to you?" I ask him. "I thought all you do is music in the summer and now you're all up in this monster business."

"Yeah, well, that was before I was a part of the Nessie Race," he informs me. "I think it's pretty groovy to be a part of the *Jug* crew. Plus, *I'm* here every summer and you leave in September. Who knows if you'll ever be back? Me and HB here might get our mugs in the history books."

"Well, just so you know, *I'm* writing a story that I need supporting characters for and you aren't even going to be one of them."

"N.I.," he says.

"What about me?" Hammy Bean asks. "Am I one?"

"Yeah, you're in it," I tell him. "You're my Ron."

"Your what?" he asks.

"My Ron," I say again. "You know, like Harry Potter's best pal?"

"Really? Who's your Harry Potter?" he asks.

"*Me*," I say. "I'm the protagonist of my own story."

"Oh," he says. "An' I'm your Ron?"

"Yep."

"Jings!" he exclaims. "I've never co-starred in anyone's story before."

"I'm going to put Quigley Dunbar the Third in it and Mr. Farquhar and Euna Begbie and the Loch Watchers and even Jasper Price. But only as the antagonist."

"Okay, I want in now too," Dax says.

I shrug with my chin in the air. "I'll consider it . . . maybe you can be my Hermione."

Hammy Bean laughs again. "Ooh, that's a cheeky shot," he says, while Dax gives him a playful slug.

"I'm no Hermione," Dax tells me. "You're going to need to come up with a whole new character for me . . . something unique and cool, like Guitarman or maybe Wolfgang. I like the idea of a one-word name for my character. It fits me, don't you think?"

I roll my eyes real big on that. "We'll see," I tell him.

The radio beeps.

"Mamo Honey to Captain Green Bean. Come in, Captain Green Bean. Over."

Hammy Bean feels for the radio and once his fingers touch the edge of it, he pulls it into his palm and presses the button. "Captain Green Bean here. Over."

"Rendezvous at the *Nessie Quest* in three minutes," she says. "Let's crack on with it. Over."

She starts the engine, and I hold my breath waiting for the loch wind to wash away the gas fumes circling me.

"*Thaaat's* a roger," Hammy Bean calls into the radio. "Strings has made it to the top o' the Great Glen and is ready to swim. Over."

"Brilliant. Bring him along," Mamo Honey tells him. "Over and oot."

Hammy Bean slams the hatch on the booth.

GONE TO FIND A MONSTER

I watch him scramble out the side door with Mac-Talla's leash in his hand as she leads the way toward the edge of the dock, with Dax following.

"Wait," I call after them. "Just so you know, I interviewed Jasper the Price Cut on Salami today and he was standing in his boat for part of the time. *That's* how close I was to the water. I might as well have been swimming in it. Ask anyone."

"Not the same," Hammy Bean says.

"Why not?"

Dax turns to me and says, "Because . . . and this is key here . . . to report on the water, you have to actually be willing to *go on the water.*"

Hammy Bean turns to face me. "Meet me an' Dax in the morn at the stroke of six o'clock. I think you're both ready for the next level of top-secret information. Even if ye havena learned all the codes yet. But you'll have to promise ye willna tell another livin' soul."

"I promise," I say.

"Me too," Dax says.

"Can ye guys cross-your-heart promise?" he asks.

"I cross-my-heart promise," I tell him.

146

"Dax?" he says.

"Yeah, whatever."

"It will be our most top-secret odyssey yet," Hammy Bean informs us, climbing into the boat.

I stand watching as the *Nessie Quest* begins to pull away from the pier. Dax cups his hands around his mouth and hollers something to me.

"What?" I holler back.

"I said, the goat soaks up the cheese with a gullet of chocolate-dipped haggis," he calls again, and then beams a wide grin.

I put my hands on my hips and give another good glare before turning on the heels of my Nikes and stomping down the pier, cursing his name all the way back to St. Benedict's, until the radio on my belt loop beeps. I don't know what I ever thought was so great about him, anyway. *Seaweed-green eyes and a one-lipped smile,* I scoff to myself, *who cares about that?* I have plenty of new feeling words to put on the page I dedicated solely to him and his stupid seaweed eyes.

Feeling word: ANNOYED in all caps.

Along with the words *Dax is a fathead!* in bubble letters *and* an exclamation point.

Beep.

"Dax the Great to Denver. Come in, Denver. Over."

I grab the radio from my belt loop. "Please tell me that is not your new handle. Over," I say.

"What's wrong with it? Over."

"Ah . . . it's *stupid*," I inform him.

"Actually, it's Strings," he says. "That's cool, right? Over?"

Back when I thought those seaweed eyes were the cutest

thing walking, I would have thought that was a pretty cool choice, but now, I couldn't care less.

The radio beeps again. "I have one more message for you," Dax says. "Are you ready for it? Over?"

I sigh. "What? Over."

"Okay, listen carefully, though. Over."

"I am," I insist. "There's no degree of listening carefully or not listening carefully. You either *are* listening or you're *not* listening and I already told you I am, so why don't you just go and say it already? Over."

Beep.

"The eagle has taken flight, but the goose still poops on the blue Subaru because she didn't take the time to learn her codes. Over and out."

I clip the walkie-talkie back on my belt loop and stomp down to the dock with my cheeks on fire.

Sci-Fi

PAGE ONE

Wolfgang Guitarman was the first to be abducted by the extraterrestrial entity residing at the bottom of Loch Ness.

Never to be seen or heard from again.

I smile at that one. Definitely a contender.

19

THERE'S NO SUCH THING
AS A POOPING GOOSE

At St. Benedict's, in the small room behind the door marked OFFICE, I print out the list of codes Hammy Bean emailed to me.

And you want to know what?

It turns out there isn't one single, solitary thing about a pooping goose *or* a blue Subaru. Not to mention goat gullets *or* chocolate-dipped haggis.

Zilch.

Zippo.

Nada.

Feeling words: *Mad rage* (aimed completely at stupid boys who are in for it big-time).

The problem is, me not knowing the codes is one thing, but it doesn't change one very important fact.

My tidbits are nowhere to be found.

Not the really important ones, anyway. The ones I need to be a serious and advanced reporter on land *and* water. Hammy

Bean and Dax were right—what kind of writer writes about a lake monster and can't even go on the water?

A lame one, that's what kind.

I decide it's all just way too big for me to handle alone and seek the help of an expert. I find her sitting cross-legged on the floor in front of the coffee table in the living room working on her journal article.

"Mom," I say, flopping my deflated body down on the red velvet couch.

"Mmmm?" she says.

Her fingers clicking the keys.

"I can't find my tidbits," I tell her.

Still clicking.

"Did you try under the bed?" she asks.

My head pops up from the rolled velvet armrest. "Under the *bed*?" I say. "What would tidbits be doing *there*?"

Still typing.

"How about your jacket pockets, then?" she suggests.

"Mom, you can't find tidbits under the bed or in a jacket pocket," I explain. "You either have them or you don't. And I don't. Get it? You've raised a tidbitless child. This is more than my twelve-year-old brain can compute. I need some real help here."

The clicking stops and her eyeballs finally focus on me over her glasses, her eyebrows crunching up.

"What did you say you lost?" she asks.

"My *tidbits*," I tell her.

"Is this another YouTube thing that I don't get?"

"No," I say.

"Syfy channel?"

"No, it's Hamish," I tell her.

She gives me a Cheez Whiz. "It's *what*?"

"It's a bravery thing."

"A bravery thing," she repeats, slipping her glasses off her nose.

"Yep," I say. "It's recently been brought to my attention that I have zero tidbits and I'm being ousted from the *Jug* because of it."

She takes in a long breath and then breathes it out again, pushing her laptop to the side.

"Huh," she says. "That is a tough one."

I give her a look. "*That* I already figured out all on my own," I say flatly.

"What I mean is, are you sure you're missing them?" she asks.

"Positive," I tell her.

"How do you know?"

"Well." I start a list on my fingers. "For one, what kind of writer won't go on the water when what they're writing about lives *in* the water? And this is your fault, by the way. You've been so focused on the feelings part of parenting that you shirked your parental responsibility on the tidbit part."

"Mmmm."

"And before you ask me how I feel about it, I will tell you . . . I feel tidbitless."

She nods. "I can see that," she says.

I throw my hands out. "So?" I say. "This is where you come in. I need some adult guidance here. That's you. So?"

"So what?" she asks.

"So lay it on me."

151

"Well." She puts her cheek in the palm of her hand and leans an elbow on the table. "I think it's best that you come up with your own answer on this one."

"It's highly unlike you to slack off on your motherly duties when I'm actually giving you the chance to tell me what to do," I say.

"How about this," she says. "I'll tell you a story about me when I was around your age."

"This isn't the story about you thinking you saw Rick Springfield at the Red Owl, buying Totino's Pizza Rolls, is it?"

She points a stern finger at me. "It was *him*," she insists.

I roll my eyes the same way me and Dad do every time she tells that story.

"But this is a different one," she tells me. "I refer to it as the Ferris Wheel Incident of 1984."

I put my cheek against the smooth red velvet of the armrest. "Fine," I say. "What do I have to lose?"

"When I was a little older than you, all my friends and I would go to the state fair every August. It's the biggest event of the year in Minnesota. I loved going. There were so many things to see and do and eat. Anyway, there was one ride at the fair that I was too frightened to go on, but it was the best ride in the fair—this humongous Ferris wheel, and I was terrified of heights."

"You were scared of a *Ferris wheel*?" I say. "Don't they go like two miles an hour?"

"That's exactly what my friends all said," she goes on. "Every year they made fun of me and every year I would search down deep for my tidbits to give that attendant my ticket and go on the ride."

"Did you ever find them?"

"It took a long time, and then one year, the year I was going into eighth grade, all my friends were lined up for the Ferris wheel, taunting me about not wanting to go with them. That's when I saw *Jeff Thomas*." She raises her eyebrows at me. "He was *the* boy."

"Did he have seaweed-green eyes and wear a jean jacket?"

She laughs. "No, blue eyes and a tan Members Only jacket."

"A member *what*?"

She shrugs and waves her hand in the air. "Doesn't matter," she says. "Anyway, I was not about to let Jeff Thomas see that I was too much of a baby to get on that Ferris wheel, so I reached down and found as many tidbits as I could muster and I *did* it. But I was terrified, thinking of going all the way to the top. So much so, I started to feel sick to my stomach."

"I know what that's like," I tell her. "So what happened? You did it and everything was fine?"

"Not exactly," she says. "Each car had four people inside. Ours had me, my best friend, Tammy, Jeff Thomas and his friend Tim Johns."

"Did he ask you on a date?"

"Nope," she says. "When we got all the way to the top, I made the mistake of looking down, and when I did my stomach started to churn. And unfortunately, before the Ferris Wheel Incident, I had eaten three foot-long corn dogs on a stick, two orders of mini-doughnuts, and a bucket of Sweet Martha's Chocolate Chip Cookies."

"You didn't!"

"I did," she says. "I threw up my state fair snacks all over the floor of the Ferris wheel car, *and* on top of Jeff Thomas's brand-new high-tops."

I throw my hand over my mouth. "That's horrible!"

"I was mortified, to say the least," she says, holding her hands over her face.

"So what happened?"

She takes a breath and smiles. "We dated all through high school."

"You *did*?"

"Yep," she says.

"Even after you blew chunks on his shoes?"

"Yes."

"So basically, you never found your tidbits?" I say. "Is that the point of this story?"

"I *did* find them," she says. "I rode that Ferris wheel."

"Yeah, but you blew chunks on Jeff What's-His-Name," I say. "I'm embarrassed for you just sitting here."

"The point is that even though I thought that was the worst thing that had ever happened in my life, it really wasn't, because he felt so bad for me he let me wear his Members Only jacket home that night. And you want to know what I did?"

"What?"

"I left my bracelet in his pocket on purpose so he'd have to call me after I gave the jacket back."

"And obviously it worked, right? You got your date?"

"I sure did."

"Does Dad know all this?"

"Oh, yeah," she says. "This was way before Dad."

"So basically you're saying that even if I blow chunks all

over the *Nessie Quest* boat and all over Dax and Hammy Bean, in the end things will work out."

"Something like that," Mom says.

I shake my head. "Is this the best you've got?" I ask. "I think you're slipping. I would die a hundred deaths if I blew chunks in front of Dax Cady."

She laughs. "You'll find your tidbits," she says. "When you're ready. You always do."

"Thanks, Mom. You always make me feel better."

"That's what I'm here for," she says, putting her glasses back on her nose.

I head back to my room and lie flat on the lavender comforter on my canopy bed, thinking about everything Mom said. I pull the walkie-talkie off my belt and push the button.

"Denver to Captain Green Bean. Come in, Captain Green Bean. Do you read me? Over."

I wait until Hammy Bean's voice comes over the speaker.

"This is Captain Green Bean. Over."

I clear my throat and read right from the page. "The crow flies at night because a secret vessel looms large across the black diamonds. Over."

First a beep and then cheers on the other end of the radio.

"Thaaat's a roger, Denver. Over," Hammy Bean says.

I can feel my grin spreading. "Rendezvous at the arch over the black diamonds, six acorns to the wind. Over," I say.

That's when I hear Dax's voice on the speaker. "Wait. Which one is that? Over."

"Read your codes," I tell him. "Oh, and one more thing. The only one pooping on a blue Subaru is Wolfgang the Guitarman. *Big-time.* Denver over and out."

20

PUDDING—HOLD THE MEAT

I end up spending that entire afternoon memorizing every stupid code on Hammy Bean's stupid list.

I mean, *every single one.*

By *heart.*

Until I can rattle each one off without even looking.

So after dinner while Mom and Dad go for a handholding stroll along the water, I decide to see if I can log another interview in my iPhone to impress Hammy Bean with my force-to-be-reckoned-with skills. With another interview and my knowing all the codes, he's going to think I'm the best reporter/secret agent he will ever have in the history of the world.

"Excuse me, Ms. Begbie," I call after knocking on the door marked 166 that night after dinner. "I'm wondering if I can interview you about your monster experiences."

The door swings open. "Cheers," she calls to me in a voice that is everything cheery.

A glorious cloud of vanilla and sugar and sweetness fills my nose.

"I was wondering if you . . . if you . . . huh, what smells so good in here?" I stretch my neck to see behind her and into the kitchen.

"Aye." She waves me inside the orange flat. "I'm makin' my sticky toffee pudding."

I swallow a gag. "Oh . . . yeah, no thanks on that. Even though it smells delicious. I have banned all Scottish puddings of any kind."

"Isna that a pity," she says with a grin, heading into the kitchen.

I follow her.

"I'm actually here to ask if I can interview you for the *Nessie Juggernaut* about the Loch Ness Monster." I show her the iPhone. "Hammy Bean hired me as a reporter for the *Jug* and I'm doing interviews, on the record, to upload for future podcasts. I'm getting Hammy Bean on the future train of technology because newsletters are so old-fashioned."

"So I've heard," she says, pulling a pan out of the oven with two orange oven mitts. "I must say, though, it's an awful shame I have to eat this sticky toffee pudding alone."

"I told you, Ms. Begbie. No bloody meat puddings for me," I tell her. "Only the chocolate kind."

She snorts. "I promise ye, there is no meat, bloody or otherwise, in my sticky toffee puddin', lass."

I eye her suspiciously. "Are you sure? Because I promise you if I eat anything like that it won't end well."

"It's just a sweet sponge wi' a caramel topping."

"*Sponge?*" I say. "In Denver we don't *eat* the sponges, Ms. Begbie. We do the dishes with them."

She laughs at that one. "Lass, a sponge is what we *call* a cake. It's a sweet cake with a caramel toppin' and, o' course, ice cream if you like."

"Oh," I say. "Well . . . I like cake. I definitely like cake."

"Ice cream too?" she asks, giving me a wink. "I just happen to have the meatless kind."

"Oh, I *love* meatless ice cream," I tell her.

"Do ye like vanilla?"

"Yes, vanilla is definitely on the list of the kinds I like."

"Take a seat, lass." She points to the round kitchen table. "I'll dish ye up some."

"Thank you, Ms. Begbie," I say, sliding a chair out from the table. "I didn't expect to get cake when I came here to interview you about a lake monster. Of all the orange possibilities I found today, this is by far the orangey-est."

I watch her while she hums and dishes up two bowls of spongy cake.

"Can I ask you something about Hammy Bean before we start the interview? Off the record?"

"O' course," she says, peeling open the cover of a carton of ice cream.

"Do you know what happened to his parents?"

She breathes in real long and then blows it out again before she answers me. "Has he told ye somethin' about them?" she asks, setting the two bowls down on the table and sliding out the chair across from mine.

"Yes, he, uh . . . well, he actually first told me they were Scottish royalty," I tell her. "And I believed him too. I mean,

158

why wouldn't I? And then he said they were with Doctors Without Borders, and then I heard him tell these tourists that they were missionaries. So I said to Dax, *Can you believe that?* And Dax says, *Well, you didn't really believe they were royalty, did you?* And I did." I take a big scoop of cake and caramel and ice cream and shovel it into my mouth. "It made me feel like a big, dumb dope too, and I'm not even the one who lied," I go on with my mouth full. "Not that I'm calling the kid a liar, but I find it hard to believe that his parents could be all those things at once. I mean, then I guess I am calling him a liar . . . but again, this is off the record."

She waits for me to swallow my bite.

"How is it?" She nods toward the bowl.

"This," I say with my mouth already full of the second bite, "is the best sticky toffee pudding I've ever had in my lifetime."

She laughs again. "Ye said you've never had it before." She takes a small scoop from the very tip of her spoon and chews it slowly.

"Still," I say, taking another giant bite.

"Hammy Bean's parents are not royalty," she says. "Nor are they missionaries or doctors. The sad truth is they didna take care o' him the way he deserved to be taken care of," she tells me.

"What does that mean exactly?"

She sighs. "Mamo Honey's daughter, Elspeth, has been a drug user for many years. And Honey has done everythin' to try to help her. Elspeth got married to a man who also uses drugs, Hammy Bean's father, Archibald. When they had Hammy Bean, they just couldna care for him properly because . . . well, they just had very bad judgment. Usin' drugs every day does horrible things to ye."

"Where are they now?" I ask her.

"We believe in London," she says. "At least that's what Mamo Honey learned a few years back. Hammy Bean doesna like to believe that his parents would choose drugs over him, so he fantasizes about all the amazin' things they could be busy doing in the world other than the truth. He likes to believe they're in London just waitin' for him. Sometimes believin' in a little fantasy helps you handle what's real."

"That's horrible," I say.

She nods.

"Do they know he's blind?"

"Hammy Bean wasna officially diagnosed until he was six months old, and by then they were gone. Mamo Honey hasna heard from them in ten years. Hammy Bean is a very special lad. He's had a hard life in his ten years."

"And they never came back?"

"Nae," she says.

"That's horrible," I say. "That's awful. That's like the worst thing I've ever heard."

"Aye," she agrees.

I take another scoop and think of my mom and dad and wonder how it would feel if they left me, and it doesn't feel good at all.

"How did he learn all the stuff he knows how to do?"

"I told ye before that I homeschool him," she says. "Between me and Honey and Hammy Bean's tenacity, we've worked it out. We also have life-skills specialists who come a few times a month. Hammy Bean is such a smart boy, with an amazin' will to live life and experience every part of it. He's surpassed his age in intelligence, charm, interest in the world . . . everythin'. Except one thing."

"What's that?"

"He feels a bit invisible."

"I can't imagine that," I say. "He seems bigger than life to me on most days."

"He is often met with silence when he interacts wi' people, so he's learned to keep to himself unless he is approached. Like in the *Nessie Quest* booth or on the tour boat. That's where he shines the brightest."

"What do you mean he's met with silence?"

"I dinnat think it's oot o' meanness, but more of a . . . *misunderstandin'*. People are unsure how to interact with him or what to say, so they just don't say anythin', which makes him feel very lonely even though he's not alone. Do ye understand what I mean by that?"

I nod. "Yes," I say. "If Britney B is out sick and I don't have anyone to sit with at lunch, I feel super lonely even though the cafeteria is filled to the brim."

"Exactly," she says.

"I suppose that's why he never wants to go out on interviews with me."

"Verra possible," she agrees. "Oftentimes when he's oot an' aboot and with others, people interact wi' the person he's with instead of him, even askin' the other person aboot Hammy Bean when he's standin' right there. And that hurts him very deeply."

"I always say words can be very powerful," I tell her. "But I suppose that applies to the ones you *don't* say too."

"You're a canny lass."

"There's this new girl at my school, Remy Prudant, who always eats lunch alone and never has made any friends, not all year. I bet she feels that way too. I can't imagine sitting at lunch without Britney B every single day. That would be quite a mare indeed."

She smiles again and nods. "Hammy Bean has taken some hard hits in life, but he never stays down for long," she says. "He always gets back up again. That's what makes him so amazin'. He's brave. The bravest lad I know."

I nod. "He's got the tidbits," I say. "That's for sure."

She gives me a Cheez Whiz. *"Tidbits?"*

"Tidbits *aplenty.*"

"Hmmm."

"Thank you for the talk and the sticky toffee pudding, Ms. Begbie," I tell her. "You know what you should do? You should call it Euna Begbie's *Famous* Sticky Toffee Pudding."

"Famous?" She laughs. "I dinna ken aboot that."

"I do," I say. "Just like at Mr. Farquhar's place. You could hang signs in the window. Like *Ada Ru from Denver says it's like she died and went to heaven* or *Dax Cady from New York City says it's right on with a side of groovy.*"

She laughs again.

"I'm glad I got to know you, Ms. Begbie," I say. "You've turned out to be one of the best orange possibilities I've found in Scotland. And not just because of your sponge and meatless ice cream either."

She puts her hand on my arm and gives it a squeeze and, with a big orange SpaghettiO grin, goes, "You are one of my best orange possibilities too."

21

A TOP-SECRET ODYSSEY
AND A WEE BOAT

We are drowning in green.

A curtain of green lush leaves and grasses and trees and moss all around us.

We rendezvoused at the arch over the black diamonds at six acorns to the wind on the dot for Hammy Bean's top-secret odyssey. I actually got there early because I was bursting to show off my new code knowledge. And not to be the one to point it out or anything, but Dax didn't show his face until six oh five acorns.

I'm just saying.

"Where are we going?" I demand, pushing branches out of my face.

It turns out that this top-secret odyssey is so top-secret that Hammy Bean couldn't even add it to the code list and, once we rendezvoused up at the bridge, he made us both cross our hearts again that we wouldn't tell another single, solitary soul.

We've walked so far through thick trees and bushes along the loch that we're all the way to the other side of the Fort Augustus beach. Lucky for us, today the clouds are in the sky where they're supposed to be, there's no rain in sight and the sun is so warm that I have my sweatshirt tied around my waist.

"We're almost there," Hammy Bean calls back to us.

Mac-Talla is leading on the leash with Hammy Bean following her, me following him and Dax following me.

He's so far ahead of me now, all I can see are bits of his captain's hat bobbing up and down between the leaves.

"How much farther?" I call up to him.

That's when Hammy Bean stops.

"Shh," he hisses. "Haud yer wheesht."

We stop too.

"Close your eyes and listen," he tells us.

I close my eyes and listen, hearing all the sounds around me that I hadn't even noticed before.

A full orchestra of noises.

Traffic swooshes from the roadway above.

The wind blows the leaves, making a sssss sound.

Trees sway and the bark cracks.

Birds sing their morning ditty.

Water laps and licks over rocks at the shore.

"I hear water lapping," I tell him.

"Exactly," he calls.

Mac-Talla barks three times and then they start to run.

"Hurry!" Hammy Bean shouts.

"Pick up the pace, Denver," Dax calls from behind me. "We're going to lose them."

164

I start to run now too and so does Dax. I can hear Ole Roy smacking against his back with each stride.

I push at more branches and leaves and trip over unearthed tree roots stretching over the path until, finally, the green curtain parts and we reach a small smooth-stone beach at the edge of the loch.

Stretched out beyond the rocky shore is a weathered rickety wooden dock with missing slats and peeling paint that bobs in the water with a bitty dinghy tied up next to it. The dinghy is supposed to be red, but the years and weather have peeled it to mostly drab gray wood with just a hint of red still hanging strong. The top is lined with small round windows. The only new thing on it is the fresh-painted letters on the back.

THE SS ALBATROSS

"Mamo Honey lets me do a lot o' things because o' Mac-Talla," Hammy Bean tells us. "But this is different. I dinna even ken what she'd do if she knew this secret."

"*This?*" I ask him.

He does a hand flourish in the direction of the boat. "It's my boat," he says with a big dimpled grin.

I point at it. "Did you say *boat*?"

"That's right." He lifts his chin high.

"Hmm . . . ," I say, examining it from the shore. "Calling it a *boat* might be a bit of a stretch."

"It's a wee boat, aye," he says.

"You've got the *wee* part right," I tell him.

"Not in my mind. When I think about it, I see a verra

165

high-tech yacht fit only for serious an' highly respected Nessie hunters."

"Sure, I can see it," Dax says with a big, toothy smile in my direction.

Fathead.

Hammy Bean takes Mac-Talla off her leash and she jumps into the boat and brings him back a dirty used-to-be-yellow tennis ball. She pushes her nose at his hand until he grabs it from her mouth.

"Go get it, girl!" Hammy Bean hollers, throwing the ball into the water.

Mac-Talla scrambles toward the end of the dock and belly-flops in after it, swimming out to retrieve it and bringing it back to the dock. Then she lays her sloppy, matted red curls down in a sunny spot, with the ball tucked safely under her chin, and closes her eyes.

"Is this thing *really* yours?" I ask.

"Finders keepers, losers weepers," he says.

"So you *found it* and basically *called it*?"

"It was abandoned," he says. "No one wanted it. No one wanted to care for it an' show it excitin' life experiences. Not until I came along. Now I care for it the way it deserves to be cared for."

"Who painted the name on it?" Dax asks.

"Cornelius Blaise Barrington, Nessie hunter extraordinaire," Hammy Bean says. "If ye want to get technical aboot it, Cornelius found it first, but it's still *mine*. I'm the captain. He said so an' we christened it that way. He even hit a bottle of cider on the side durin' the official christenin' ceremony."

"Right on," Dax says.

"So what's an albatross . . . *exactly*?" I want to know. "It's some kind of bird, right?"

"Not just some bird, ye ken. It's a mighty bird," Hammy Bean tells us. "One that spends most o' its days flyin' the skies of the world above us, circlin', watchin' . . . and wishin'."

I look at Dax and he looks at me.

"Wishing for what?" I ask.

Hammy Bean shrugs. "Lots o' things."

"What about this Cornelius guy?" Dax says. "Has he actually ever seen the monster?"

"Not yet."

"How long has he been searching for it?" I ask.

"For more years than I've been alive," Hammy Bean tells us.

"*Thaaaat's* not exactly a great track record," I say.

"Yet *you* still won't go in the water," Dax informs me, stepping aboard the wee dinghy and guiding Hammy Bean to the edge of the pier so he can hop inside too.

"A discovery is meant to be discovered only when the time is right to discover it," Hammy Bean says.

I think about that.

"Hey, that's pretty good," I say. "It's got pop."

"It's actually a quote from the one an' only Tobin Sky himself."

Dax sits down on a bench at the back of the boat and slips Ole Roy off, setting it on the bench next to him. "Do you really take this thing out in the middle of the loch?"

"Aye," Hammy Bean says. "Nessie is oot there." He points

to the water. "But I always go out wi' Cornelius. That's his one rule. An' one day, we're goin' to take this thing all the way oot to the ocean."

"The ocean?" I say, eyeing the wee boat, which doesn't look seaworthy enough for a rain puddle, let alone the ocean. "How would you get this thing to the ocean from a lake?"

"There's a river that connects Loch Ness to the Moray Firth, which takes ye right to the North Sea. One day I plan to sail all the way to London."

"What's in London?" Dax asks.

Hammy Bean doesn't say anything, but I know the answer to that one.

"Are ye comin' aboard or aren't you? I have things to show you." Hammy Bean calls up to me, my Nikes still planted firmly on the dock.

The headlines run through my brain like the neon news crawl signs in Times Square.

DENVER GIRL PRESUMED EATEN ALIVE
BY A LAKE MONSTER AFTER SINKING TO THE
BOTTOM OF THE LOCH IN A VERY WEE VESSEL

"Come on." Dax holds a hand out to me.

"Yeah, I promise we won't leave the dock," Hammy Bean says.

I pace the rickety boards and chew my bottom lip.

A wake from a passing boat in the middle of the loch hits the posts of the dock and makes it sway beneath me.

I hold my arms straight out to balance myself.

Hammy Bean pushes the button on his watch. It calls out the time: *"Twelve-thirty,"* the voice announces.

"You have a talking watch too?" Dax says.

"That's right." Hammy Bean holds out his wrist. "And I named it as well. In honor of Dax, I've named all *my* important things."

"Right on, HB," Dax says.

Hammy Bean holds up a black digital watch strapped to his skinny arm. "Dax and Ada Ru, meet Tavish Tick. And this"—he holds up his slick, shiny walking cane—"is Tadhg Cane."

When Hammy Bean says *Tadhg*, he Mr. Mews horks the last part of it.

"Tag?" Dax repeats.

"Tadhg," Hammy Bean horks again. "Kind o' like *tag* wi' a *k* at the end o' it."

"Yeah, but that time you spit on me." Dax wipes at his face.

Hammy Bean giggles. "That's when ye know you've said it right."

"Tadhg," Dax horks.

"Brilliant!" Hammy Bean exclaims. "It means *philosopher*. I picked that one because he knows all the places to take me."

"Nice," Dax says.

"Twelve thirty-two," Tavish Tick announces.

"Come on, Dax." Hammy Bean holds two arms straight out to find his way through the door to the inside part of the boat. "At this rate, we'll never get to it."

"See you in there." Dax gives me the same toothy smile as I watch them head inside.

I pace the dock.

Up.

And then down it.

Up.

And then down it.

And then I think of Mom's Ferris wheel, take a deep breath and jump with all my might, landing my Nikes flat on the deck of the wee boat. But once I do, it rocks like we're sailing through a hurricane and I spread my arms out on both sides of me to balance.

Hammy Bean and Dax lean out the door.

"Well done!" Hammy Bean tells me.

"Yeah, but now she looks like an airplane trying to take off," Dax says.

"An airplane?" Hammy Bean asks him. "Airplanes have wings, right?"

"Right," Dax says. "Her arms are out like she's trying to fly."

I slap my arms down and give him a good glare.

"Do the wings on a plane move up and down like a flyin' albatross?" Hammy Bean asks.

Me and Dax stay silent for a minute.

"No," I say. "They're steel. They stay straight out all the time and glide through the air. It's the motor that propels the plane so the wings don't need to flap."

"Aye, that makes sense," he says. "I always wondered that an' never asked. And I've never flown on an airplane. So are *her* arms straight or flappin'?" he asks Dax.

Dax laughs. "A little of both."

Hammy Bean laughs too.

"They are not," I snap.

"Hurry now." Hammy Bean curls a hand to wave me inside. "I have a lot to teach you."

The three of us wedge ourselves inside.

"*This* is the cockpit an' ye can call it kind of the salon too," he says.

"What's a *salon*?"

"On a boat, it's the livin' area. And since this is the only area for livin', this is it. It's a combination cockpit and salon."

"But it's so tiny," I tell him.

"I didn't say it was a *grand* salon," he says. "It's a wee salon, but a salon nonetheless. An' that motor on the back. The Kommander 5000 is so powerful, it can take ye all the way to Russia if you like."

"Is the motor new?" Dax asks.

"Nae," Hammy Bean says. "But Cornelius Blaise Barrington, Nessie hunter extraordinaire, can fix anythin'. Above us"—he points straight up—"is a second floor, or technically a small observation platform ye can crawl out onto."

I giggle at that one.

"An' this"—he reaches out to find three tiny dark television screens mounted on an area near the helm—"is my ultra-sonar equipment. Well, Cornelius's, anyway. He mounted it in here for us to use when we take the boat oot."

"And Mamo Honey doesn't know about any of this?" I ask.

"Are ye kiddin'?"

"How is the sonar used?" Dax asks.

Hammy Bean's finger finds a single button on the side of

the screen and he holds it down until the screens come to life. "It's vital monster-huntin' equipment for the loch," he explains. "Watch this."

The screen flickers with a neon-green light and then there's a graph of numbers along the bottom and up the left side. Soon, more color splotches show up between the lines.

"Okay, so what do all these colors mean?" I ask.

"The sonar is measurin' what's beneath us."

"Like with a camera?"

"Nae," he says. "With sound. The sonar makes a ping, and its sound wave bounces off solid objects and records their shapes on the screen."

"Whoa," I say. "Seeing with sound."

"Aye. The loch is twenty-three miles long, one mile wide an' seven hundred an' eighty-eight feet deep. It's twice as deep as the North Sea, so really, it's almost like an ocean. The thing is that an underwater camera can only capture up to twenty-seven feet because the water's so black. So most investigators also use sonar. Even the Loch Ness Project an' all the real scientists associated with that search use sonar."

"That is awesome!" Dax tells him, leaning in closer to see the screen.

"Look at these." Hammy Bean motions in the direction of the wall next to the screens. "Do ye see pieces of paper taped to the wall?"

"Yes," I say. "They're oval-shaped colors."

"Exactly," he says. "Our sonar made these discoveries."

"You found shapes?" I say.

"We call them targets. We're not sure what it was the sonar measured, but it captured something that was ten feet long.

And when we went over it again, it was gone, which means it was alive an' movin' under its own power. It wasn't a rock or something that's inanimate and doesna move."

"*Ten . . . feet . . . long?*" I whisper from behind my hand.

"That's right."

"That's what you meant at the booth that day," I say. "Even though you haven't seen Nessie with your own eyes. You've *heard* her."

"Aye."

"Euna Begbie says when Nessie breaks the surface you hear the bubbles first."

"That's exactly right."

Then I feel something brimming up inside me, and I know exactly what it is too.

"Captain Green Bean." I stand tall and salute him with a straight hand to my forehead. "I'm ready to hear her too."

"Aye, aye," he says. "The question is . . . did ye memorize all the codes?"

I take a deep breath and clear my throat. "The fairy swims by night, but only the swans will be victors of the spoils."

Dax and Hammy Bean cheer and clap.

"Well done!" Hammy Bean exclaims.

"It's about time," Dax says with that one-lipped smile of his.

I look Dax right in his seaweed eyes and say, "And just so you know . . . I found out there is no such thing as a pooping goose or a blue Subaru."

Dax's one-lipper turns to a full-on two-lipper that spreads all across his face.

"Team Nessie Quest," Hammy Bean starts. "You're both

ready for yer next mission. My Mamo Honey lets me stay over wi' Corny on Saturday nights, but what she doesna ken is that we go out on the boat at night. Some people say Nessie is nocturnal, yet not one person is oot here searchin' in the dark . . . except us."

"And you want us to come with you?" Dax asks.

"Aye," Hammy Bean says. "We're a team now. So will ye commit to helpin' me find definitive evidence? Without it, the Loch Ness Project will never take any of my research seriously. Are you really and truly a force to be reckoned with?"

"I'm in," Dax says.

"That's pure tidy, Dax!" Hammy Bean exclaims. "What about you, Denver?"

"I'm in it, *big-time*," I tell him.

22

SIX ACORNS AND SHAGGY CATTLE

I think long and hard about how best to present my case to Mom and Dad.

One parental veto is all it will take to throw a wrench in the whole plan.

And with my luck it will be my parents' veto that does it.

At dinner that night I try real hard to pay attention to Dad while he talks all about his class at the university, but I'm much too busy worrying to concentrate. How in the world am I going to find the right words to ask for permission to camp out with Dax and Hammy Bean on Saturday night so we can slip out to meet Corny on the SS *Albatross* and go searching for Nessie?

"You're sure quiet over there," Mom tells me, taking a bite of mac and cheese.

"Oh, yeah . . . well, I had a big day," I say.

"Does that mean you've secured all your supporting characters?" Dad asks.

"Yep," I tell him. "I've found my Ron and lots of supporting characters. I'm just trying to figure out how best to start it."

"What about your Hermione?" Dad asks. "Have you found her?"

I smile real big. "Kind of," I say, and then giggle. "It's Dax, although he's not exactly on board with it, but that's just his too bad."

"So, now that you have your characters, Ms. Harriet Potter, what's next?"

"Well." I clear my throat. "I'm glad you asked because I would like permission to go camping overnight with Dax and Hammy Bean next Saturday night for a nighttime Nessie search."

They both breathe in slow and look at each other, which only means one thing. I'd better start doing some fast talking.

"It's only for one night," I say. "We will set up the tent right out there." I point toward the tall arched window. "It's for research purposes and you always say research is the most important thing, right, Mom? Like for your journal articles? Right?"

"Well . . . yes, but—" she starts.

"You'll be able to look out the window at any time and see us out there. It'll be totally safe. You said so, right? Because you don't believe in the monster anyway."

"Hmmm, I don't know if it's a good idea," she says, folding her hands in front of her face and resting her chin on them. "Zuma?"

Uh-oh. This is not good.

Not to be parentally paranoid, but in my past experience

on Tennyson Street, that particular gesture on Mom's part is a signal to Dad that they need to be on the same page and that page begins and ends with a big, fat no.

I hold my hands out. "Wait," I say. "Before you say no can I just say one more thing?"

Mom nods.

"You told me to make the best of my time in Scotland and I finally am. I found my story, Mom. And it's out there." I point toward the loch. "Euna Begbie said tourists always leave things behind that she keeps stored in the cellar and she has both a tent and a cooler for us to use."

"What about sleeping bags?" Mom asks.

"*Sleeping bags?*" I say. "Who plans on sleeping? It's a land excursion to find the elusive Loch Ness Monster. There will be no sleeping. We have research to complete. *Research.* How can we do that asleep?"

"Uh-huh, well, I think—"

"Mom," I interrupt again. "Please think hard about this before you decide to squelch my young enthusiasm with a parental veto, because it may scar me for life."

"Are you done?" she asks.

I think about it.

"One more thing," I say with my finger in the air. "I'd also like to say that . . . um, the thing is . . . okay, here's the thing . . . ummm . . . actually . . . hmmm, yeah, I guess that was it."

My radio beeps.

"Captain Green Bean to Denver and Strings. Captain Green Bean is a go for p.m. duty. Over."

"Who's that?" Dad asks.

"Hammy Bean," I say. "His Mamo Honey said yes and he's going to want to know your answer too."

Dad raises his eyebrows. "Why didn't he just say that?"

"It's code," I tell him. "You know, because of . . . *Nessie Race spies.*" I whisper the last three words.

Dad raises his eyebrows at Mom. "Nessie Race spies?"

Beep.

"Strings is a go for p.m. duty. Over," Dax calls into the radio.

"Rendezvous on Saturday night, black diamonds, six acorns to the wind of obscurity," Hammy Bean instructs. "Denver, do ye read? Over."

"See that?" I say. "They both have permission now. Please don't let me be the only one left out. I have to be there. I'm the first-string reporter for the *Nessie Juggernaut.*"

"And what does Dax do?" Dad asks.

"He's just creating Hammy Bean's podcast intro, but Hammy Bean has already promoted him and given him a radio and a handle and everything and before you know it, Dax will be in and I'll be out. Just like with that sneaky Emmanuelle Penney, always trying to one-up me. I know she's moving in on Britney B for best-friend status as we speak."

"Adelaide Ru—" Mom starts.

"I knew it," I mumble, slumping down in my chair with my arms crossed. "I knew you'd say no and now I'll be the laughingstock of the whole team. They'll make up all these codes about a pooping goose and laugh and laugh. Hammy Bean will oust me and even take away my walkie-talkie and make Dax his first mate."

"A pooping what?" Dad asks.

I sigh. "Goose—" I start.

"Can we please stay on track here?" Mom interrupts.

"What? I shouldn't ask about a pooping goose?" Dad says.

"About the overnight," Mom says, and then hesitates.

Here it comes.

The big, fat, hairy no.

"I think it'll be fine, Libby," Dad says to Mom.

I suck air, sit up straight in my chair and slap my hands flat together in Mom's direction. "Please, Mom? Please? It's a super-important component of making the best of Scotland and you're the one who said I should do that. This is me doing that and I need to do this to do that."

I know she's thinking hard about it because she's chewing on her bottom lip the same exact way I do when I'm thinking hard about something.

"Oh, all right," she says, and then holds up one straight finger. "But there will be rules."

I pop up from the table and throw my arms around her neck. "Thank you. Thank you. Thank you," I say, bombarding her cheek with kisses.

"Hey, what about me?" Dad protests. "I said yes first."

I run over to his side of the table and smooch on him for a while too.

Beep.

Hammy Bean's voice comes over the radio.

"Denver. Come in, Denver. What's your status? Over."

I grab the radio off my belt and push the button.

"Denver's *in*. Rendezvous on Saturday night, black diamonds, six acorns to the wind of obscurity. Over."

"*Thaaat's* a roger, Denver. Over an' oot."

Then Dax comes on the radio and says, "Saturday night will fly in the sky, but the Highland cattle will still need a haircut. Over."

I roll my eyes.

"What does that one mean?" Dad asks.

I throw my hands in the air. "Nothing," I say. "The kid just makes things up."

"It's all made up?" Dad asks. "Even the pooping goose?"

"Pooping goose and hairy cow yes, but not everything."

"So what does the rest of it mean?"

"You have to be an official employee of the *Jug* to be briefed on top-secret codes." I put a hand on Dad's shoulder. "Only Team Nessie Quest gets to know them."

"Ahh," he says. "I understand."

"Can I be excused?" I ask, darting out of the dining room before my permission is officially granted.

"Hey, come back! You haven't finished your dinner!" Mom calls after me.

By the time I hit the hall I'm in a full-on run, slipping and sliding on the hardwood floor in my white socks. "Can't!" I call back to her. "My stomach is too excited to eat!"

23

A SECRET AGENT MISSION

With one tent firmly tied to the ground, three lawn chairs, one portable fire pit, a single bag of marshmallows and a well-worn game of Clue, we're set for our very first undercover operation: our Saturday-night Nessie hunt.

It's two against one.

Me and Hammy Bean against Dax.

We whisper together, back and forth. First me to Hammy Bean, then him to me, until we figure out the hidden combination.

"I think that might be it," I whisper.

"Are you sure?" he asks.

"Are you?" I say.

He thinks about it.

"It's Miss Scarlet . . . in the library . . . wi' the candlestick," Hammy Bean calls out during our fifth go-around.

Dax has won three games and we've won two.

This is the tiebreaker.

"Nae! It's the wrench . . . no, wait, it's the candlestick," Hammy Bean says.

"Is that your final answer?" Dax wants to know.

"Wait," I say. "I really think it's the wrench. Say wrench."

"I need your final answer," Dax says.

Hammy Bean sucks in a long, deep breath. "Wrench," he finally says.

Dax opens the envelope. "It's the candlestick!"

Hammy Bean jumps out of his lawn chair. "I knew it!" he shouts. "I was the one who said candlestick first!"

"Yes." Dax grins. "But you didn't say it *last*."

"I call an official reconsideration," Hammy Bean says.

"Judge's rule?" Dax calls out into the darkness, and then listens to the silence. He points a thumb toward the ground. "Loser!"

Hammy Bean busts a gut laughing. "Dax, yer bum's out the windae!"

"Yeah," I say giggling. "Yer bum's out the windae."

"You don't even know what that means," Dax tells me.

"I know, but it sounds like you."

"It means you're full o' nonsense," Hammy Bean tells us.

"See?" I say to Dax.

Dax just one-lips me and reaches for Ole Roy.

"Fancy another game?" Hammy Bean wants to know.

"*No*," Dax and I say at the very same time.

"We've roasted marshmallows, eaten all the cheese sandwiches and played Clue six whole times and it's only eight-thirty," I say. "What time are we rendezvousing, anyway?"

"Shh!" Hammy Bean hisses. "Haud yer wheesht or someone will hear ye."

I look around. "Not likely," I tell him. "There's no one even out here but us."

"Nessie Race spies are everywhere," he whispers.

"Did Euna Begbie have any other games in her cellar?" Dax asks.

"No," I say.

"I brought Braille Uno." Hammy Bean pulls a deck out of his Windbreaker pocket.

"Can't do it, HB," Dax tells him, plucking on his strings. "Uno's for babies."

"Fine," Hammy Bean says, popping another marshmallow from the bag and sitting back in his lawn chair.

We listen as Dax plays his beautiful music, the sun sinks behind the rolling green hills and a crisp breeze makes the flames in our fire pit dance and crackle.

"Did Corny at least give you an approximate number of acorns on the oak tree that blows in the morning breeze?" I ask him.

He holds his ear to the sky and listens and then finally decides.

"Aye," he says. "But first we at least have to wait until the last parental roll call o' the night."

"The *what*?" I ask.

"Hello!" Mom calls from the shadows.

I let out a shriek.

"Sorry to scare you," she says. "How's everyone doing out here?"

"Mom, you scared me half to death." I look over at Hammy Bean and he's got a big I-told-you-so smirk going on between the dimples.

"Oh, well, just checking in," she says, standing by the fire. "Anyone need anything else before we go to bed? More cheese sandwiches? I can put a few slices of ham on there too for anyone who's interested."

I stand up from my lawn chair and grab her hand, pulling her back in the direction of the abbey.

Except she's not budging.

"Mom," I tell her. "We're working."

- "Oh, I know, I know." She pulls her sweater tighter and shivers. "It's just getting chilly and I'm double-checking to see if there isn't a change of heart out here. Mamo Honey called earlier and I told her I'd check in on you all one more time and give a call back."

"We're *Juggernauts*," I remind her. "Forces to be reckoned with. And forces . . . *never* have second thoughts."

"Right, yep . . . and you remember all the ground rules, though, right?" She looks back and forth at us, waiting for an answer.

Hammy Bean jumps up from his chair and salutes her before he spouts off Mamo Honey and Mom's rules in clear, crisp order.

"No water expeditions. Stay at least three meters clear o' the shore at all times. Radio you if we need anythin'."

As part of the camping-out agreement, I have surrendered my walkie-talkie to Mom so that we have a lifeline if anything comes up. Hammy Bean surrendered his to Mamo Honey. Both set to channel seventeen to avoid security breaches regarding any top-secret communications.

That all means we have one radio left set to channel five.

Mom pulls my radio out of her jacket pocket and holds

it in the air. "Don't worry about waking us if you need anything," she tells us.

I pull on her sleeve again. "Mom," I whisper. "You're being totally embarrassing right now."

"I don't think so, Mrs. Fitzhugh," Hammy Bean hollers in our direction. "I think it's nice that ye care so much." He gives her a wide dimpled smile with his chin high in the air.

Brownnoser.

"Mom, we got this," I assure her. "I promise it will be fine. If we have a problem, Dax will radio, okay?"

"All right," she says. "I'll leave you all to it, then."

"Good night, Mrs. Fitzhugh," Hammy Bean calls out.

"Good night, then," she says, and gives Dax a good, long once-over. "Good night, Dax."

He looks up from the guitar. "Have a groovy night, Mrs. F."

Mom hesitates and then says, "Okay, then. See you all in the morning."

I watch her until she disappears into the darkness and then I slink back into my seat.

"Oh my god, she's so embarrassing," I mumble.

"I think your mam is pure barry," Hammy Bean tells me. I look over at him, hugging his knees on top of his lawn chair, his cheeks pink from the flames. "I wish my mam an' da were here more to worry aboot me that way."

"When's the last time you saw them?" I ask.

Dax rolls his eyes to the sky.

"Oh . . . ummmm, maybe May?" Hammy Bean says. "Aye, yes . . . definitely May. They brought me this T-shirt."

He opens up his tweed suit coat to show us a T-shirt with a

big green Nessie on the front and the words HIDE-AND-SEEK CHAMPION on the bottom.

"That's a good one," Dax says. "Real cool, HB."

"They think it's great that I want to be a famous crypto-zoologist when I grow up," Hammy Bean says. "Just like the one an' only Tobin Sky. They really love me. A lot."

"What's so great about this Tobin Sky, anyway?" Dax asks.

"What's not so great aboot him?" Hammy Bean says. "He's just like me, I mean he was when he was my age. He started his own cryptozoology business when he was a kid. He lived in this small town in California known for its Bigfoot sight-ings, so he opened his verra own Bigfoot detective agency."

"Did he ever find a Bigfoot?" I ask.

"He an' his partner, Dr. Lemonade Liberty Witt, went on to make a lot o' great discoveries, includin' the Sky-Witt video, which still hasna been debunked to this day. It's the most definitive evidence to date. Now he teaches crypto-zoology at Berkeley and she's a veterinarian in San Francisco, but they're still partners when it comes to expeditions. An' ye wanna talk aboot famous? They're famous. Ye just know they go to the store in a limo to get their bananas because the Sky-Witt video is the best of a Bigfoot there has ever been. They're so well respected in their research that the Loch Ness Project invited Tobin Sky to speak in Inverness two years ago aboot the science o' findin' hidden creatures."

"That's the group Mamo Honey used to work with," Dax says.

"That's right," Hammy Bean says. "The Loch Ness Project has the most esteemed group of scientists searching for Nessie."

"But she quit," I say.

"Aye," he says.

"Why?"

"She doesn't like to talk about it," he says. "All I can say is that it had to do with an incident on the water."

My eyes open wide. "I bet she had a close encounter with the monster."

"Nae," he tells me. "That wouldna make her quit. Mamo Honey is the bravest scientist on the face of this earth when it comes to creature discovery. She would never be scared off by the monster."

"So what was it?" I ask. "Oh, wait . . . does it have anything to do with that old locked-up garage behind your house?"

"How do ye ken aboot that?" he asks.

I shrug. "I saw it." I point to Dax. "I mean . . . we did. Right, Dax?"

"Mmm," he says, picking at his strings again.

"It's just curious is all I'm saying," I tell Hammy Bean. "What needs to be locked up so tight with a super-thick chain and padlock? Like no one would ever in a million years get it open—"

Hammy Bean leans forward and gets real serious.

"That's a top-secret bobble that is so Nessie sensitive I can't even let *the Jug* crew know aboot it. Do ye understand? All I can say aboot it is that it's our ace in the hole. But she has to be the one to decide it, no one else."

Beep.

"Team Nessie Quest, do ye read?" a voice calls into the darkness on Dax's radio. "Come in, Team Nessie Quest. Over."

Finally, the amazing Cornelius Blaise Barrington, Nessie hunter extraordinaire.

Dax grabs the radio from his belt and pushes the button.

I check my watch. Exactly eleven acorns on the oak tree that blows in the morning breeze.

"Team Nessie Quest here," Dax says. "Strings, Denver and Captain Green Bean all present and accounted for. Over."

"The corn is poppin' and the secret vessel looms large on the black diamonds. Over."

"Roger that, Corncob," Dax calls into the radio. "Buttered and salted? Over."

"*Thaaat's* a ten-four, Strings. Over and oot."

Hammy Bean leans toward me, finding my arm and grabbing it tight. "Our first undercover mission as a team," he screeches in a whisper. "It's goin' to be brilliant! Epic! Grand in all proportions! They'll name me the greatest crypto-zoologist in all o' Scotland. The Loch Ness Project will ask me an' Corny to be a part o' their group o' scientists and Tobin Sky will be beggin' to do our podcast after tonight."

I laugh. "How can you be so sure tonight is the night?" I ask him.

Hammy Bean zips up his Nessie Quest Windbreaker all the way to his chin.

"Because," he says. "Everythin' has changed for me now an' it's all down to you. My mates . . . the best mates any lad could ask for."

I look at Dax and he looks at me.

"Now, come on, you right numpties, haud yer wheesht and let's git gaun!"

24

BUTTER AND SALT
AND A WHOLE LOT OF POP

Cornelius Blaise Barrington, Nessie Hunter Extraordinaire.

Talk about a character that pops.

Not to mention a force to be reckoned with.

I find this out when our feet finally hit the first weath-ered board of the rickety pier housing Hammy Bean's wee boat. Since Mac-Talla stayed home with Mamo Honey, Hammy Bean held on to my elbow and stayed an arm's length behind me so that he could feel my steps and know where to go.

"Hello, the SS *Albatross*!" Hammy Bean shouts out when he feels the dock underneath his feet.

A blinding flashlight beam finds us at the dock and then a booming voice follows like a lightning bolt through the dark.

"Hello, the shore!"

Cornelius is a looming figure making the wee boat even wee-*er* than the first time I saw it. Under his weight, it's a wonder the thing stays afloat. Cornelius is way taller than Dad but probably about the same age, with wide shoulders and chiseled features that make him look more like a carved statue of a mythological god than just a plain old man.

"Ahoy there! I am Cornelius Blaise Barrington," he announces in a deep, booming voice. "But ye can all call me Corny. So nice to meet the new crew. Cheers! Ye look like you're ready to find a monster."

"Oh, we are!" Hammy Bean tells him. "This is Dax an' Ada Ru—they're my mates."

"Welcome! Welcome!" Corny calls, and then, with a strong hand, he gives us each an alley-oop onto the wee boat. When he takes my hand, his fingers cover it completely and his alley-oop is so strong, it almost lands me in the water on the other side of the boat.

Once we're all aboard, we huddle in the salon. Corny has to duck his head way down to even fit in the door.

Inside we're elbow to elbow. It's a good thing Dax left Ole Roy in the tent because Ole Roy would've definitely had to sit this one out.

"Captain Green Bean," Corny announces. "How would ye like to assign the crew for this mission?"

"Dax," Hammy Bean announces. "You're assigned to port side. Ada Ru, you are assigned the starboard side. Corny, ye take the bow an' I'll monitor the sonar."

"Aye aye, Captain." Corny gives him a salute.

"Team Nessie Quest, do ye believe we can do it?" Hammy Bean calls out.

"Maybe," I say.

"It could happen," Dax says.

"I hope so," Corny says.

Hammy Bean shakes his head and lets his chin fall to his chest.

"That's not very enthusiastic," he informs us. "I said, do ye believe we can find the monster?" He shouts it this time with his finger to the sky.

Dax looks at me and I look at Dax and we both look at Corny.

"Say *I believe!*" Hammy Bean exclaims.

Corny holds out one finger, then two and then three, and on three me, Dax and Corny shout a booming *I believe!* in Hammy Bean's direction.

"See? Was that so hard?" Hammy Bean says, and then busies himself with the knobs on the tiny sonar television screens.

Corny turns the key and starts the Kommander 5000.

"All right, crew, are ye ready to be a part of our Saturday-night midnight sonar sweep?" he asks. "Tonight's mission is the waters near the Urquhart Castle."

"Um, excuse me, please." I raise my hand.

"Aye?"

"Just one question. You've got life jackets on board, right?" I ask. "I mean, if we're going out in the middle of this lake in the dead of night, we should have life jackets, right?"

Dax sighs and whispers, "Don't be a baby."

"I'm not being a baby," I insist. "I'm here, aren't I? There's nothing wrong with being safety-conscious. Am I right, Corny?"

"Aye, right ye are, lass, it's maritime law. There are plenty o' life jackets in the benches at the stern o' the boat. Everyone needs to have one on before we leave the dock."

I turn to Dax and give him an I-told-you-so stink eye.

"See," I say. "It's not just me, it's *Mary's Law*."

25

SUBTERRANEAN SNOOZE BUTTON

Dax is staring at me with his hands on his hips and his eyebrows crunched together. "Are you seriously that big of a baby?" he asks, jutting a chin toward my life preserver.

"What?" I say. "*You're* wearing one."

"Yeah, one . . . not *two*."

"Lads and lass," Corny interrupts us. "We are going to do a sonar sweep in the bay oot front o' the Urquhart Castle." Corny turns the wheel, pulling away from the rickety dock. "It's where we've had our best hits on the sonar."

There are dim lights on every side of the boat and scattered lights along the shore and way off into the hills, but the water and the air and the night are pitch black.

I keep my face glued to the starboard side with Dad's camera in the on position as the SS *Albatross* glides smoothly through the glassy water. There isn't a single noise other than the Kommander 5000's low hum beneath the surface as it propels us forward at a very slow speed.

Hammy Bean is standing in front of the sonar, chewing on his pinky nail, ears glued to the pinging sounds coming from the tiny screen.

"Dax," he calls out. "Anythin'?"

"Negative," Dax says.

"Ada Ru?"

"Nope," I say.

"But ye have yer camera ready, right?"

"Roger that," I say.

Corny guides the SS *Albatross* back and forth over the waters of Urquhart Bay as we watch wide-eyed at our posts.

Sweeping back and forth.

Until finally, at two acorns and about the gazillionth sweep, Corny says, "I think she's sleepin' in tonight."

"I thought this thing was supposed to be nocturnal," Dax says.

"So you're saying even subterranean reptiles can push the Snooze button," I say, following my remark with a loud *HA!*

No one laughs.

Especially not Hammy Bean, who has a scowl on his face like no one's business.

"Corny," I ask, "do you think the monster could be just a plain old fish?"

"The sturgeon theory."

"Right," I say.

"I've studied everythin' aboot this loch for over twenty years an' I know, based on the water temperature, depth, ecosystem and more, that there is only one option."

I hold one finger up. "One?"

He nods. "It must be a new species or possibly a combination o' already cataloged species an' one not yet identified."

"So, like a cross between two different kinds of animals?" I ask.

"Aye," he says. "Since the lochs are connected to the North Sea by the river, it verra well could be a combination o' sea creatures; however, it would have to be able to survive in both seawater and freshwater at the same time. The big question is, how does it evade capture or detection every time? The loch is large an' deep, but there has to be more than that. The question is what?"

"But that information is still classified," Hammy Bean says.

"What information?" I ask.

"The banana is yet to be skinned and it's still growin' on the vine," Hammy Bean tells Corny.

"Hey," I say. "That one isn't on the list either."

"That's because it's classified," he tells me.

"Well, when are we going to call it a night because the monster isn't cooperating? I'm tired, and Dax is already asleep."

Dax's head pops up. "I'm not sleeping."

"Being a Nessie hunter isna for the faint o' heart," he tells me. "Ye have to be a warrior. A force to be reckoned with. So man yer post. In all this time you've been blabbin' ye might have missed yer chance."

∾⟡

By three-oh-five acorns, I can barely keep my eyes open and Dax's head is bobbing. Corny makes the final decision to end the hunt and motors the SS *Albatross* back to the rickety dock while Hammy Bean hangs his head in defeat.

All in all, there are pros and cons to our midnight search with the larger-than-life Cornelius Blaise Barrington, Nessie Hunter Extraordinaire.

Pro: I'm alive.

Which is kind of a big one.

Pro: the SS *Albatross* didn't sink to the bottom.

Another big one.

Con: Team Nessie Quest investigators found diddly squat.

And that's a big con to have. Especially for Hammy Bean.

After an entire night of scanning the loch for a monster, we don't have anything to show for it.

Not one single target hit.

I'm disappointed for sure, but on our way back to the tent Hammy Bean is one surly green bean.

Dax on one end, me on the other and Hammy Bean in the middle. After no one says anything for a real long time, I try my best to lighten the mood.

"Maybe they really were sleeping," I suggest, looking back and forth between the boys. "I mean, they have to sleep sometimes, right?"

Silence.

"Look at it this way," I say. "We've got more time to hunt together as a team. I mean, if we found definitive proof tonight, what would we do tomorrow? Right? Right?"

"Not even one target hit," Hammy Bean mutters. "That's just bloody terrible science. Bloody awful is what it is. How will anyone ever take me seriously if I dinna come up with fresh an' credible evidence?"

"Who's anyone?" I ask him.

"The Loch Ness Project," he says. "They'll never consider me more than just an amateur hunter without any real proof."

"Give it time," I say. "We'll find something significant, I can feel it. Just because we didn't find anything orange today doesn't mean we won't find it tomorrow."

Euna Begbie's words of wisdom finally seem to do the trick and his mood brightens as we make our way over the bridge and down the dock.

"I sure could eat another cheese sandwich," Hammy Bean says when we hit the edge of the Highland Club grounds.

"Wolfgang here ate the last one," I tell him. "But there's probably some marshmallows left in the bag."

"I'm serious, do not make me your Hermione," Dax insists. "Say it with me . . . *Guitarman*."

"I don't need a Guitarman," I tell him. "I need a Ron"— I put a hand on Hammy Bean's shoulder—"a Harriet Potter"—I point to myself—"and a Hermione," and I point a thumb in his direction.

Dax stops.

"Hey." He juts a chin ahead of us toward the grounds where we set up the tent. "There's a light there. Did anyone leave their flashlight on?"

I stop too and stretch my neck to see darting flashlights in the darkness where we left our empty tent.

One.

Two.

Three.

Four long lights, darting across the lawn of the abbey.

"Oh no," I whisper.

"What?" Hammy Bean asks. "What is it?"

I sigh a deflated sigh. "They're up . . . and they're looking for us."

"Not cool," Dax says.

Hammy Bean turns to us both, pointing a single quaking finger in our direction. "Ye crossed yer hearts," he says, his voice shaking. "Ye promised the most ultimate promise. There's nothin' stronger than that. Don't ye dare be a wee clipe."

"What's a wee clipe?" I ask.

"Someone who goes back on their ultimate promise an' tells," he says, tears balling up inside his eyes and perching on the bottom ledge of his lashes.

I put a hand on his shoulder. "I'm no wee clipe, I'll tell you that," I say. "We won't say anything, right, Dax?"

"No way, HB. We've got your back. The person who'd do something like that is the lowest of the low."

"I canna lose the SS *Albatross*," he whispers. "I just canna. I'd be gutted—it's my whole life. I have to win the race, an' if I lose that boat, I willna even have a chance to matter. I need that boat. It's my wings."

That's when I know for the first time that Hammy Bean isn't just talking about the Nessie Race. He's talking about a whole lot more. It's also when I know that no matter what, I am going to do my best to help him win that race.

In any way I can . . . but, you know, with double the life preservers.

26

THANK GOD FOR YOUTUBE

So as it turns out, Dad *does* get mad.

Like with-all-caps-in-a-feelings-journal mad.

A Crayola masterpiece on the living room wall doesn't bring something like that to the surface, but when you sneak off in the dead of night in a whole other country and they wake up to do a surprise late-night parental roll call on you and you're gone for hours . . . it's a whole other story.

He was *mad*.

I mean *big-time*.

Like red-in-the-face and voice-booming and go-to-your-room-until-further-notice mad.

Even using-my-whole-entire-name-without-going-short-in-any-form-whatsoever mad.

It was a brutal scene.

Especially after we pled the Fifth in a silent Team Nessie Quest pact to never give away the secrets of the SS *Albatross*.

Me and Dax crossed our hearts for Hammy Bean and we meant it. His secret was safe with us.

He didn't hire any wee clipes. All I can say now is thank God for YouTube and skateboarding dogs.

The bulldog's name is Otto and he set the Guinness World Record for his skateboarding ability on all fours. I'm not sure if they have a special book just for dogs, but either way, he's in there and he's real good too.

With the exception of some texting with Britney B for Tennyson updates, by the end of the week, I had clocked more than a hundred videos on my laptop and I was still going strong.

Solitary confinement will do that to a person.

Feeling word: *Bored*. Bored out of my gourd.

Unless I think about Dax when he's wearing that jean jacket with the peace sign on the back of it. Then my feeling word changes, but I'm keeping that one to myself.

"Adelaide Ru?" Mom says, tapping on the door just before lunch. "What are you doing?"

"Watching puppies fall asleep in funny positions," I tell her, lying on my stomach in the middle of my bed, still in my pajamas with my chin on my palm.

She squints at the laptop screen from the doorway. "Please turn that off," she says.

"But, Mom, the next one up is a pug that says *I love you*," I tell her. "He actually *speaks* the words. Like a person?"

"Come on out," she tells me. "I need your help on something."

"N.I.," I tell her.

"N.I.?"

"Not interested," I say.

"Come on," she says.

"Wait, let me just show you this one where a guy does a magic trick for a baby orangutan. It's totally brill—"

"I said *turn it off*," she says in her I-mean-it voice.

I close the laptop, drag myself off the bed and follow her out to the kitchen. "What else am I supposed to do in there, stare at the walls?"

"I'm springing you from your jail cell so you can help me with the grocery list," she says, sliding a hip onto one of the stools at the breakfast bar. "I need to get some things from Ness for Less and you can help."

"Does that mean I'm sprung from solitary confinement for good?" I ask, leaning my chin on her arm.

She smiles. "Dad's getting there."

"But I at least have permission to once again interact with the general population?"

"For today."

"I hope you know that Britney B has just informed me that Mr. Mews is now walking on a leash on a regular basis," I tell her.

"See, I knew Mr. Mews could rise to his challenge as well," she says. "Didn't I say that?"

I sit up and pop a grape into my mouth from the bowl of fruit on the breakfast bar.

"So does that mean I can go with you to the store too and see Quigley Dunbar the Third?"

"And to lunch at Farquhar's too," she says.

I breathe a sigh of relief. "Thank God," I tell her. "I thought I'd lose my mind locked up in that room."

"Well, the door wasn't locked and it's been less than a week, but I suppose I can understand." She gives me a sympathetic look. "But don't forget that you're the one who caused this." She points at me. "Don't try to make me feel guilty about your punishment."

"I know it," I sigh. "But there was important research that had to be done. Hammy Bean needs to remain significant in the Nessie Race . . . for more reasons than you even know."

"I'm so glad to hear you've made the best of Scotland," she says. "And are making such special friends here. However, there were ground rules about Saturday night to keep you all safe."

"I know, I know," I say. "I get it. But when will I be completely off punishment? You have to admit, 'until further notice' is more than a little unfair. I mean, if I'm being honest about it."

"You scared Dad," she tells me. "I've never seen him so scared."

"He looked *mad* to me," I mumble.

"He was mad once he knew you were okay because we were scared that something might have happened to you. Do you know how much we love you?"

I sigh again and lay my chin back on her arm. "Yes," I say.

"Do you know what we would do if we ever lost you?"

"No."

"Well, neither do I," she says. "Parents protect their children—that's our job and that's why there are rules."

I think hard about all of it and I can't help but wonder what it feels like for Hammy Bean not to have his parents want to protect *him*. Even though he has his Mamo Honey, I know he wishes his parents cared enough about him to jail him inhumanely just the way mine do.

I wrap my arms around Mom's waist and feel her arms wrap around me. Tight.

Feeling words: *Loved the way I deserve to be loved.*

"I'm sorry," I tell her. "I really and truly am."

"Thank you," she whispers at the top of my head.

"But could you at least ask Dad if he has an inkling about when he'll stop being mad so I can keep gathering my research?" I ask her.

She squeezes me even tighter. "I'm sure he'll come around."

"I sure hope so, because there's a story here, Mom. A story that's never been written before, and I'm the one who must write it."

"The lake monster story?"

"Yeah, there's definitely a lake monster in it," I tell her. "But there's so much more too."

"So . . . tell me."

I shake my head. "Not yet," I tell her. "But soon."

"Okay, go on and get dressed."

"Woo-hoo!" I exclaim as I run toward the hall, slipping and sliding on the wood floor in my white socks. "I'm getting a double-sized basket with extra flat fries and two sides of top-secret-recipe tartar sauce."

27

MAKING THE IMPOSSIBLE POSSIBLE

"Captain Green Bean to Team Nessie Quest, do ye read? Over."

My eyes peel open and my hands scramble in the dark, searching for the walkie-talkie as I squint at the clock on the bedside table.

Four-twenty.

Are you kidding me?

"Do ye read me, Team Nessie Quest? Over."

My fingers find the radio and I grab it.

"Don't you ever sleep? Over?" I ask him.

"Not when important Nessie discovery work is to be done. Would Roy Mackal sleep? Would Tobin Sky? No, because we are dedicated to our cryptid discoveries. Over."

"Who's Roy Mackal? Over?"

"A professor from Chicago who came here in 1969 an' was convinced Nessie was most likely a type of sea cow. Over."

"Oh, right. The sirenian."

"Brilliant, Denver. You've turned out to be a great reporter/ secret agent. Over."

"Did you ever have a doubt? Over."

Silence.

"Hello? Over?"

Laughter. "Never. Over."

"So Mamo Honey obviously gave you your radio back. Over," I say.

"After more than a wee bit o' convincin'. Over."

"My sentencing consisted of life without parole," I say. "*Buuuut* I think they may be softening. Over."

"*Thaaat's* a roger, Denver, because there's been a major sightin'," he tells me. "A tourist got a picture this week. Is there any way ye could go oot and investigate? Over."

"*Thaaat's* a big-time negative," I tell him. "They're still pretty mad. I don't see that happening. Over."

"Can ye at least ask? Over."

"Why? What's the big deal about it?"

"First, it was taken at the Urquhart Castle!" he exclaims. "Exactly where we were . . . *Saturday night*. Over."

I sit straight up in bed and stare at the speaker. "Are you kidding me right now? Over?" I ask.

"Nae. Over."

"I *knew* she overslept!" I exclaim. "I told you that, didn't I? She pushed the Snooze button on our important mission."

"Aye, yes," he says. "Ye said it. Tourists from Germany got a picture and it's all over the internet already. Can you Google it?" he asks. "An' tell me what it looks like? Over."

I slip out of bed, grab my laptop off the dresser and open it, wincing from the light of the screen in the darkness.

"What do I type in? Over?" I ask him, my fingers poised above the keyboard.

"Type in *Loch Ness Monster seen at Urquhart Castle, Scotland.* Over."

I carefully type the words one letter at a time.

"What's taking so long? Over."

"Urquhart Castle isn't exactly easy to spell," I tell him.

He waits, and on my third try, I get it.

"Here it is!" I exclaim into the speaker. "A German family was on the beach and they saw something in the water . . . with a wake behind it too!" I say, reading the article. "A wake as big as if it were a small ship. Over."

"The picture," Hammy Bean says. "Tell me what it looks like? Over."

I click on the picture and it expands to fill the screen, my *wow* coming out in a whisper.

"Wow what? Over?" he cries.

"Well, it's far away, but there's definitely something there. And it's long too. Over."

"Well? What does it look like? Over?"

"Like something real long and big and slippery and it's flipping and flopping and coming out of the surface of the water. Like a snake or eel or something. Over."

"Is there a neck protruding from the surface? Over."

"Mmm . . . no. More like a bunch of humps weaving in and out of the waves. Over."

"But is it the be-all and end-all o' Nessie discovery? Like, will this picture go down in history as definitive proof? Over."

"No way," I tell him. "There's definitely room for more . . . definitive-*ness.*"

He breathes a sigh of relief into the speaker and then says, "Is there any way ye can meet me at twelve acorns on the oak tree that blows in the morning breeze? I have somethin' to show ye. It's too top secret to share on the radio. Over."

"That's also a big, fat hairy negative," I say.

"But . . . I'm runnin' oot o' time. Over," he tells me.

"What does that mean?"

"Will ye please just ask? Over."

"Roger that," I say. "Denver over and out."

❧

Dad Googles the picture on his phone at breakfast.

"It's Nessie," I tell them over pastries from a Wee Spot of Tea and Biscuits and fresh cheeses from the Connage Highland Dairy just past Inverness.

"Hmmm." Dad squints at his phone. "I don't know, Ruby Ring."

"Let me see it." Mom hops up from her chair at the kitchen table and leans over his shoulder. She squints too and then says, "Zoom in."

He does.

I find a spot over his other shoulder as he pans in closer, dragging his thumb and pointer finger over the tiny screen.

"Yeah," he says flatly. "Looks like seals to me."

I throw my hands out. "Seals? Are you kidding me?" I exclaim. "If you saw it on the bigger computer you wouldn't say that."

"Looks like seals to me too," Mom agrees.

I huff air out of my mouth.

"Look here." She points. "And here too. It looks like seal pups playing in the water, don't you think, Zum?"

"Yep," Dad says.

I sigh and slide back in my chair, taking a bite of orange scone. "You guys have no imagination whatsoever. If that's what happens when you grow up, I'm happy to stay a kid."

Dad smiles at me then and leans in closer, his elbows on the table. "I knew this guy once who said he would never grow up and you want to know what happened?"

I smell a joke.

I just stare at him and chew my scone. "No," I say.

"He grew up anyway, became a professional photographer and snagged your mom away from this geek in a Members Only jacket."

Mom laughs at that one.

"If you really still had the heart of a kid like me, you'd believe that picture is real," I tell him. "But you're a Muggle, tried and true. That's what adulthood does to you."

"RuRu, did you know that I spent my entire childhood searching for the perfect picture of that thing?" he asks me.

I suck air. "I knew it!"

"Just like you're searching for your story to write. I searched to tell a story with my lens and I never found the soul in Loch Ness that I was looking for."

"And you gave up because you stopped believing?"

"After that many years of never seeing any signs of the monster . . . yes, I would say I started to question the truth of it all, and then one day it just became ridiculous."

I point a finger at him. "I knew it that day at Uncle Clive's.

You knew far too many scientific facts about it to be a full-on nonbeliever."

"I *don't* believe it," he says, smiling and shaking his head. "You weren't listening."

"Oh, I heard you loud and clear," I tell him. "And when I'm done with my story you are going to be a believer again. Bigtime."

"Mmm-hmm, well, I'm off to work," he says, pushing his chair back from the table.

He kisses Mom on the cheek and then me.

I throw my arms around his neck and give him a giant squeeze.

"Good luck today," he tells me in my ear, and then leans down so we're eye to eye, putting a heavy hand on each of my shoulders. "The best part of the story," he says, "is when the *impossible* becomes possible. Now go out and make it happen."

"Brill, does that mean I'm officially forgiven?"

He smiles his big smile at me, the one with all the teeth, and heads toward the door.

"Tatty bye," I call after him. "Have a pure barry day at university, Da!"

Mom smirks at me over her coffee mug. "You're really digging into Scotland now, aren't you?"

I shrug. "When in Rome," I say, dancing a newly-found-freedom jig. "Or in this case, Fort Augustus."

I give Mom a big kiss on her cheek and then pull my radio off my belt loop.

"Denver to Captain Green Bean, do you read? Over?"

Beep.

"Captain Green Bean here. Over."

"I'll meet you at twelve acorns on the oak tree that blows in the morning breeze!"

"Brill!" he calls into the radio, and then real loud he says, "Thank you, Mrs. Fitzhugh! Over."

Mom just smiles and sips her coffee.

28

~~~~~~~~~

THE HUMMINBIRD HELIX COMBO

"Hello, the SS *Albatross*!" I call out when I hit the first weathered board on the rickety dock.

Mac-Talla barks from the water.

"Hello, the shore." Hammy Bean peeks his head out of the wee salon.

Mac-Talla climbs out of the water at the shore, drops the soggy tennis ball at my feet and gives me a Loch Ness shower while she shakes herself dry.

"Ew! Yuck!" I say, covering my face with my arms. "I already had a shower this morning, Mac-Talla!"

Her tongue swipes my cheek as I pick up the tennis ball and throw it as far as I can.

Mac-Talla darts to the end of the dock and belly-flops in after it.

"So, what was so top secret?" I ask him, jumping onto the wee boat.

"Promise ye willna tell?"

I squeeze in through the wee salon door and stand next to him.

"Let me show ye somethin'. See this?" Hammy Bean points to a brand-new tiny television screen set next to the sonar.

"What is that?"

"It's a Humminbird Helix Combo."

"What's a Humminbird Helix Combo?"

"It's only the most advanced electronic boating device known to man. It has both advanced sonar *and* an audio GPS system. I can program over twenty-five hundred way points and up to forty-five routes when we get a direct hit so we can go back to the same exact location."

"Yeah? So?"

"So wi' this, I can go oot on my own."

"Wait, what? That's not the agreement," I tell him. "Corny told you he had to go with you."

"Corny's workin' wi' Mamo Honey on the *Nessie Quest* today, so I need ye," Hammy Bean says.

I point to myself. "Me?" I say. "No way, you're not dragging me down with you again. I was subjected to YouTube videos for a week on account of you. Where did you get that thing anyway?"

"I bought it on Amazon."

"How did you pay for it?" I ask. "I mean, it looks real expensive."

"I've been savin' my allowance for a year."

"And Mamo Honey doesn't know about this part of it either?"

"Ada Ru," he says. "Nessie is oot there. The German tourists saw her in the exact spot we were searchin'. We need to have a sightin' o' our own. An' I need ye to be my first mate!"

"Why can't you just wait for Corny?"

He sighs. "Because I'm runnin' oot o' time."

"What does that mean?"

"I heard that the Loch Ness Project is goin' to start two new unprecedented searches. A DNA sweep and an underwater drone. If they find definitive evidence, then . . . well, the race is over. And so is my shot at bein' a serious scientist. Please."

Hammy Bean is waiting for my answer and so is Mac-Talla, a true and loyal mate sitting tall next to Hammy Bean, her tail sweeping back and forth across the wee salon's floor-boards. I can see the headline now:

**TWO KIDS, ONE DOG AND THE
HUMMINBIRD HELIX COMBO SINK
TO THE BOTTOM OF LOCH NESS**

That's when he reaches out to put a hand on my arm.

"Ye think I dinna ken that no one sees me as a contender in the race?"

"People think you're a contender," I assure him.

"No . . . no, they dinna," he says. "At least not until you and Dax. You are everythin' to me."

Beep.

"Strings to Team Nessie Quest, do you read? Come in. Over."

Hammy Bean grabs the walkie-talkie from his belt.

"Captain Green Bean here, an' Denver too. Over."

"The three-headed slippery serpent has come to the surface and the Three Bears have the goods. Over."

Hammy Bean drops the radio on the deck and stands there stuck in time like a Tin Man without his oilcan. And I don't have one to unstick him with.

I unclip my radio from my belt. "What is it? Over."

"Can't say," Dax tells me. "There's no code for it. Over."

"Just say it, then," I tell him. "Over."

"I heard from QDT that the BBC *Highlands & Islands Edition* is on their way to the beach now. What's your ten-twenty? Over."

"The red dog sees all, but the vessel looms large across the black diamonds. Over."

Silence.

Beep.

"Alone?"

"It's not what you think," I tell him. "We're on our way. Rendezvous at the arch in twenty acorns. Over."

"Copy that," Dax says. "You're not supposed to be out without Corncob. What are you thinking? Over."

"That's affirmative, Strings," I call into the radio. "Twenty acorns on the oak tree that blows in the morning breeze. Denver out."

I clip the radio back to my belt and look up at Hammy Bean. Big tears form on his bottom lashes and topple down his cheeks.

"It's probably nothing," I assure him, pulling myself up on the dock next to him. "I mean, discoveries are made all the time, photos are taken every day, but it doesn't mean they're the most definitive thing."

He stands there with his chin pointed toward the loch.

"Ye don't understand. The Three Bears have the goods," he repeats. "The goods is somethin' way better than just a photo or a video. It's actual physical evidence. The BBC *Highlands & Islands Edition* doesna come oot unless it's real news. They must have something big."

"Like what . . . *exactly*?"

"Dunno," he says.

"Still, it might not be so bad."

"Try bloody awful," he mumbles.

29

THE NO-GOOD THREE BEARS

The BBC *Highlands & Islands Edition* sets up right in front of the Fort Augustus beach. The news of the discovery travels as far as Inverness and everyone who's anyone shows up for it.

Including Uncle Clive, Aunt Isla and Briony.

Granted they were invited to dinner at our place anyway, but still.

The news crew consists of one woman holding a microphone and two men, all in Windbreakers with BBC HIGH-LANDS & ISLANDS EDITION written on the back.

I glance around at the crowd of spectators, which includes Jasper Price; Cornelius Blaise Barrington; Mr. Farquhar; Mr. and Mrs. Kumar, who own a Wee Spot of Tea and Biscuits; Quigley Dunbar III; Euna Begbie; and Mom and Dad. Even Tuna Tetrazzini shows up for it.

I wave Dax and Mamo Honey over as they push their way through the crowd. Hammy Bean is beside Mamo Honey, holding her elbow.

"You guys made it," Dax whispers to me. "Going out alone? What were you thinking?"

"We didn't actually go, plus you don't even understand," I tell him. "He's running out of time."

"What is that supposed to mean—"

Mamo Honey comes up behind us and puts her hand on my shoulder. "The clishmaclaver is that they found *prints in the mud*," she whispers.

"Wait, what?" I say. "Nessie prints? Since when does a lake monster have *feet*?"

Hammy Bean reaches a hand out and finds my arm. "Is there a tall, skinny guy here with a long gray beard and a tweed jacket?" he asks me.

I stretch my neck and scan the crowd.

"He's probably wearin' a woolen Scottish flat cap."

"Hmmm, no," I say. "Why? Who's that?"

"Haud yer wheesht, please," the male reporter without the camera calls out to the crowd. "We're on in five," he says, holding five fingers at the woman, and then counts down, hiding a finger with each number.

Four.

Three.

Two.

And then he points to her with his final finger.

She smiles a dark-lipstick smile into the camera. "Thank ye, Gage, we are lochside in Fort Augustus at the edge of Loch Ness. As many know, this large body of water is synonymous with a well-known monster by the name of Nessie. I'm here today with three Loch Ness locals known as the Loch Watchers, a team taking part in what the locals here call the Nessie

Race, an unofficial competition to find the most definitive evidence of the monster first. They claim to have discovered solid evidence of the elusive Nessie's existence on the bonny, bonny banks of Loch Ness." She turns to the three men. "Please, one at a time, introduce yourselves."

The cameraman pans over them.

Lord Grunter, the Duke of Buttcrack, and Sir Farts-When-He-Laughs are lined up, all of them in their flat caps and nubby navy wool sweaters, with binoculars hanging around their necks.

Lord Grunter clears his soggy throat. "I'm Cappy McGee."

The Duke of Buttcrack keeps one fist clutched tight to his belt and leans toward the microphone. "Norval Watt."

And finally, it's Sir Farts-When-He-Laughs's turn. "Sterling Jack, ma'am."

"Thank you all for being here with us today. Please tell us what you've found."

"Oh, ah . . . thank you," Lord Grunter says. "Today we've found definitive proof that a monster lives and breathes in the waters of our very own Loch Ness." He looks at the other men and they nod. "We found actual prints in the mud."

Sir Farts-When-He-Laughs waves the woman closer to the edge of the bank where there is a patch of dried mud. "See here." He points. "These are prints we found early this morning."

The woman leans in close to the dirt while the man with the fingers directs the cameraman to get a closer shot.

"They are three-toed prints wi' large claws," the Duke of Buttcrack says.

"We've never seen anythin' like this before and we're here every day, sunrise to sunset," Lord Grunter says.

"And how can you be so sure they're from our very own Nessie?" the woman asks the men.

"For one, we don't know of another species that has a three-toed foot wi' a large claw," Lord Grunter tells her.

"And secondly," Farts-When-He-Laughs adds, "the toes are webbed, see here? And history tells us that webbed toes possibly indicate a type of plesiosaur dinosaur from the late Triassic period."

"Or a new species altogether," Lord Grunter interjects.

"Oh, yer bum's oot the windae, Cappy McGee." Farts-When-He-Laughs chuckles, giving one solo toot, and then turns to the woman and says, "We don't tend to agree about what Nessie might be."

Hammy Bean leans closer to me. "What does it look like?" he asks.

I shrug. "Exactly what they're describing," I tell him. "A three-toed footprint in dried mud. And it looks like there are giant claws at the top of the toe."

Hammy Bean huffs air out of his mouth and puts his chin on his chest.

The man with the fingers makes circular gestures to the lady and she gives another wide lipstick smile toward the camera. "Thank you, Loch Watchers, for your keen investigative skills and for sharing this amazing discovery with us. This is Mysie Maccrum, out at the bonny, bonny banks of the Fort Augustus beach with an outstanding discovery pertaining to one of the greatest mysteries of Scotland. Today's discovery could just be the clue that determines once and for all what really is swimming down in the depths of the Loch Ness. Back to you in the studio, Gage."

"It's okay," I tell Hammy Bean.

"Aye, they dinna even ken what made those prints," Mamo Honey adds. "They're just makin' a connection to the plesiosaur prints found up on the Isle of Skye a few years ago. They could be dog prints for all they ken."

"Yeah, HB," Dax chimes in. "It's bunk."

Hammy Bean sighs. "Ye all dinna understand," he says. "It was on the BBC. Now the whole world believes that the Loch Watchers have conclusive evidence, whether it's true or not."

"It will happen for you too," I say. "You said so yourself. A discovery is meant to be discovered only when the time is right to discover it, right? Isn't that what your great cryptozoologist Dr. Tobin Sky says?"

"Aye," he mumbles. "But maybe I'm not the one meant to discover it."

30

SCRUMMY AND TIDY
AND BARRY, OH MY!

That night after the newscast, Uncle Clive, Aunt Isla and Briony come to our St. Benedict's flat for an all-American dinner, including hamburgers with cheese and hot dogs with sauerkraut and relish.

After I give Briony a tour of the abbey, we find Dax and Ole Roy coming down the steps.

I actually hear Briony suck air when she sees him.

"Hey," he says.

"Oh, hey," I say.

He's wearing his jean jacket.

"You going somewhere?" I ask him.

"Ness for Less," he tells me. "QDT is working tonight and I have some new stuff to play for him."

Briony gives me an elbow in the ribs.

"Um . . . yeah, so . . ." I give a limp wave in her direction. "This is my cousin Briony—"

"Howzitgoan." She stands real tall, beaming at him with all her teeth showing. "I'm Briony, Ada Ru's cousin."

I wave a hand in his direction. "I just told him that," I say.

But she's not even listening because she's way too busy mad eyeballing Dax in his jean jacket with the peace sign and smiling with far too many teeth showing to be normal.

"How old are ye?" Briony asks Dax.

"Thirteen," he says.

"Wow, I really like your jacket . . . um, that's really cool."

And then the worst thing happens.

Dax gives her his smile.

The *one-lipped one.*

The one he smiles at *me.*

"Well, we better get going, then," I say, curling my arm around Briony's and trying to pull her up off the step.

Briony slips her arm away from mine like a ninja and keeps on smiling her crazy smile. "I see ye play the guitar?"

"Yep," he says.

"Yeah, yeah . . . he plays, he sings . . . da, da, da, let's get going or dinner is going to get cold."

"I play the piano," she gushes. "And I sing too. I'm in choir in school. D'ye wan' to hear me sing? I mean, mebbe I could sing for ye sometime—"

That's when I give her a mighty yank by the back of her sweater to really get her attention.

Which it does, because she gives me a very dirty look.

"We really have to go, Dax," I say, stumbling up the steps as I pull on her arm. "Have fun with Mr. Dunbar the Third. We'll see you later."

"Right," Dax says, bounding down the steps.

"Hey," Briony complains. "What's wrong wi' ye?"

"I was doing that for you," I tell her. "I hate to be the one to tell you this, but you totally embarrassed yourself back there."

She puts two hands on her hips and gives me an angry stare.

"Emmmmmbarrassing," I say.

"That lad is pure tidy," she tells me. "I mean seriously barry."

I know I'm going to be sorry for asking her, but I do it anyway. "What is that supposed to mean?"

She puts her hands on the banister and stretches her neck to sneak another peek at Dax through the spiral of the staircase.

"He's utterly wonderful is what he is," she gushes. "And ye see him every day, ye jammy lass?"

"Mmm," I say, shaking my head. "Wonderful? Not sure I'd use that particular word. I mean, you know . . . he's *okay.*"

"Are ye well radge?"

"I don't think so," I say.

But I don't tell her what word I wrote in my feelings journal that first day I met Dax or what I think about him when I see him in that jean jacket with the peace sign on the back. Those words are for no one's eyes but mine. That's why my feelings journal has found its new home under the mattress.

But it doesn't mean I *like* the kid or anything.

I mean, do I think he's cute? Sure, he's cute in an obvious sort of way with the seaweed eyes and the one-lip smile, but that doesn't mean I *like* him. Do I think he's cool and smart and really good at playing the guitar and funny and a little bit weird . . . oh, and do I like the way he uses people's initials instead of their full names or what it sounds like when he says my handle on the radio or how he shakes his hair out of his eyes when he's playing the guitar? I mean, yeah, I suppose I do . . . but it doesn't mean I *like* him, *like* him.

"You know," I say, "he's . . . well, I would say he is a little . . . it's like this, he's . . . he's like a . . . this is what it is, okay? He's like a, um . . . a—"

"I think someone would like to winch with our lad Dax."

"I would *not*," I snap. "Wait. What is that?"

She smiles real wide this time and puckers her lips up into the air and makes kissing noises.

"First of all"—I point a sharp finger in her direction—"*that's* just plain gross, and secondly, you couldn't be more wrong."

She's still smiling.

I point to myself. "You think *I* have a crush on *that* kid?"

"Quite right, and I think he fancies ye too," she says. "I saw the way he looked at ye when he said goodbye. I think he might want to nip on ye too."

"Okay, there will be no winching or nipping of any kind," I tell her. "Plus, he doesn't like me, he makes fun of me all the time."

"That's exactly what lads do when they like ye." She starts up the steps.

I think about that and follow her.

"I don't think so, because when Tad Garrett liked me in fourth grade, he gave a note to Britney B to give to me and it said *Do you like me?*, with a no box and a yes box. I checked the yes box and we were officially boyfriend and girlfriend for three weeks. But we ignored each other the entire time.

And then I heard three weeks later he asked Emmanuelle Penney the same question and she had checked yes. So then he ignored her."

"What's your point?"

"The point is he never made fun of me once. He just never talked to me."

"Aye, lads can be well radge. But I still think there's somethin' happenin' between you and Dax."

"Well, there isn't," I tell her. "I have no feelings about that kid whatsoever."

"So ye keep prattlin' on aboot."

"Listen," I say. "I would know if I liked that kid, which I don't. And I know for a fact that he's not pure barry or toody."

"*Tidy*," she corrects me. "He's pure *tidy*. And, I might add, downright scrummy."

31

~~~~~~

ONE POCKETED KIT KAT BAR

After Uncle Clive, Aunt Isla and Briony have gone home, I lie in my bed staring at the ceiling. That's when it comes to me. Exactly what might raise Hammy Bean's spirits.

A killer article.

One that is so stellar, he's going to want to read it word for word on the very first podcast and maybe even interview *me*.

The one and only Tobin Sky will have to settle for second place.

I would bet any money on it.

It'll be the breakthrough Hammy Bean's been looking for.

I spend the entire week working on it and finally email it to him on Friday, letting him know I'm on my way to the *Juggernaut* office. But I stop at Ness for Less for a Coke and a Kit Kat bar first.

"Hello, Mr. Dunbar the Third," I call when the bell on the door dings.

Dax is on the counter again playing his guitar and I know I hear my name in the words he's singing right before he stops.

My Nikes halt dead in their tracks and I point a finger at Dax.

"Were you just singing about me?"

"*No,*" he insists.

But I can't help but notice his cheeks getting a shade pinker.

I don't know what Briony is even talking about. Maybe I think he's cute and maybe I like the way he looks in his jean jacket and maybe the tips of my ears feel hot sometimes when his seaweeds meet mine, but that doesn't mean I *like* him, like him.

"Good mornin', Ms. Ada Ru," Quigley Dunbar III calls back to me. "Here for yer regular Coke an' a Kit Kat bar?"

"That's right," I tell him, heading to the refrigerator and grabbing a can of soda. "I'm on my way to see Hammy Bean today. I wrote a killer article that I hope he's going to want to read on the very first podcast."

I slide the can of Coke and the Kit Kat bar onto the counter.

"That will be one pound an' thirty-one pence, please," Mr. Dunbar III says.

I take the coins from my pocket and pick the ones I need and put the others back.

"Dear girl, ye should have a jacket on today, yer arms are filled wi' goose bumps, lass."

"Yeah," I say, rubbing them down. "It was warm and sunny yesterday."

"The weather changes quickly here because of the mountains," Dax says.

"I'll be okay," I say.

"Here," Dax says, setting Ole Roy to the side and shrugging his jean jacket off his shoulders. "You can wear mine if you want."

"Ah . . . you mean . . . that? I mean, y-your . . . your *jean jacket?*" I point to it hanging in his hand.

He shrugs. "Yeah, why not?"

"Oh . . . well, I wouldn't want you to get cold."

"I'll be okay," he says. "Here, take it."

I slip one arm in and then the other. It's still warm and smells like him. Like soap and whatever he shampoos his hair with, which is sweet and spicy and a little bit tropical. The shoulders are too big and the arms reach well below my fingers.

It's perfect.

"Thanks," I say.

"Yer change, lass," Mr. Dunbar III says, handing me a few coins.

"Oh . . . thank you," I say, dropping them into the pocket of my jeans.

"So . . . did you want to come with me to see Hammy Bean?" I ask Dax.

"Yeah, sure," he says, jumping down from the counter and swinging Ole Roy around to his back. "Later, QDT. Thanks for the tips. You said key of G instead of E, right?"

"Aye, I think G would be best," Mr. Dunbar III says, and then waves a hand to us as we're on our way out the door. "Tatty bye, kids."

228

"Hey," I say. "How far have you gotten on the Harry Potter series?"

"I'm on book seven, but don't say anything. I just started it."

"Oooh, that's a good one," I tell him. "Don't worry, though. I won't give any spoilers."

Once the door of Ness for Less closes behind us, Dax grabs the sleeve of the jacket and drags me over to the side of the walkway.

"I have to tell you something," he whispers.

"Hey," I say. "What are you doing?"

"You will never in a million years guess what I found out," Dax tells me.

I open my eyes wide at him.

"What?"

"Guess."

"I'm not going to guess," I tell him.

"Come on, just one guess," he says.

"You said I won't guess it anyway, so just tell me."

"*One guess,*" he says again. "What will it hurt? Come on, I gave you my jacket."

"Fine," I say. "Ummmmm . . . you're done with Hammy Bean's intro."

He makes an annoying buzzer noise. "Wrong," he says. "Not even close. Try again."

"Oooh!" I clasp my hands together. "My intro? Did you finish *mine*?"

"Almost, but no, that's not it either."

"Really? You're almost done? Is that what you were singing to Quigley Dunbar the Third? In the key of G?"

"You're changing the subject," he informs me.

"What's the subject?"

"What you'll never guess in a million."

"Just tell me already," I say.

He looks to the right and then the left and places two palms on my shoulders, just like Dad does when he's setting me up for one of his jokes.

"I found out why Mamo Honey quit the Nessie Race."

I suck air. "Get out!" I whisper with wide eyes. "You know the top-secret bobble that is so Nessie-sensitive, Hammy Bean can't even let the *Jug* crew know about it?"

"Yep," he says.

"Tell me," I say. "Wait . . . I bet you anything it has something to do with what's padlocked up in that old garage in the back of their house, doesn't it? Doesn't it?" I stand on my tiptoes and bounce up and down. "I know it does! Does it?"

He looks to the right and then the left again and then leans even closer to me, which causes me considerable knee weakness.

"QDT told me the whole deal," he says. "But he swore me to secrecy, so you have to swear too."

"I swear." I make a crossing motion over my heart. "Hope to die," I tell him.

"It has to do with a yellow submarine and a near-death experience."

"Wait a second," I say then, putting my hands on my hips. "Is this a joke? Like the whole pooping goose thing? A yellow submarine flies in the wind while the goose poops on a Subaru?"

His laugh comes up in a burst. "No, but that's good."

"So you're being totally serious?"

"Totally serious."

"Swear?"

"Swear."

My eyes open wider and I suck air.

"So that's what she's got locked in the shed?" I ask. "An actual submarine?"

"It's got to be what's in there," he says.

"Wait, aren't submarines supposed to be super huge, though?"

"I guess this is a smaller version or something."

"That's crazy," I say. "So . . . what was the accident?"

"I don't know all the details, but I found out there was an accident with the yellow submarine and she almost died from it. Which is why she doesn't like to talk about it. After it all happened she decided Hammy Bean was more important than anything else. And if something happened to her, who would take care of him? You know, because of his parents and everything. So she quit the Loch Ness Project and that's when she started the *Nessie Quest* business. Even though she was considered the top investigator by scientists all around the world. She had even suspected that a portion of the loch was a hundred feet deeper than the rest. But because of the accident, she was never able to prove it."

"Whoa," I say. "Did someone actually save her?"

"Yeah, she almost drowned," he tells me. "The submarine started to take on water, like six hundred feet below the surface. And you'll never guess who saved her."

"Who?"

"*Corny.* She radioed for help and he was there. I guess he ended up having to give her serious CPR and everything."

"Cornelius. Blaise. Barrington." I say each word slow and careful.

"Yep," says Dax, nodding.

"No wonder they call him *extraordinaire*," I say. "This story is getting *good*."

"Epic," he says. "But you still have to give me a part cooler than Hermione."

"Fine," I say.

"Right on," he calls out. "Are you thinking Wolfgang or Guitarman?"

I start walking and he scrambles to follow me. "I mean, I'm fine with either one, really."

I roll my eyes even though I can't help but grin way wider than I want to.

And when he's not looking, I slip my Kit Kat bar deep inside the pocket of his jean jacket just like Mom did with Jeff What's-His-Name.

32

STUCK IN THE OZONE

I ring the old-fashioned doorbell and then crack open the red door of Tibby Manor and poke my head inside. "Hammy Bean!" I call.

"He's upstairs, love," Mamo Honey hollers back to me from the kitchen.

Me and Dax stop in the doorway of the kitchen and find her. Mamo Honey is at the table writing numbers in a leather-bound notebook.

"Cheers, Mamo Honey," I tell her.

"Hello, kids," she says.

"What are you doing?" I ask her.

"Oh, just the books for the business," she says.

"I just wanted to say sorry again for the other night. We really didn't mean to make you worry."

She smiles and scribbles more numbers. "I appreciate that, lass, but I have a feelin' ye may not have been the instigator o' that wee excursion."

I smile too. "I suppose he's just like you in a way, huh?"

"Aye, I'm afraid our love for cryptozoological mysteries is in the blood," she says.

I look at Dax and he looks at me.

"So I—I heard that, um, you . . . you, well, were a great explorer in your time."

Dax smacks my arm.

"Is that right, lass?" she says, writing down another number.

"A famous one," I go on.

"Well, I dinna ken aboot that."

"You were probably the only female explorer, though, huh?" I say. "I mean, of that time."

She stops writing and looks at me. "Aye, an' it was a challenge," she says. "A wonderful one. But that was in the past."

"Yeah . . . I heard that you . . . ah, that you . . . ah . . ."

Dax smacks me again and shakes his head.

". . . you didn't want to do it anymore," I say.

"Aye, it was time," is all she says.

"Have you ever thought about starting up again?"

"Oh, no, dear, my time is past. There are plenty o' new explorers oot there to find new answers. It's their time now."

Hammy Bean's feet stomp in the hall above us.

"Are ye comin' up here or aren't ye?" he calls down at us from the top of the stairs.

Mamo Honey gives us a big grin then. "He's been anxiously awaitin' yer visit this mornin'," she tells me.

I wrap my arms around the back of her shoulders and she turns to look at me.

"What was that for, lass?"

"For all the orange possibilities you discovered in your

time," I tell her. "And all the ones you help Hammy Bean explore. I'm just happy I get to be a part of it."

She holds her arms out to me, enveloping me in a warm hug.

"Thank ye," she tells me, and reaches for Dax's hand. "Hammy Bean hasna ever had a friend like you and Dax. Ye have made a big difference in his life. An' not because ye treat him like he's special or different in any way—it's because ye *don't*. He's just one o' ye, and that has changed things for him in a way that has made him smile down to his toes—and I havena seen that in . . . well, I guess I've never seen it."

"*Hello?*" Hammy hollers from the top of the steps. "Are ye comin'?"

"He doesn't sound very happy right now," I say to Mamo Honey.

"I'm sure you kids can cheer him up."

∽

Hammy Bean is behind the desk, his fingers racing on the keyboard. His computer voice names each letter he types.

Dax finds his leather chair in the corner and starts his strumming.

"Did you get it?" I ask him.

Hammy Bean stops typing and leans back in his too-large leather office chair. "Aye," he says. "I got it this mornin'."

"And you read it?"

"Aye, I listened to it twice."

I wait for it.

But he just sits there, his fingers intertwined on the back of his head, not saying a single word.

"Well?" I demand.

"Mmmmm," he finally says. "There's something not quite right about it."

Dax stops strumming.

I stop breathing.

My heart stops beating.

"Pardon me?" I say.

"It's . . . it's . . . missin' somethin'."

"*Missing* something?" I repeat.

What is he even talking about?

"What's it missing?" I ask.

"Emmm . . . *pop*," he says, and goes back to typing.

I put my hands on my hips.

"*Excuuuuse* me? I wrote my tail off in that article. It's popping all over the place. Did you read the whole thing? I mean, the part about Roy Mackal and his research about the Mokele-mbembe? It took me hours to learn all of that. I wrote about the real possibility of an actual living dinosaur in the Republic of Congo today. I'm sorry, but that's cryptozoology gold right there."

"Ummm, yeah, well . . . my mam and da always say, *Reach for the stars*," he tells me, his fingers paused over the keyboard. "An' I think ye havena reached quite far enough. So I think ye need to keep workin' on it."

"Oh," I scoff. "Your *parents* tell you that?"

I hear Dax blow air out his mouth behind me.

"That's exactly right," Hammy Bean tells me. "They say, *Hammy Bean, nothing can stop ye, so you reach for the stars, son.*"

I can feel my face burning and my brain steaming.

"That's what they say?"

"Aye, and I think ye only reached as far as . . . say, the ozone layer, but it needs to go higher." He leans forward and starts typing again. "Think Venus or Mars."

I stand there like a steaming pot, watching his blurry fingers while fast and furious letters spew out of the speaker with each key he presses.

"Venus, huh?" I say. "I think you're just crabby because you haven't found any evidence and you're taking it out on me."

"Nae!" he snaps. "Maybe ye just think ye can do anythin' an' maybe ye canna."

"Well, who made you the king of good writing?"

Hammy Bean stops typing, Dax stands up and swings Ole Roy around to his back and I stand seething.

"I'm the editor in chief of the *Nessie Juggernaut*," Hammy Bean informs me.

"Yeah . . . well, you're not the boss of me."

"Ah, actually . . . I *am*," he says. "That title makes me the boss. Ye work for me, remember? An' if ye want to be a writer like ye say ye do, you have to learn to take criticism."

"*Criticism?*"

"That's right. I'm afraid that sometimes the truth hurts."

"Sooooo, I'm going to take off," Dax says, stuffing his hands in his jeans pockets and heading toward the door.

"The *truth*?" I say as Dax's feet echo down the hall and then the stairs. "Let's talk about the truth if you're such a big fan of it."

The red Tibby Manor door slams below us.

"What's that supposed to mean?" Hammy Bean wants to know.

"It means your mom and dad are not Scottish royalty," I

say. "Nor are they missionaries in the Congo. They don't work for Doctors Without Borders or even as earthquake relief volunteers in Haiti or some other far-off place."

Hammy Bean slams the laptop closed with a scowl. "What do *ye* know aboot it?"

"*Everyone* knows," I tell him. "You want people to look at you like you're some amazing scientist, but you tell ridiculous stories that no one even believes. Do you know what that makes you?"

He doesn't say anything.

"A liar, that's what," I inform him.

I stand there staring at him.

Tears well at the bottom of my eyes first.

And then his.

Hammy Bean wipes at them with the back of his hand and stands up straight, putting two palms flat on the wooden desk. "My mam an' da are good people doin' good things in the world!" he shouts at me. "And I can prove it too. Now on yer bike, *mate*."

"What?"

"Git oot."

"Fine by me," I say, turning on my Nike heels and stomping out of the room.

33

BOILED-NOODLE STINK

Even more tears come before I hit the last stone step in front of Tibby Manor.

Dax and Ole Roy are waiting for me on the curb.

I wipe the tears from my face with Dax's jean jacket sleeve and keep on walking while he scurries to catch up to me.

"So what happened?" he asks.

"Nothing," I snap.

"Something happened or you wouldn't be crying."

I wipe at the steady stream. "I'm not crying."

"Well, you should tell your face that," he says.

I stop and look at him. "I told him, okay? I told him."

Dax sighs big and looks up to the graying clouds, shaking his head.

"I told him he's a liar and everyone knows it too and if he wants to have friends here he'd better stop it."

Dax's eyes meet mine. "Mmm, not cool," he says.

"Someone had to have the tidbits to say it," I say. "You sulked out of there like a big, fat, hairy chicken."

"Yeah, but *why* did you do it?" he demands.

"Because," I say. "He shouldn't be running around here lying to everyone under the sun. It's not right and someone needed to tell him so."

"That's not why," Dax says.

"Yeah, it is," I insist, wiping my nose across the sleeve of his jacket and leaving a big wet streak.

"But you didn't go in there planning to say that," he says.

"Fine then, you tell me why, since you're the king of knowing everything about anything."

"Because you were getting back at him for ripping on your writing."

"No." I shake my head. "That's not it. He should be telling the truth."

"He did," Dax says. "He told you your article stank."

"It didn't stink," I insist. "You stink."

He raises his eyebrows at me. "That's random."

"Yeah, well, I've been meaning to tell you," I say. "You smell like . . . *boiled noodles* and you say *groovy* way too much to be normal."

"Feel better?"

"*No,*" I snap, starting back down Bunioch Brae.

"You know, for someone who claims to know the power of words, you've got some learning to do about them," he calls after me.

I stop again, turning to face him.

"What is with you and that stupid guitar, anyway? If you

love it so much, why don't you just go and marry it already?"
I tell him.

Then I pull his stupid jean jacket off my shoulders and
throw it at him.

We both stare at it lying in the middle of the road.

"You know I'm right," he tells me. "You may not like it, but
you know it's true."

"You think you're so smart!" I yell back. "But you aren't.
You're just a fathead with a weird hippie vibe and a know-it-
all New Yorker attitude who thinks the world revolves around
you and no one else."

He gives me his stupid one-lip grin. "Yeah, but I'm right
too."

"Yeah . . . well . . . just so you know, someone *real* important dies in book seven—"

"Hold it right there," he says, his one lipper slowly disappearing and his seaweeds narrowing. "There is nothing lower
than an unsolicited spoiler and you know it."

34

A ONE-WAY TICKET TO TENNYSON

Back at the abbey, I race up the heavenly steps toward flat 402 and slam the front door with all the might I can muster.

"Scotland bites it!" I call out, flopping my worn-out body down on the red velvet couch with my Nikes still on.

Mom is sitting at the coffee table in front of her laptop, her legs tucked under her. She stops typing, looks up at me and takes her glasses off.

"Shoes," she says.

I kick them off and they land on the wooden floor with two loud thumps.

"Now," she says. "Can you calmly tell me what's going on?"

The tears start up again. "I really don't think so," I say. "It's too horrible."

She gives me a sympathetic smile. "Try."

"Mom, there's no way I can stay here until September. *No way.* In fact, I'd like to leave by sundown if possible."

I pull myself up from the couch and stomp in my socks to my room to start packing.

She shows up in the doorway while I'm pulling my suitcase from the closet. "How about we take a breath," she says in that voice.

I point a finger at her. "Don't therapize me!" I tell her, unzipping my suitcase and shoving a sweatshirt inside it. "This is an emergency. Code Black. DEFCON One. I need out of this place, pronto."

She sits down on the bed next to my suitcase, watching me pack my underwear.

"I would just like to talk with you, and I think we can accomplish that with no one shouting," she says. "Let's take a breath together." She covers my hand with hers.

And it's that hand on mine that makes the floodgates open and so many tears start to fall that I can hardly breathe. My whole body feels tired and I let it collapse on the bed next to her. Streams of wet, sloppy tears slide down my cheeks and around my chin, inside my ears and down my neck.

"Take a deep breath for me," she says.

"I don't want to breathe," my throat chokes out at her. "I just want a plane ticket home. Why aren't you listening to me?"

Her arms are warm and safe as she strokes my hair and rocks me just a little. Right this minute, I wish I could be a baby again, when things weren't so hard and Mom could fix absolutely everything. Now when I make the mess, I have to clean it up and I have no idea how to do that.

Especially not after *this* mess.

"Talk to me," she whispers into my hair. "Maybe I can help."

I hide my face in her arm. "Not this time," I tell her. "I did something horrible."

"Try me," she says. "You can tell me anything."

"You'll hate me," I tell her. "Maybe even disown me. Leave me to fend for myself, a pirate on the high seas."

"I promise there's nothing you could ever do or say that would make me hate you. I might not like what you did, but we all make mistakes. Maybe if you trust me, we can talk it out and come up with a solution together."

I pull away from her and wipe my nose across my forearm, but she lets it go just like she did with the shoe pile by the couch.

I stand facing her. "Okay, but I don't want you to look at me when I tell you," I say.

She raises her eyebrows. "What would you like me to do?"

"Turn around," I say. "It'll be easier to tell you if you're not looking at me."

"Okay." She turns her gaze toward the two skinny stained-glass windows filled with faces. More eyes staring at me.

Judging me.

"I—I . . . I told Hammy Bean that . . . I know he's been lying this whole time . . . lying about his parents."

"Okay," she says to the window.

"I mean, I *told* him."

She turns to face me then. "I don't understand."

"Hammy Bean has been lying to everyone about his parents," I tell her.

"They aren't missionaries in the Congo?" she asks.

"No," I say. "Or the Scottish royalty."

"Well, sure, there's been no Scottish royalty since—"

"I know, I know. 1745."

"So where are they?" she asks.

"Euna Begbie told me they take drugs and Mamo Honey took Hammy Bean away to keep him safe and raise him right. They live in London and Hammy Bean doesn't even know them."

"Oh no," Mom breathes out, putting her hand on her heart.

"And I told him I know all about it. I told him he's a liar and that everyone else knows it too."

She raises her eyebrows again. "I see," she says.

I stare at her. "You hate me now, right?" I ask her.

"Of course not," she says. "Come back over here and sit."

I sit back down on the bed and we face each other, both of us cross-legged. Me with my chin in my hand and my elbow on my knee.

"I yelled it at him," I say. "I didn't even say it nice. I said it mean because he was mean to me about my writing for the podcast."

"Mmm," she says. "What did he say about it?"

I throw my hands out. "He said it had no pop," I tell her. "Can you believe that one? No pop. *Me*? I'm all about the pop. I ooze pop. Pop is everything to me," I scoff again. "No pop," I grumble.

"I can see why that upset you," she says.

"That's just a big, fat lie. *He* doesn't have pop. *Him*. And he's no Ron either, I'll tell you that. As far as my lake monster story goes, he's out. Why aren't you making the call to book my flight?"

"So he gave you some criticism on your writing and you got mad and said some things that you wish now you hadn't."

"In a nutshell," I say. "But worse, you know, because I said those things to him about his mom and dad. Not to mention, I told Dax he smelled like boiled noodles and then threw his jacket down on Bunioch Brae." I bury my head again. "It's too bad to fix. I want to go home, please. Britney B would never say I didn't have pop. Never."

"Okay," she says. "Your feelings are hurt."

I nod.

"And there are words that have been said and you can't take them back."

"And if you really loved me, you'd book that ticket."

"I suppose leaving is one option."

I breathe a sigh of relief. "Could you book me a window seat?"

"I didn't finish," she says.

I drop my chin in my hand.

"Even though it may be an option, I don't know if running away from the problem is the best idea."

I throw my hands out. "Mom, a Ferris wheel story isn't going to cut it this time," I tell her.

"I agree," she says. "But do you really think leaving on a plane in the dead of night is going to fix it?"

"Yes. I really think it will."

"Mmmm," she says, pausing for a long while. "Words have been said that have hurt someone. Will being home in your room or going to Parisi on Italian Wednesdays or sleeping over at Britney B's really change that?"

I sigh. "I s'pose not."

"This is the night that Mamo Honey has her class in Inverness, and Hammy Bean is supposed to come over for dinner, right? What if you talked to him and told him how you feel about what happened? And maybe even apologized for words that hurt him."

I sigh. "No way. I *can't* talk to him about it."

"And why is that?"

"Simple," I say. "I don't have the tidbits for it. Plus, I think I'd be much better at pretending it didn't happen. You know, sweep it under the rug."

"Is that what we do in our family?"

I sigh again. "No."

"You've been finding tidbits left and right this summer, so I'm pretty sure you'll find them for this too. Maybe you just need a day, but they're in there. I'm sure of it."

"You may be right about everything else, but I really think you're wrong about that one," I tell her. "All I feel is tired out and limp and droopy."

"Everyone makes mistakes, especially with our words, but the best thing we can do is to go back and at least try to clean them up the best we can."

"Fine," I tell her. "I'll look for my Hammy Bean tidbits. But I'm warning you right now, I really don't think they're in there."

35

GOOEY GRILLED CHEESE
WITH A SIDE OF SORRY

At six o'clock Hammy Bean doesn't show up for dinner. At six-thirty I call him on channel five.

"Come in, Captain Green Bean, do you read? Over."

Silence.

I try him on channel seventeen.

"Denver to Captain Green Bean. Over."

Silence.

"Dax," I call then. "Are you there? Over?"

Nothing.

They're freezing me out.

They hate me and there are no words that will fix this mess. Mom doesn't get it. I wish she'd booked that ticket when I asked her to.

We wait to eat until six forty-five and then me and Mom eat our grilled cheese while Dad goes to Tibby Manor to see if Hammy Bean is there, even though no one answers when we call on the phone. Each bite of gooey cheese makes me feel like I'm choking on the words I said to Hammy Bean earlier in the day.

When Dad comes home to tell us that no one answered the door at Tibby Manor either, Mom leaves a message on Mamo Honey's cell phone.

"Maybe Hammy Bean ended up going with her to class," Mom says.

After dinner, Mamo Honey calls back to tell us that Hammy Bean went to Farquar's Famous Fish for dinner with Dax. Mom and Dad feel a whole lot better, but I can't help but wonder what those boys are saying about me.

By nine o'clock I'm in my flowered nightgown on the red velvet couch cuddled up between Mom and Dad as he reads chapter sixteen, "Through the Trapdoor," of *Harry Potter and the Sorcerer's Stone*. With Dad reading and doing all his different voices, it makes me forget for a few minutes everything that's happening. Especially when he does his Voldemort, which makes actual goose bumps pop out on my arms every single time.

Spending time right in between Mom and Dad, which is my most favorite place in life to be, makes me feel even worse about what I've said to Hammy Bean because I forget sometimes that I have the very best parents in the world and not everyone has that. I lay my head against Dad's arm and hold Mom's hand while we listen to Dad do voices.

The phone rings right after the grandfather clock in the hall announces that it's fifteen acorns past nine.

Mom gets up to answer it while Dad keeps reading and it's right at the part where Harry, Ron and Hermione are at the trapdoor that we hear that something's not right.

In fact, something is *very* wrong.

"Um, no," Mom says. "We haven't seen him at all tonight, Honey. Did you call the Cadys?"

Dad stops reading midsentence.

I look up at Mom and she's looking at me.

"Uh-huh . . . uh-huh. Adelaide Ru?" Mom says. "If Hammy Bean's not home, do you know where he might be?"

My heart is beating hard.

Pounding in my chest.

Hammering in my ears.

I swallow. "No," I say. "Why? What's wrong?"

"He wasn't home when Honey returned from her class and no one is answering at the Cady flat."

The half a grilled cheese that made it into my stomach doesn't feel so good anymore and neither does the hot chocolate with extra marshmallows that Mom made me for our story.

"Where else might he be?" Mom asks Honey.

She listens.

"Uh-huh . . . uh-huh. I don't know," Mom says. "I'll ask her. Adelaide, when is the last time you spoke to Dax?"

I just blink at her with wide eyes and don't say a thing.

"Adelaide Ru?" she says. "Answer me."

∾

As it turns out, I am a wee clipe after all.

I cave, plain and simple.

I blab, *big-time.*

The lowest of the low is what Dax will call me.

Hammy Bean will most certainly strip me of my position

and force me to relinquish my walkie-talkie too. He'll probably never speak to me again and regret making me his very first reporter/secret agent for the *Nessie Juggernaut*.

But I don't blame him one bit.

I cross my heart and then blab his most ultimate bobble. I'm the worst secret keeper in the history of secret keeping. I totally renege on a cross-your-heart-hope-to-die. And everyone who's anyone knows there is nothing more sacred than a cross-your-heart-hope-to-die. *Nothing.*

But Mom and Dad don't exactly see it the same way.

"I cannot believe you kept this from Honey," Mom is saying to me from the front seat of the rental car on the way to the rickety dock where Hammy Bean keeps the SS *Albatross*. "Haven't I always said you can tell me anything?"

"But, Mom, I crossed my heart on this one," I tell her.

She just shakes her head and stares out through the rain racing across the car window. "That's nonsense."

She doesn't get it.

"It's *his* wee boat, not mine," I say. "What are you yelling at *me* for?"

She snaps her head in my direction. "Because you're *my* daughter and I thought you knew better than this."

"You don't understand." I try again. "I crossed my heart and everyone who's anyone—"

"Don't." She points a finger at me. "Hammy Bean's and Dax's safety is at stake here and that takes precedence over some childish dare."

"I mean . . . *technically* it's not a dare," I explain. "It's more like a—"

She holds a hand up. "Please, just stop," she says.

I cross my arms over my chest and stare out the rainy window.

"Where is it?" Dad asks, squinting through the windshield.

"Just past the McLean's Farm sign on the right," I tell him.

Dad pulls the car off the road. Wet leaves slap against the windshield as he rolls to a stop. I push open the back door. The lights on Mamo Honey's *Nessie Quest* tour van shine bright behind us, and behind that is Mr. and Mrs. Cady's BMW. I watch as Mamo Honey pulls herself out from behind the steering wheel, forgetting to even turn the engine off and fly toward me in her yellow rain slicker and matching hat, her wet curls stuck to her face.

"Where is it?" she demands. "Where is it?"

"This way," I say, taking her hand and pulling her through the wet, sloppy leaves. Raindrops click on the hood of the rain jacket that's zipped up over my flowered nightgown and my bare feet squish inside my Nikes as I lead her down the embankment through the soaked leafy branches.

"Can you still see them?" I hear Mrs. Cady call to Mr. Cady.

"It's through here," I call back to them, waiting until I hear their footsteps sloshing through the wet ground.

When we finally all reach the edge of the rickety dock, I stop on the first weathered board, but Mamo Honey runs to the very last one, shining her flashlight out on the water.

"Wh-where is it?" Mamo Honey demands.

The SS *Albatross* is gone.

"Where is the boat?" Mrs. Cady asks when she reaches the dock. "I thought you said the boat was here. Where is it?"

"I—I guess . . . it—it's gone," I say.

"Oh my God," Mrs. Cady gasps, dropping her face into her palms.

"I canna believe this is happenin'!" Mamo Honey cries into the rain. "How did he even get a boat? Someone must have helped him do this. Was it you?" She spins to me, shining the light in my eyes.

"N-no," I say. "He had the boat before I got here. He showed it to me. It wasn't my idea. I promise it wasn't."

"Well, then ye must know who did this."

Uh-oh.

I can't reveal another bobble.

I can't.

I won't.

"Adelaide Ru," Mom says. "Answer her."

"Where is it?" a breathless Mrs. Cady calls out when she hits the dock, with Mr. Cady behind her.

"They're gone," Mamo Honey announces. "Gone, oot there somewhere!" She points to the loch.

"Adelaide Ru," Dad says in a voice I've never heard before. "Where did Hammy Bean get this boat?"

The rain is pelting our coats harder now and they're all standing there staring at me.

Waiting for answers.

Answers I can't give them. Answers I crossed my heart not to ever reveal. But they're answers that could help save Hammy Bean and Dax from sure danger.

"What's that?" Dad shines his flashlight at something at the end of the dock.

Mamo Honey's light bounces left, then right, then back again until the beam finds it.

A hat.

Hammy Bean's way-too-big captain's hat.

Mamo Honey bends down to pick it up and hugs it to her middle.

"Adelaide Ru," Mom says. "You aren't doing anyone any favors by keeping secrets."

Tears roll down my already-rain-soaked cheeks, and when my words make it past my throat, they come out in a croak. "B-but . . . I promised."

36

DECLASSIFIED . . . *BIG-TIME*

So I do it again.

I blab another one.

I'm a wee clipe supreme, the teller of sacred and classified secrets. A blabbermouth of bobbles big and small. A snitch. A stoolie. And a big, fat fink wrapped into one twelve-year-old girl. I cross my heart and hope to die on Hammy Bean's secret and then spewed it all over town. I'm a menace to society of all things confidential. If he ever speaks to me again, it sure won't be to tell me anything even remotely classified.

And I deserve it.

All of it.

I *am* the lowest of the low.

When I finally blab about Cornelius Blaise Barrington giving Hammy Bean the SS *Albatross*, Mamo Honey is fit to be tied. Not to mention Mom and Dad.

I will surely be sentenced to far worse than a week of solitary for this one.

Pound.

Pound.

Pound.

Mamo Honey slams a fist on the door of Corny's lochside camper van. A small motor home with a large wooden sign on the front of it that says *Nessie Hunter.* "Cornelius Blaise Barrington!" she hollers. "Open the door this instant!"

The smooth stones on the small stretch of beach outside Fort Augustus are especially slippery in the rain with just wet Nikes hanging on to bare feet with loose laces.

"Knock again," Mrs. Cady calls to her.

"Wait, Mamo Honey," I say. "I told you Corny won't let Hammy Bean go out by himself."

She stares hard at me. "So he's *never* asked ye to go oot alone?"

At first, I don't say anything. But then I break. "He asked once, but I said no."

For some reason, that didn't make her feel any better.

Or Mrs. Cady either. "Knock again, Honey," she calls, louder this time.

Mamo Honey slams on the door with her fist again.

Pound.

Pound.

Pound.

"Cornelius Blaise Barrington!" she calls and pounds again. "I ken you are in there! Yer lights are on!"

I stand behind her on the stoop, with Mom and Dad and Mr. and Mrs. Cady standing on the rocky beach below. I close my eyes and hope with all my might that he doesn't answer the door. That Cornelius Blaise Barrington, Nessie hunter extraordinaire, is out in the boat with Hammy Bean and Dax.

I hope with all my might that they aren't alone.

But when the door cracks open just enough for us to see Corny peek two blue eyes out at us, all the air I was holding in my lungs escapes, making me feel more deflated than anything else.

"Honey," he says, opening the door wider. "Ada Ru? What are ye doin' here so late?"

"Hammy Bean and Dax are gone," I tell him before Mamo Honey even has a chance to say the words.

"What do you mean?"

"The SS *Albatross*," I say. "It's gone. And neither of them are answering on the radio."

Corny puts two flat palms on top of his head. "Ahhhh—"

"I'm sorry, I had to tell her," I say. "I had to. They made me."

"How could ye, Cornelius?" Mamo Honey asks him. "He has no business havin' that boat, and ye ken it."

"It's not what ye think. We go oot on it together," Cornelius tells her. "He's never taken it oot without me. That was the agreement."

She points an angry arm toward the water. "Well, tonight he's out there without you, isna he?" she says with anger flashing in her eyes, even though her voice cracks on the very last word.

"It's okay," I say. "He has the Humminbird Helix Combo."

They all turn to me and stare.

"What is that?" Mr. Cady asks.

"It—it's an advanced s-sonar and . . . and . . . GPS," I explain.

Mamo Honey huffs a blast of hot air out of her lungs. "Cornelius! How could ye?" she exclaims again.

"I didna do that!" he tells her. "I dinna even ken what that is. We just had the regular sonar setup and we went out together. That was the rule. That was always the rule."

"Well, where did he get somethin' like that, then?"

They both stare at me again.

"Online," I say. "It—it came in the mail."

Cornelius takes his bright yellow slicker from a hook near the door and begins to slip it over his gigantic shoulders. "Keep the heid," he tells Mamo Honey. "I know this loch better than anyone. I will find them, I promise ye that."

Then I remember something horrible.

Terrible.

Absolutely and completely dismal.

"Unless . . . ," I start.

"Unless what?" Mamo Honey says.

"I just remembered something," I say.

Mamo Honey puts her strong hands on my shoulders. "What did ye remember?"

I look at Mom and she shakes her head at me. "No more secrets, Adelaide Ru. You tell Mamo Honey everything you know."

I swallow hard.

Mamo Honey's eyes are filled with worrying tears, and her brow furrowed with fear.

Waiting.

"The Moray Firth," I tell her. "He said something about the Moray Firth leading out to the North Sea."

Mrs. Cady gasps, and Mamo Honey closes her eyes and shakes her head.

"What do you mean?" Dad demands.

"He wanted to take the boat to London one day," I say.

"Oh my God, Gary," Mrs. Cady says to Mr. Cady, grabbing his hand.

"*London?*" Dad says. "What for?"

Mamo Honey drops onto the ground like an emptied sack and Mom bends down quickly at her side, wrapping her arms around Mamo Honey's brokenness.

"It's where his parents live," Mamo Honey says, and then drops her face into her palms and cries, her shoulders shaking with every sob that comes out of her.

37

WINGS

Words.

They torture me all night with dreams of all the awful ones I spewed all over Hammy Bean and Dax. Horrible, despicable words chasing me through leafy branches and pulling me down in black waves.

It's words that wake me the next morning too, my eyes opening to a strange ceiling with an antique chandelier hanging in the center of the room. Dad's coat is covering me and Tuna Tetrazzini is curled up in a ball in the crook of my arm. I push the coat aside and sit up, rubbing my eyes and watching all the pictures from last night flood my brain, reminding me all over again of the real-life nightmare that's way worse than any dream could ever be.

Voices float around me.

Mumbles and whispers along with dishes clanking and cups clinking. I'm on my feet in an instant and I scramble into the Tibby kitchen with Tuna Tetrazzini on my heels.

"Are they back?" I demand.

Mamo Honey, Mom and Dad, and Mr. and Mrs. Cady are all sitting at the table, sipping hot tea with bleary eyes and somber faces. Minus one Cornelius Blaise Barrington.

"No, honey," Mom says.

"Well, what are we doing just sitting here?" I say, pacing the kitchen floor. "We have to do something."

"The police are oot lookin' today," Mamo Honey says. "They're searchin' the waterways now. Unfortunately, the rain an' fog are makin' the search difficult. But I'm hopin' they come through that door any minute."

"Well, Mac-Talla is with them," I say. "She won't let anything bad happen."

"Dax should've known better," Mrs. Cady says, while Mr. Cady bites his bottom lip and stares out the window. "He usually has better judgment than this. Maybe we gave him too much freedom here."

Mr. Cady puts a hand on her arm.

"I'm sure they'll be fine," he whispers, glancing at his wristwatch and biting his lip again.

Mamo Honey just shakes her head, creating invisible circles onto the surface of her teacup. "I would never have let him go oot on that boat."

"He loves that boat," I tell Mamo Honey. "He says the SS *Albatross* gave him his wings."

"I havena hidden him away," Mamo Honey says. "Even though I wanted to, just to keep him safe from the world. But I kent he needed to be oot in it. I kent that," she tells Mom.

Mom puts a hand on top of Honey's and nods.

"But he's a bird," Mamo Honey says. "He wants to fly all

261

the time, in every different direction. No matter how much I've wanted to keep him in my nest, I've let him fly and fall again and again until he fell less and less. But he never stops wantin' to soar. He is an unstoppable force sometimes."

"He's an albatross," I whisper.

"The albatross," she says, "spends its life circlin'—"

"I know," I say. "Flying the skies of the world above us, circling and watching from afar . . . *wishing*," I whisper, tears starting to leak from the corners of my eyes.

I swallow hard and take a deep shaky breath.

"Mamo Honey," I choke. "I have something else to tell you . . . and I'm afraid it's . . . it's worse than the wee boat."

"What is it, love?"

"I think it's all my fault. I think he left b-because of me."

"What do ye mean?"

"I told him I know he's been lying about his parents," I say. She doesn't say anything.

"It's worse than that," I say. "I told him . . . that everyone knows it too."

She stays silent for a very long time. Such a long time that my legs start to ache as I stand there waiting for her anger.

The fury.

The lashing out.

The horrible words.

"He doesna deserve all that's happened to him in his life," she says softly. "But he's never once complained." She smiles and wipes another rogue tear. "Not once. He's a strong an' verra brave lad. An' so full of love." Her voice cracks. "He should have parents who wanted to stand up for him. Give him everythin' he deserves. Love. A home. A family. I knew he lied about his parents. He was . . . *devastated*, ashamed that they dinna love him more than the drugs. It was somethin' I couldna protect him from because it was his truth. As much as I dinna want it to be."

I reach out and find Mom's hand resting on her leg under the counter. Her fingers wrap around mine and she holds them tight.

"I'm sorry," I tell Mamo Honey. "I didn't mean to say it. I was mad at him and that made me say things I didn't mean and wouldn't have said if I'd been thinking with my whole brain."

"He looks up to ye, Ada Ru." Mamo Honey smiles up at me.

I swallow a big lump. "He does?"

She nods.

The black makeup that usually sits around her eyes has found its way into the cracks below her bottom lashes like tiny black veins.

"Your friendship wi' Hammy Bean has been one o' his greatest treasures," she says.

I swallow the tears welling in the back of my throat. "He said that?"

"Aye," she says. "He's said it . . . every day since he's met you an' Dax."

"He's been a good friend to me too," I tell her. "He's made my time here in Scotland better than I ever thought it could be."

More tears find their way down my cheeks as I wish with all my might there was something more I could do than just wait.

And then it comes to me.

Words.

Later that morning, when we return to the abbey, I sit down at my laptop to do what I do best.

Write.

I choose my words carefully and with purpose and feeling. And it's my feelings that actually help me find the right words.

The right line.

The right paragraph.

My fingers race across the keyboard.

Until I reach the end.

It's what I will share with the whole town. So they can know Hammy Bean like I know him. So they'll know he matters, and not as an albatross existing only on the outskirts, but as one of them.

And a true and serious contender in the Nessie Race.

So that when he and Dax make it home things might be different for him.

After I'm all done, I print out as many copies as the printer behind the door marked OFFICE at St. Benedict's will print and then I pass it all around town.

Everywhere.

TO MY FORT AUGUSTUS FRIENDS

Words may seem innocent enough, but I'm here to tell you that they're a way bigger deal than most people know.

They are so powerful, in fact, that they can change you in a single, solitary second.

Words can propel you so high that you could fly straight

up to the sky blue. Or can seem so heavy on your shoulders that you think you'll never stand straight again. And there's one reason for that.

Words make us *feel*.

And feelings are everything. They control who we are and how we live and every single choice we make.

My name is Adelaide Ru Fitzhugh and I'm asking for your help. Two of my very good friends are missing and they need to be found.

Hammy Bean Tibby lives in Fort Augustus, as some of you know, and Dax Cady is an annual summer visitor to St. Benedict's. I hope you will all join me with thoughts and hopes and prayers that they come home safely.

But I also hope you will join me in remembering that the words you say and the words you don't say have an equal impact in this world. And everyone deserves to feel good about who they are and what they do. Please join me in making sure the words we share are positive ones that lift people up and are never too heavy to carry.

Believe me . . . you'll be glad you did.

Thank you, Ada Ru Fitzhugh

38

~~~~~~~~~~~

IPX5 WATERPROOF RATING

After lunch, I lie on my bed, staring at the gray camouflage walkie-talkie.

I pick it up and push the button.

"Denver to Captain Green Bean. Come in, Captain Green Bean. Over," I say into the speaker.

Silence.

"Please come in. Over," I whisper.

Nothing.

I want to hear his voice tell me to memorize my codes and call me a right numpty for not doing it. I want to hear about his latest top-secret bobble or sighting to investigate.

"Strings," I say. "Do you read? Over."

Silence.

"Team Nessie Quest," I whisper again. "Please come home. Over."

I cradle the radio in my arms, waiting for them to answer, until my eyes can't stay open anymore. But even though my eyelids refuse to stay up, my brain won't let me rest. Dreams about the inky waves in the loch swallowing Hammy Bean and Dax whole taunt me.

Moody, murky waves, thrashing them.

Darkness beneath the surface, sucking them deep.

Low-hanging clouds and rain hiding them like a dark, dusky secret.

"Adelaide Ru," Mom whispers, shaking my shoulder gently.

My eyes peel open.

"There's someone here to see you," she tells me.

I sit straight up. "Wh-what?" I rub my eyes. "Is it . . . is it—"

She nods and smiles.

I throw the covers to one side and dart out of bed, my bare feet slapping the floorboards down the hall and around the corner.

They're there.

Sitting side by side in front of the fireplace.

Two extra-wet Nessie hunters and one sloppy red dog drying in the heat of the flames.

Dax and Hammy Bean, both wrapped in big, fuzzy blankets and Mac-Talla sleeping on the floor next to them, her grubby tennis ball under her chin, too tired to even give me a sniff.

Dad's in the kitchen heating up water for tea while Mamo Honey, Mr. and Mrs. Cady and a curiously damp Cornelius Blaise Barrington sit at the kitchen table.

I squeeze in between the bedraggled boys and throw an arm over each one, pulling them to me.

"What were you thinking?" I ask them.

"What can I say?" Hammy Bean dimples me with that big grin of his. "There was evidence to be found."

I laugh and squeeze him close to me.

"I'm so sorry," I tell him. "I didn't mean . . . I didn't mean any of it. I know more than anyone how important words are, and I used mine in a horrible way. You're my friend and I'd just die if you wanted to take away my walkie-talkie for what I did."

"Ye want to be my mate even after ye ken I lied about my mam and da?"

"Are you kidding me? *Yes*," I say. "I know why you did it and I should never have said those things to you. I was mad about what you said about my article and I took it out on you. I didn't mean any of it."

"I'm sorry too," he tells me. "I shouldna lied to ye. I've told those stories for as long as I can remember—I dinna ken why. I guess it's better than sayin' the truth."

"I totally get that," I say. "Mates for life or longer?"

"Mates for life or longer." He holds out a hand and I shake it.

"*Hello?* What about *my* apology?" Dax says then.

I turn to face him and he's one-lipping me.

"*Boiled noodles?*" He raises his eyebrows at me.

"What's boiled noodles?" Hammy Bean asks.

"She said that's what I smell like," Dax says.

"*Boiled noodles?*" Hammy Bean says again. "That's random."

Dax throws his arms out. "That's what *I* said."

"Plus, ye smell more like a pure hearty beef stew than pasta."

My laugh comes out in a burst.

"*Beef stew?*" Dax reaches over me to give Hammy Bean a punch in his arm.

"I'm sorry," I tell Dax. "I'm sorry I said all the things I did."

"What about the spoiler?" he asks.

"Definitely the spoiler."

He shrugs and gives me his one-lipper again. "It's cool."

"Please promise me one thing," I say to them both. "No more solo excursions."

"Dinna fash," Hammy Bean tells me. "The SS *Albatross* sank oot past Urquhart Bay."

I gasp. "What did you do?"

"Dax got us all to shore an' Corny found us as we were hikin' back toward home."

"Oh, man, so . . . the boat is gone?" I ask.

"Sunk," Dax says.

"Oh no, your wings," I say.

"Aye," Hammy Bean agrees.

"And the Humminbird Helix Combo?"

Hammy Bean leans real close to me and whispers in my ear. "Can they hear us?" he asks.

I give a nonchalant glance toward the kitchen, pretending to scratch my chin on my shoulder just in case someone's looking. But Mamo Honey, Corny, Mr. and Mrs. Cady and Mom and Dad are all too busy sitting at the table, sipping on hot tea from mugs and snacking on plates of goodies from a Wee Spot of Tea and Biscuits to notice.

"No," I whisper back. "Why?"

"You'll never guess what we found," he tells me.

"What?" I ask.

"A long time ago, Mamo Honey discovered a part o' the

loch that dips down to over eight hundred and fifty feet deep," he says. "She thinks it's where there may be a lair or even tunnels oot to other lochs an' maybe even to the North Sea."

"What's a lair?" I ask.

"A nest or cave or area where the Nessies live."

"How do you know all this stuff?" I ask him.

"I've listened to every single report she's written aboot it," he tells me. "In the attic, she has boxes and boxes o' writings dated all the way back to the sixties, an' five years ago she uploaded all those files to the computer."

"And you found this spot she wrote about?" I say.

"Sure did." Hammy Bean grins big. "With the help o' the Humminbird Helix Combo."

"So, I don't get it," I say. "What now?"

"I can show ye right where it is," Hammy Bean says. "She found the coordinates first an' we found the spot oot there in the SS *Albatross* last night. Well, me, Dax an' the Humminbird Helix Combo. We were right on top o' the dip and measured it on the sonar. *Nine hundred feet!* That's fifty feet more than Mamo Honey's original findings."

"But the Humminbird Helix Combo sank with the boat?" I say.

"It's okay," he says. "It has an IPX5 waterproof rating."

"What does that mean?" Dax asks.

"I'm not exactly sure," Hammy Bean says. "But it sounded good when I read it online. So I'm hopin' one day to get it back from the bottom of the loch an' maybe it will still work with the coordinates we programmed."

"And how do you suppose you'll do that?" I ask him.

"It would have to be a scuba situation o' sorts," he tells me.

I roll my eyes. "I missed you, you little know-it-all," I tell him.

"Yeah?" He dimples me again.

"Definitely," I say.

"Did you miss me?" Dax asks.

I turn to face him and shrug. "I suppose," I say, trying not to grin too big.

"We need to go back oot there," Hammy Bean informs us.

"And how do you expect to do that without a boat?" Dax asks.

Hammy Bean sighs real loud. "Do I have to be the one to think o' everythin'?"

39

OFF THE RADAR

Beep.

"Team Nessie Quest, do ye read me? Over."

My eyes pop open and I glance at the antique clock.

Five-thirty.

In the morning.

It's been two weeks since Hammy Bean sank the SS *Albatross* and he's been on that radio every single day before six acorns.

"I sure hope you're manning this radio because I told ye that here at the *Jug*, Nessie news never stops. Do ye read me, Team Nessie Quest? Over."

I yawn and stretch and reach to grab the radio lying on the bed next to me.

Lucky for me, all is back to normal, including my reporter/secret agent position at the *Jug*. Dax's sentence has been converted to spending more time on family excursions now and again since *the incident*.

Team Nessie Quest will have to pretty much stay off the radar for a while, especially since Mamo Honey has Hammy Bean on an every-thirty-minute walkie-talkie check-in.

In secret, I think Hammy Bean has something up his *Nessie Quest* Windbreaker sleeve, but for now he's keeping it on the down-low.

But one thing is for sure—after Hammy Bean's voyage to the bottom of the loch, the other teams have a newfound respect for him as a serious contender in the Nessie Race.

And that's been obvious in more ways than one.

I push the button on the radio.

"Don't you ever sleep?" I ask him. "Over."

"The famous sturgeon makes his bloody pudding next to the black diamonds while the best mates eat famous fish with extra tartar sauce. Over."

I laugh. "How is that Nessie news? Over."

"Are ye in or are ye out? Over."

Beep.

"Copy that, Strings is in with a double chips order since the Pooping Goose always eats all my fries. Over."

"I *know* you're not talking about me," I tell Dax.

"You forgot to say *over.* Over," he informs me.

"*Thaaaat's* a roger. Rendezvous at twelve acorns on the oak tree that blows in the morning breeze. Over an' oot," Hammy Bean says.

~

"Howzitgoan, Ada Ru and Hamish Bean," Mr. Farquhar calls out when we step inside Farquhar's Famous Fish House.

Hammy Bean's cheeks turn bright pink and he says, "Me?"

"Aye, lad. Good afternoon to you!"

"H-hello," Hammy Bean calls back. "I mean good afternoon."

"Mr. Farquhar," I say. "We will have three baskets of your famous fish and three Cokes, please."

Tuna Tetrazzini rubs against my leg and I give her a scratch on her back.

"Three?" Mr. Farquhar asks. "Ye must be hungry, lassie."

"Our friend Dax is coming too," I tell him.

He nods and pushes buttons on the cash register. "Three orders o' famous fish, no bloody meat," he calls out to the kitchen, giving me a wink. "That will be twenty-six pounds seventy-five."

"With extra homemade tartar sauce on the side, please," I tell him, handing him the bills Mom gave me for our lunch.

"Of course, lass," he says, putting the bills inside the drawer.

"Hey," Dax says, coming up from behind me.

"I got you an order too," I tell him. "On me. Well, Mom."

"Thanks," he says. "What's up, HB?" He gives Hammy Bean's arm a punch.

Hammy Bean smiles. "I'm *groovy*," he tells Dax.

"Right on." Dax one-lips him.

Hammy Bean holds out a fist and Dax bumps it with his own and then they fan out their fingers and shake them.

"Wait, what's that?" I ask.

"A secret handshake," Dax tells me.

"For the *Jug*?"

"No," Dax says. "Just us."

"Why can't *I* know it?" I ask.

"Sorry," he says. "You have to belong to the club."

"What club?"

"The club you belong to when your boat has sunk and you're freezing and you have to keep your mind off it while you make your way home."

"Got it," I say.

"There's an open table in the front window for ye kids." Mr. Farquhar points to the front of the shop.

Me and Dax slide ourselves onto stools at the table and I tap the stool next to mine.

"Here, Hammy Bean. You can sit next to me."

He finds the stool with an outstretched hand, sets his cane to the side and then slides on top of the seat.

Beep.

"Mamo Honey to Captain Green Bean. Checkin' in. Over."

Hammy Bean sighs and grabs his walkie-talkie off his belt loop. "Captain Green Bean to Mamo Honey. The fish floats at the top with tartar sauce on the side. Over."

I laugh. "That's your new code for Farquhar's Famous Fish House?"

He laughs too. "Nae, I'm the fish. Because I'm banned from water contact," he explains. "I'm the one floatin', ken? It's a wee guilt trip I have goin'."

"Ah," I say. "Is it working?"

"Nae."

"Yeah, they don't work in my house either," I tell him.

"Roger that, Captain Green Bean. Over an' oot," Mamo Honey calls into the radio.

"I suppose you're done investigating for a while," I say.

He just smiles like a little evil genius and says, "The wheels are in motion."

"What wheels?" I ask.

"Haud yer wheesht," he tells us. "I've got an idea. An' like all good ideas, it will take time. Something verra excitin' is on the horizon."

"Orange exciting?"

"Pure barry orange," he tells me.

"Whoa," I say. "That's a lot of orange. Can you at least give us a hint?"

"Sorry," he says, shaking his head. "It's a super-top-secret bobble an' I have to make sure everythin' is perfect before I can reveal it."

"Here you go, lads an' lass." Mr. Farquhar sets down three baskets o' famous fish and chips. "Cheers!"

Hammy Bean leans in close to me. "What is happenin'?"

I blow on a fish stick. "Why?" I ask.

"Mr. Farquhar has never talked to me before."

"Never?"

"Never," he says. "He talks to Mamo Honey when I'm wi' her, but he never talks directly to me. I quite like this change."

The bell on the door rings and the Loch Watchers pile into the shop in single file, arguing loudly.

"You're a right numpty, Sterling. How could a species that large survive on the amount of salmon in the loch?" Norval Watt is saying.

"With those steep contours on the sides o' the loch, there's every possibility that caves or tunnels exist that could reach all the way oot to the North Sea, leadin' to some form of subsea network," Sterling Jack replies.

"Yer bum's oot the windae!" Cappy McGee exclaims. "That's never been proven."

"Hello there, Loch Watchers!" I call out to them with my mouth full of famous fish. "Haven't you decided what it was that made the prints in the mud yet?"

"It's still a matter of ragin' debate," Sterling Jack tells us.

I give them a slow nod. "I know exactly what you mean about that."

Cappy McGee makes his way over to our table and leans an elbow next to Hammy Bean. "Say there, lad," he says, putting a hand on his shoulder. "Ye find anything oot there that ye'd like to share wi' us?"

Hammy Bean grabs his napkin and wipes the tartar sauce from the corner of his mouth. "No disrespect, but not a chance, sir."

A big, booming laugh comes out of all three men, with one solo toot.

Cappy McGee pats Hammy Bean's shoulder with a big grin. "I'd be gobsmacked if ye did, lad," he says. "Gobsmacked."

All three men head over to the counter to talk with Mr. Farquhar.

Hammy Bean leans in close again. "They've never talked to me either," he whispers. "What's goin' on?"

That's what makes me wonder if the words I shared when the boys went missing had anything to do with this change of heart. If maybe, just maybe I helped bridge a gap.

"Maybe it took them time to learn just what a force to be reckoned with you really are," I tell him.

"Do ye think so?"

"Totally, little dude," Dax says, chewing on a chip.

"Hey, Hammy Bean!" Mr. Farquhar calls from the counter. "These men up here are worried about what ye might have discovered oot there at Urquhart Bay the other night."

"My lips are sealed," Hammy Bean calls back.

Norval Watt holds up his can of soda to toast us at our table. "Cheers, Team Nessie Quest! May the best team win!" he calls out.

Hammy Bean shoots the men two of his deepest dimples yet. "Oh, dinna fash, we will."

We all laugh and so do they.

With one solo toot.

40

~~~~~~

COOL BLUE WITH WHIPPED-CREAM CLOUDS

After lunch, with our bellies full, me, Dax, Hammy Bean and Mac-Talla lie in the sun on the aging planks of the rickety dock.

Minus one wee SS *Albatross*.

I actually miss it, if I'm being honest.

Me and Dax are staring up at the clouds and taking turns describing the shapes to Hammy Bean as we try to decide what they look like.

"And it has a spout," I say to Hammy Bean. "And a handle on the other side."

"A teapot," Hammy Bean guesses.

"Yep," I say.

Dax wrinkles his nose up at the sky. "No way. It looks more like a catcher's mitt to me."

"Oh, yer bum's oot the windae!" I exclaim. "That's a teapot, see the handle and the spout?"

"Mmmm, I'm sticking with catcher's mitt," he says.

"Maybe a catcher's mitt with a spout."

He laughs.

The fluffy clouds swirl and swim in slow motion, morphing and melding into new shapes above us. "I wish you could see the clouds today," I finally say to Hammy Bean. "It's a perfect blue sky. No gray at all."

"The loch is a moody one," he tells us. "The weather comes down quickly from the mountains an' it's ever-changin'."

"If I had my camera with me I'd take a picture of the sky because the blue is so pretty and I want to remember this day for a long time. *Click.*"

"What's that?" Dax asks.

"My dad's camera makes this amazing clicking noise when I push the button that means I've captured something in a blink of an eye. Something very special. A moment in time that will never, ever be reproduced. And if you're really good, you can even capture the *soul* of the picture."

"What does yer soul look like today?" Hammy Bean asks, propping his head on his elbow.

"A bright blue sky with fluffy white clouds."

"Aye, but what do clouds actually look like?" Hammy Bean asks.

I prop my head then too and stare back at him. "What do they look like?"

"Right, I've never seen them before," he says. "Describe yer picture to me."

"Well," I say. "The clouds are white—"

"Wait. What's white?" he asks.

"Um, well, it's like . . . it's like there's no color at all," I say. "Except next to the blue sky, they're stark."

"So what's blue?"

"*Ummmm?*" I think hard about his question. "It's like this . . . give me your hand."

He sits up and holds out his palm.

"Come with me." I scooch over to the side of the dock with his hand in mine. "Put your hand in the water like this," I say.

We reach down together, touching the water just below the boards.

"That's what blue is," I tell him. "What does it feel like to you?"

He moves his hand back and forth through the water like an oar. "It's cool," he says.

"Yep," I say.

"An' refreshin' and smooth and it makes goose bumps pop oot on my skin too."

"That's exactly what a perfect blue sky looks like," I tell him.

"And what aboot the clouds?"

I squint while I stare up at them again. "Do you remember when we were roasting marshmallows that night at the tent? I mean, you should, you ate like seven."

He rubs his belly and laughs. "Oh, I remember them well," he says.

"Clouds are like when the marshmallow is roasted just right with crisp outsides and a mushy center," I say.

"No way," Dax says.

"Well, what do you think they look like, then?" I ask.

"Clouds are like a huge mound of whipped cream on top of a hot piece of sticky toffee pudding. Constantly changing shape because they're melting from the heat of the cake."

"Yeah." I point to Dax. "That's right, clouds are a mound of whipped cream. That's definitely what they are."

Hammy Bean reaches his hand out toward me then. "Where are ye?" he asks.

I grab his hand.

"I liked what ye wrote about me," he says. "And about how important words can be. Mamo Honey read it to me."

"Yeah?" I say.

"Thanks for stickin' up for me."

"I just wrote how I felt," I tell him.

That's when he reaches up and finds my cheek with his fingertips. "This," he says, "is what kindness looks like."

I beam down at him with my insides filling up and over with love for everything about Fort Augustus and all the people who have become like family to me.

Especially Hammy Bean Tibby.

"And you," I tell him, "are a force to be reckoned with. Don't let anyone ever make you feel anything different."

41

~~~~~~~~~~

NESSIE JUGGERNAUT

For the next few weeks, Team Nessie Quest lies low and stays out of trouble. Instead of nighttime searches, we work on getting the *Nessie Juggernaut* podcast ready to go live.

I've been writing and conducting interviews around town.

Hammy Bean has been practicing his announcer skills, and he's getting legit good too.

Dax has been putting the finishing touches on the intro.

Mom has gotten everything up and running for the podcast and showed us how to upload interviews and edit them. We have all the interviews I've done uploaded and edited and we've added some voice-over copy to them too. They're all ready to go live when Hammy Bean finally makes up his mind on what his debut podcast will be.

Dad even did a cool graphic for a logo.

NESSIE JUGGERNAUT
WITH HAMMY BEAN TIBBY

It's going to be epic orange.

Right this minute, we're waiting on Dax at the *Nessie Juggernaut* office for the big intro reveal. I have Hammy Bean's computer all ready to record it and then upload it to play at the beginning of every show.

Dax is all out of breath when he shows up ten acorns late with Ole Roy on his back and a spiral notebook in his hand.

I give him one pointer finger before he even makes it through the doorway of the office. "Don't tell me you're not ready," I say.

"I'm ready," he says, getting comfortable on his same comfy leather chair in the corner and picking at the strings on Ole Roy. He turns the knobs on the handle to find just the sound he's looking for.

"Okay," he finally says. "I'm ready now."

Hammy Bean sits back in his leather desk chair and I slide a hip onto the armrest.

We wait.

Dax clears his throat.

He strums once and then stops and looks up at us.

"You know," he says, "it'd be cool if you didn't look at me while I did this."

"What do you want us to do?" I ask.

"I mean, I don't sing for people very often and . . ."

I grin big at him. "Are you saying you haven't found your share-your-own-words-in-front-of-people tidbits yet?"

He one-lips me. "Okay," he says. "I'll give you that one. You found yours and I have to find mine. I get it."

He takes a deep breath.

He strums for a long while as Hammy Bean and I wait. And then after a whole bunch of music with no words, he finally starts:

Nessie Juggernaut is a place for facts you can score,
with your host, Hammy Bean.
He's got the facts you're looking for,
if what you want is a real monster scene.
Hammy Bean is the boss,
with his wings, watch him fly.
Like the mighty albatross,
he takes his flight through water and sky.
In his search for Nessie high and low,
he'll never lead you astray.
No hoaxes, no lies, no, no, no,
join Nessie Juggernaut today.

Then Dax looks up at us and in an announcer voice says, "Here's your host, the Amazing Hammy Bean Tibby, crypto-zoologist extraordinaire."

He takes a deep breath and stares at us.

"Well?" he asks.

Hammy Bean pops up from his chair and so do I, and we both give Dax a standing ovation.

I even give him a *whoop whoop* and wave my fist in the air.

"That was so good," I tell him. "*So* good."

He shrugs. "Yeah?"

"Totally," I say. "Epic."

Hammy Bean says, "I love it! I love it! I love it! That's the best intro anyone could have ever made for me. The best intro anyone could ever ask for. Thank ye, Dax. Thank ye for writin' that for me. Sing it again!"

"We have to record it," I remind Hammy Bean.

"I know, but I want to hear it again."

"You heard the kid," I tell Dax. "Play it again."

The smile that spreads across Dax's face is a two-lipper and then some. I'd say he's smiling way too big to be normal, but he's so pure tidy when he does it, it sure doesn't matter to me.

"What about *my* intro?" I ask him before he starts.

"I'm working on it," he says. "You're a . . . ah . . . *complex* subject to write about."

"What does that mean?"

"It means . . . I'm coming up with just the right words for you."

And maybe it's my imagination, but those seaweeds hold mine a little longer than they usually do.

Feeling word: That's private.

42

~~~~~~~~~~

A SEARCH FOR THE END

"Captain Green Bean to Team Nessie Quest. Come in, Team Nessie Quest," Hammy Bean calls from the walkie-talkie. "Do ye read me? Over."

I shove my head under the pillow.

So, I know I *said* I missed hearing his voice over that speaker, but I take it back. I would seriously miss hearing it a lot more at like . . . say, eight acorns. Or even nine, after my Wee Spot of Tea scone and English Breakfast tea with extra cream and lots of honey.

"Denver, you'd better be listenin' is all I have to say because you're the first-ever *Nessie Juggernaut* employee and bein' a reporter/secret agent means bein' on call at all times, day or night, in case a story breaks," Hammy Bean says. "An' right now, a story is about to *explode*, so you had better pick up that radio right this minute. It's aboot the banana. Over."

I sigh and pick up the walkie-talkie lying on the bed next to me and push the button. "This had better be good."

"Ye forgot to say *over*. Over."

"Hammy Bean!"

"Okay, okay. Believe me, ye willna be disappointed," he says. "I've got a big assignment for ye, and I mean *big*. Humongous is what it is. So you're goin' to need to reach down deep and find all the tidbits ye can muster. Do ye understand? Over."

I yawn. "Uh-huh," I say.

"This assignment is too sensitive to say any more than I've already said on air," he goes on. "The airwaves are just not secure enough and this is a top-secret bobble if there's ever been one. I mean over-the-top top-secret. Do ye understand what I'm sayin' to ye? Over."

I sit up and stare at the speaker. "Banana secret? Over?"

"Exactly," he says. "Over."

"I dinna think I can wait. Over."

"I tell you, I can't say this over the airwaves," he says. "It's not secure enough. Over."

"Give it to me in code, then. Over."

Silence.

"Hello?" I say.

"Fine . . . The yellow fish . . . swims deep . . . but a sand bottom an' the darkest crevices are where ye will end yer final journey of discovery. Over."

"What about the banana?"

"I tell ye, this is new code."

But before I can push the button to answer him, my bedroom door creaks open and I shriek.

"Everything okay?" Mom whispers from the doorway in her robe and slippers.

I drop the radio and it lands on the floor with a thud.

"Wh-what? Oh, yeah," I say, scrambling out from under the covers and lifting the bed skirt to look for it. "It's just Hammy Bean," I tell her, snatching the radio out from under the bed. "He has a new assignment for me. Wr-writing . . . I mean, just writing. On land. Y-you know . . . copy for the podcast."

The speaker beeps. "Denver? Do ye read? Over."

I push the button and stare at Mom. "Momma Bear is out of hibernation and on a hunt for cheese and crackers. Over," I say, grinning big at Mom.

Mom gives me a suspicious look. "Is that supposed to be about me?"

"Nope," I say.

"Roger that," Hammy Bean says. And then he shouts, "Good mornin', Mrs. Fitzhugh! Over!"

She lifts one eyebrow at me. "I hope you're not planning anything bananas with all these secret morning codes."

"Bananas? Me? No way, I learned my lesson the last time. So we're cool, I mean like freezing cold. We're so freezing, in fact . . . you know what it is? It's like arctic weather, really . . . and like I'm a polar bear—"

She holds a hand up. "Got it," she says, standing there a few more seconds before sliding her baffies to the kitchen to start the coffee. I listen to the opening and closing of cupboards and the sound of Dad starting the shower in the hall bathroom with his typical morning chorus of "Singin' in the Rain."

"Momma Bear is back in the den but still open to sniffing out crackers and cheese, so proceed with caution. Over," I whisper.

"Affirmative. Over."

"So . . . what did you say again about yellow fishes? Over?"

"I said the yellow fish . . . swims deep . . . but a sand bottom and the darkest crevices are where you will end your final journey of discovery. Over."

I grab my code sheet from the bedside table drawer and check the list.

"There isn't a single thing about yellow fishes or dark crevices on here. Over," I inform him.

"I already told ye, it's brand-new. It's an ultrasecret and extremely important new assignment that you must gather up all your tidbits to experience. Over."

"Like how many are we talking? Over?"

"I need ye to be my first mate. Over."

"So water, then? Over?"

"Don't be a wee bairn. Over."

"I'm not a wee bairn," I insist. "Wait. What is that?"

"A baby. Over."

"I'm not a baby," I say.

"Rendezvous at the arch at six an' a half acorns on the oak tree that blows in the mornin' breeze. An' not a minute later. We can't alert the Three Bears to the plan. Or Price Cut on Salami either. Are ye a *Juggernaut* or aren't ye? Over."

"I *am*," I assure him. "I mean, I *think* I am. Over."

"Are ye a force to be reckoned with? Over?"

I bite my lip. "Maybe. Over."

"I knew I should have asked Strings. Over."

"*No,*" I insist. "I'm a force. I'm a force. A way stronger force than Dax any day because I'm talking to you at five acorns and he didn't even answer. That's how strong a force I am. Over."

"You want to be a part o' somethin' bigger, right? Over."

I take a deep breath and sit straight. "*Thaaat's* a roger, Captain Green Bean," I say. "You can count on me. I'll meet you at your arch at the stroke of six an' a half acorns."

"An' bring yer camera. Over."

"Roger that," I tell him. "I'll be there with my camera *and* my tidbits. Denver over and out."

⁓◦⁓

After my Wee Spot of Tea scone and English Breakfast tea with far too much cream and honey, I grab Dad's camera and scramble for the door.

"Where are you going at this hour?" Mom asks me from behind her cup.

"Ah . . . sorry, that's official *Nessie Juggernaut* business," I tell her.

She takes a sip and eyeballs Dad. "Did you hear that, Zum? Official *Nessie Juggernaut* business," she says.

He looks up from the *Inverness Courier*. "Ru Ru," he says, curling his pointer finger at me, "come here. I have some top-secret information for your mission."

I roll my eyes. "I don't need a joke for my mission."

"It's not a joke," he says.

"It's not a story about a Ferris wheel, is it?"

"Nope," he says. "Not that either."

I sigh and drag my Nikes toward his kitchen chair.

He wraps one arm around my waist and pulls me close, his mouth next to my ear, and whispers, "The yellow fish . . . swims deep . . . but a sand bottom and the darkest crevices are where . . . you will end your final journey of discovery."

I suck air. "How do you—"

He smiles that smile, the one with all his teeth. "I've always said, the best part of the story is when the *impossible* becomes possible. Go find the end of your story today. Find it for both of us."

"I will," I promise him.

"Maybe you can even change my mind," he says with a wink. "Maybe I'm not a complete and total Muggle . . . *yet*."

"Sorry to be the one to break this to you," I tell him. "But you've definitely turned."

"Still, maybe you can give me something to hope for?"

I consider that. "I'll do my best," I tell him. "Bringing you back from your Muggle status will prove to be my greatest challenge yet."

He salutes me. "Godspeed," he says.

I stand up straight, salute him back and then run out the door. "Tatty bye!" I holler over my shoulder.

As I run down the heavenly stairs the crack of orange possibilities is just showing its bald head through the stained-glass faces, and I know it's a sign that today is the day. I use both hands to push open the tall wooden doors of the abbey and run as fast as I can to the arch. I'm ready for my most important assignment as a *Nessie Juggernaut* reporter/secret agent to date.

My biggest orange hope for today?

That I don't blow chunks like Mom did all over that Ferris wheel.

43

~~~~~~~~~~

A BANANA AND A VW VAN

I'm the very first one at the bridge.

That's how big a force I am.

Today the morning air is crisp and cool and the black waters of the loch are smooth and calm. The ovens at a Wee Spot of Tea and Biscuits are already busy pumping its sweetness into the sky, but Ness for Less is still dark. The walkway in front of Farquhar's Famous Fish House waits patiently to be swept, and covered tour boats bob alongside the dock, still fast asleep and before a day of tourists hop aboard hoping for a glimpse of a monster.

Even the Loch Watchers haven't clocked in for their lochside shift.

Then, at twenty-five after six acorns, I finally see Hammy Bean and Mac-Talla running along the sidewalk, racing in my direction.

"Hey!" I call. "Where've you been?"

When they reach me Mac-Talla jumps up on me, putting one paw on each shoulder and giving me a sloppy, wet tongue facewash.

"Hey, girl," I say. "Did he get you up at five too?"

She just keeps licking my cheeks and then starts with bitty nibbles on my earlobes.

"Okay, okay!" I giggle. "That tickles!" Then I ask Hammy Bean, "So why were my mom and dad suspiciously in the know this morning? Did you have something to do with that?"

"Had to be done," he says. "Sometimes top-secret bobble intel must be shared for the sake o' the hunt."

"What's that supposed to mean?"

"Just wait!" he squeals. "Just wait until ye see this! It's going to be epic beyond belief."

"Epic orange?" I ask.

He grins dimples at me. "Big-time," he tells me. "Just wait."

"For what?"

"Haud yer wheesht," he says, tilting his head. "It's coming."

I look to the left and then the right.

Nothing.

"No one is coming," I inform him. "They'll be turning onto the main road in four, three, two, one . . ." He points toward Bunioch Brae.

That's when headlights beam in the early-morning fog and creep slowly in our direction.

Mac-Talla barks three times.

"Haud yer wheesht, lass," he tells her. "Don't ye be a wee clipe."

I watch as an old tan-and-rust Volkswagen van with tattered red-and-green-plaid curtains hanging at the side windows pulls up next to us. The backside of the square van is wallpapered with aged and faded bumper stickers. It's the exact same van that Mamo Honey posed with in that black-and-white picture hanging in the hall of Tibby Manor. Except much older and way more rusted. Behind the van is a large, flat trailer pulling something way bigger than Hammy Bean's wee SS *Albatross*. But whatever it is, it's covered by a large black tarp.

The driver's-side window rolls down halfway and the one and only Cornelius Blaise Barrington gives me a larger-than-life smile with a whole lot of pop.

"Howzitgoan, lad an' lassie," he calls.

I move toward the van and curl my fingers over the top of the window.

"Corny," I say. "What's going on?"

And that's when I see Mamo Honey just past him, sitting in the backward passenger seat wearing an old gray sweatshirt that says THE LOCH NESS PROJECT on the front of it. Her red curls are tied up tight under a red scarf.

"Good mornin'." Mamo Honey waves.

"Mamo Honey, what are you doing here?"

"I felt like it was a day to find some orange possibilities," she tells me with a wink.

"Always," I say. "But what's under that tarp?"

"Mamo Honey agreed to take *Little Yellow* oot for an excursion in the loch!" Hammy Bean bursts out. "Can you believe it?"

Uh-oh.

I swallow hard. "Did you say *Little Yellow*?"

"Mamo Honey's submarine back from her days o' exploration," Hammy Bean says.

"I—I, ah—" I stutter.

"Before ye say anythin'," he interrupts me, "I warned ye that you'd have to look down deep for your tidbits for this one. Remember?"

"I know, but—"

"In." He points to the van.

I start, stepping backward while Corny jumps out and slides the side door open for us. Inside the van is a long bench along one side, with a miniature kitchen on the other. I watch Mac-Talla climb in, followed by Hammy Bean. They find places to sit on the bench, scooching over to make room for me.

"Hurry on now," Hammy Bean instructs me, patting the seat beside him. "Ye can do this."

"Yes, I can," I say, taking a deep breath and pulling myself up into the van.

Corny slams the door tight and climbs back up into the driver's side.

"Here we go, Nessie hunters!" he announces, putting the van into drive and pulling ahead.

Hammy Bean is beaming.

Mac-Talla is panting.

My stomach is churning.

"I'm so glad ye found your tidbits for this," Hammy Bean tells me.

"Don't get crazy," I say. "I'm still looking."

"Well, you've got twenty-five minutes until we get there."

"Get where?"

"To Urquhart Bay," he says. "That's where we're going to take her down."

I swallow again. "Take who where, now?"

"*Little Yellow.*"

"The broken submarine from September sixth, 2011?" I whisper.

"It's all right," he tells me. "He fixed it."

"Who?"

"Corny did."

Corny is fussing with the radio while Mamo Honey is telling him to watch the road.

"Is he really qualified to be a submarine fixer?" I whisper.

"That's a very valid question," Hammy Bean says, bobbing his head up and down.

I blink at him. "That's all you've got?" I throw my palms out toward the VW roof.

He reaches out a hand and finds my knee, giving it a pat. "Don't worry," he says again. "Cornelius Blaise Barrington, Nessie hunter extraordinaire, can do *anythin'*."

❧

Next to the rickety dock, *Little Yellow* looks like a much larger and way rustier banana, bobbing in the water with round windows lining the side of it. There's a big round hatch on the very top, where Mamo Honey, Corny and Hammy Bean climb inside it, and a long, skinny tube sticking out of it that looks like a bent telescope.

Hammy Bean calls it a periscope and says it's a telescope to use underwater.

I watch the banana from the dock as it bobs in the waves. *Pacing.*

The thing is that once I climb inside, Corny will close that hatch and sail this broken banana boat straight to the bottom.

On purpose.

Mamo Honey and Corny are down below getting things ready while Hammy Bean hangs out the glass hatch door on top of *Little Yellow* waiting for me to find my submarine tidbits.

"A told ye, didna I?" he demands.

"Don't *rush* me," I tell him, still pacing the planks. "And just for the record, you said *on* the water tidbits, not *underwater* tidbits."

"What's the difference?"

"There's a big difference," I inform him.

"Ye have yer two life jackets on," Hammy Bean tells me. "What else do ye need? We have to get this thing down before the *Nessie Race* spies spot us."

"Corny," I call.

Corny peeks out of the round windows. "Yes, lass!" he shouts through the glass.

"You're sure you fixed this thing up good, right? You didn't have any extra parts left over?"

"You've asked him that three times already," Hammy Bean reminds me.

"Absolutely, love," Corny tells me. "It's one hundred percent safe. Ye just climb on in when yer ready."

"And gas too, right? You've gassed it up and whatnot?"

"*Gas?*" Hammy Bean exclaims. "Are ye kiddin' me?"

"I promise ye that we will have yer toes back on this dock in no time," he tells me.

DENVER GIRL IS SUCKED OUT OF SUBMARINE WINDOW DEEP WITHIN THE LOCH NESS NEVER TO BE SEEN AGAIN

44

A BOBBING BANANA

Going down into the depths of Loch Ness in *Little Yellow* seems to happen in slow motion, with Corny calling out the depth levels as we descend into blackness. Bubbles rush at every window like we're floating in a bottle of carbonated soda.

I'm wedged between Hammy Bean on one side and Mamo Honey on the other.

"One hundred feet," Corny calls.

Deeper.

Bubbles rushing.

My ears popping.

"Four hundred feet," he calls.

Deeper.

"Six hundred feet."

"My ears are plugged," I tell Hammy Bean.

"Swallow," Hammy Bean tells me. "That will release the pressure."

"Seven hundred fifty feet," Corny calls out. "We're at the bottom. I will motor on toward Urquhart Bay now."

"The coordinates are 57.33212 degrees north latitude by minus 4.44348 degrees east longitude," Hammy Bean tells him, his fingers brushing across a Braille note that he's pulled from his pocket.

"Aye, aye, Captain," Corny says, tilting us to the right.

I study Mamo Honey. She looks like the inside of a jack-in-the-box ready to pop.

"It's been a long time since you've been in the race," I say to her.

She takes a deep breath and nods.

"Happy to be back at it?" I ask her.

When her eyes meet mine, I see tears at the rims.

"More than I can possibly say."

"What word would you use to describe the feeling?" I ask her.

She thinks hard about my question. "Alive," she says.

I nod. "Good word," I say.

"Ada Ru," Hammy Bean says to me. "We should be near the dip in the bottom o' the loch."

"What do you want me to do?"

"Get yer camera ready."

"Aye, aye, Captain," I say, pressing my palms against one of the round windows and getting so close that my nose fogs up the glass. Mamo Honey sits at the periscope, which can turn in different directions outside the ship according to which way she turns the handles on the inside.

Outside the glass, the water is hazy, dark and murky,

allowing me to see just a short distance in the lights beaming out from *Little Yellow*.

"Remember I told ye that visibility is only about twenty feet? It's because o' the peat that grows along the banks. It turns the water that black color. So look for bubbles," he tells me. "That's the first sign."

"I saw bubbles on the way down!" I exclaim.

"That was just air in the water as we descended," Corny explains. "Now that we're down here, the only bubbles you'll see will be a Nessie callin' card."

"Roger that," I call up to Corny in the front of *Little Yellow*.

"What are ye seein'?" Hammy Bean asks me.

"The movement of the ship seems to make the sand from the bottom of the loch mix with the water," I tell him.

"It's silt," he says.

"Well, there's a lot of it, squishing and squashing around," I say. "Making it real hard to see. And what's weird is there's hardly any vegetation. If the Nessies were vegetarians, they'd surely starve to death."

"Keep watchin'," Hammy Bean instructs. "We're almost there."

After maybe ten more minutes of floating forward, Corny says, "We are at the coordinates, Captain Green Bean."

"Ada Ru," Hammy Bean says. "Man the hatch window with your camera as well, just in case Nessie swims over us."

"Aye, aye, Captain."

Mamo Honey's eyes are wide in front of the periscope while Corny steers the ship and Hammy Bean stands near me with his hand on my arm.

"To the left, Corny," Mamo Honey directs.

Little Yellow turns a slight louie.

"Do ye see anythin' yet?" Hammy Bean asks me.

"Just silt," I say.

"It should be here." Mamo Honey leans toward the screen.

"Wait. I see it!" I shout. "It's there, more left, Corny. I see a dip in the bottom."

Little Yellow turns.

"Got it," Corny calls.

Corny moves *Little Yellow* in the direction of the dip in the bottom of the loch. When he's right on top of it, he begins to lower us farther.

"Eight hundred feet," he calls out.

We sink even deeper.

"Eight hundred twenty-five."

Deeper.

"Eight hundred fifty."

"Isna this amazin', Ada Ru?" Hammy Bean squeals. "No one has ever proven this before. My Mamo Honey found it first an' I found it second with the sonar, but no one has ever gone down into the depths o' the crevice."

"Eight hundred seventy feet," Corny calls out. "And we still havena reached the bottom."

My ears are popping again and my head feels like someone is pressing against it. I swallow again to clear my ears.

"Nine hundred, an' there's more to go," Corny tells us.

"Keep on!" Hammy Bean exclaims with a finger in the air.

"We are currently at nine hundred fifty feet! This is unprecedented," Corny calls back to us.

"Ada Ru," Hammy Bean says. "What do ye see?"

I squint, my eyes searching through the darkness and the silt, and then I see something.

"Port side!" I shout.

"I've got it!" Mamo Honey exclaims, peering through the periscope. "Come here, lass."

I stand next to Mamo Honey and place my cheek against hers as we watch the periscope screen together.

"What is it?" Hammy Bean exclaims. "What do ye see?"

"We've found it, lad," Mamo Honey tells him.

"It's a cave," I tell him. "A big one too. Gigantic, even."

Hammy Bean shoves his video camera in my direction. "Start recordin'!" he shouts. "Start recordin'!"

I grab the camera and fumble with it until I find the red Record button and push it, focusing the lens out the portside window.

"Are ye recordin'?" he asks.

"I'm recording! I'm recording!"

Corny rushes to look out another portside window while I get the footage. "Well, I'll be," he marvels.

"It's the lair o' the Loch Ness Monster," Hammy Bean says. "I just know it is. We've solved one of the greatest monster mysteries of all time. They've theorized for years about where Nessie could hide. There've always been questions about there being an underwater cave-and-tunnel system that connects the lochs and allows them to access the North Sea. This is the proof. An' we've got it on video."

"My mom and dad are not going to believe this," I say, still recording. "Who needs an underwater drone or a DNA scan when you have Honey Tibby and her banana boat?"

"Team Nessie Quest," Hammy Bean says, "welcome to Nessie Manor."

45

A POPPING BANANA

Things are popping all over the place.

First off, I found my underwater tidbits.

Pop.

Second, the famous Nessie investigator Mamo Honey is *back.*

Pop.

And third, Team Nessie Quest has surely taken the lead in the Nessie Race.

Big-time pop.

And I know Dax can feel it too when we show him the video from *Little Yellow* at the *Juggernaut* office the very next day.

"That"—Dax points to Hammy Bean's computer—"is the grooviest thing I've ever seen. I mean, seriously."

"I recorded it," I tell him, with my chin in the air. "Me."

Me and Dax are standing over Hammy Bean watching

the video I shot, which Hammy Bean uploaded to his talking computer.

"I can't believe I missed this," Dax says, leaning closer to the screen.

"Guess you weren't manning that radio twenty-four seven like a dedicated *Nessie Juggernaut* employee should," I say.

"Play it again," Dax says.

"You've watched it four times already," I tell him.

"So?" he says. "I'm goin' to watch it five. Or seventeen. Just push Play again."

Hammy Bean pushes a button and the computer spouts, *"Play."*

And the video starts again.

"Not to brag or anything," I say. "But my cinematography *is* kind of stellar. I mean, I'm not talking an Oscar nomination, but still. I definitely think I got the soul of the shot. Look at how I pan in here, you know, for dramatic effect."

Dax rolls his eyes at me. "Give me a break," he mumbles under his breath.

"Out of the hazy waters," I say in my very best podcast host voice, "it appears for the first time in history. The actual lair of the Loch Ness Monster has been discovered by the one and only Hamish Bean Tibby and recorded by storyteller Adelaide Ru Fitzhugh. Unfortunately, Dax Cady slept through the whole darn thing."

Hammy Bean laughs. "Boy, ye *are* a writer," he tells me. "I canna wait to read yer story."

"You'll read it?" I ask.

"Are ye kiddin'? Why wouldna I? I'm your Ron, right? An' there's a monster in it?"

"Yeah," I say. "And—"

"Don't say it," Dax warns me.

"Don't worry," I say. "I was never going to make you my Hermione. I definitely have another part for you."

"Your Ron?"

"No way," Hammy Bean protests. "Ye canna be her Ron. *I'm* her Ron!"

"Okay, okay," I say. "You can both be my Ron."

"How are you going to make that happen?" Dax asks.

I shrug. "It's fiction. I can do whatever I want."

"I'm still thinking Wolfgang, though," Dax says.

I roll my eyes.

Beep.

"Mamo Honey to Captain Green Bean. Come in, Captain Green Bean. Over."

"I thought she was just downstairs making lunch," I say.

"She is," Hammy Bean says, reaching for the walkie-talkie on the desk. "Captain Green Bean here. Over."

"You'd better be sittin' down for this one," Mamo Honey tells him. "Over."

Dax and I look at each other.

Hammy Bean scoots his leather chair tighter under the giant wooden desk. "Roger that. What is it? Over."

"The BBC *Highlands & Islands Edition* news is on their way! Over and out!"

Something epic is happening.

Something amazing.

Something legit stellar and one of a kind.

The Loch Ness Project will be begging Hammy Bean to join them after this for sure.

And I'm a part of that.

Me.

Ada Ru Fitzhugh, *Nessie Juggernaut* reporter/secret agent.

46

~

ALBERT TOD

When word gets around town about the Team Nessie Quest discovery, almost all of Fort Augustus shows up for the BBC *Highlands & Islands Edition*. Including Hammy Bean in a tweed flat cap and bow tie just like Mr. Quigley Dunbar III.

"Are there a lot o' people here?" Hammy Bean asks me as the news crew sets up for the interview in front of Farquhar's Famous Fish House.

"A ton of people," I tell him.

"More than the time with the Loch Watchers?"

"Way more," I say. "There's even a new tour boat called the *Nessie Trek (The Real Story of the Loch Ness Monster)* docked with a man and two boys standing out front of it."

"Well, that's well radge," he says, tugging on his bow tie.

"English, please," I say.

"It's crazy," he tells me. "Because it's Kagen Bootsman, his boys, Bates an' Bowie. They dock oot of Drumnadrochit an' are the only tour that tells their passengers Nessie doesna exist."

"*Veeeery* interesting," I say.

"What about the guy with the long beard?" Hammy Bean asks. "Do ye see him?"

I stand on my toes and scan the crowd until I see a tall, rail-thin man with a long gray beard and a tweed coat leaning against a light post.

"I think so," I say to Hammy Bean. "There's a skinny guy with a long beard standing alone in the back."

Hammy Bean sucks air. "A long *gray* beard?"

"Yeah," I say.

"Tweed jacket an' a flat cap?"

"Yeah," I say. "How did you—"

"That's Albert Tod," he says. "He's the leader of the Loch Ness Project."

I gasp and grab his arm. "Oh my God, you did it," I tell him.

"*We* did," he says.

The news crew is finally ready and the crowd is even bigger. Everyone from town is there and then some. Even Mr. Farquhar shows up dressed for the occasion, standing out in front of Farquhar's Famous Fish House with a spanking clean apron without even one grease stain on his belly.

Hammy Bean is no albatross today. He's right smack-dab in the middle of everything, and I've never seen his dimples deeper.

He's *famous.*

The woman with the dark lipstick is back, along with the same two men. The cameraman and the guy with the fingers.

"An' we're on in five," the finger guy says, holding up five fingers and then counting down.

Four.

Three.

Two.

One.

He points to the woman.

She smiles her dark-lipstick smile into the camera. "Thank you, Gage. We are lochside in Fort Augustus at the edge of Loch Ness . . . for a second time this summer, with yet another amazing story about our Nessie. In Scotland, the enduring story of Nessie has become more than folklore and legend about a prehistoric sea monster, it is a story enshrined in our current Scottish culture. I'm here today with a very special investigator"—she puts her arm around Hammy Bean—"with an incredible find. More incredible than any before it. Please tell the viewers your name, lad."

Hammy Bean is beaming brighter than I've ever seen him shine, and I couldn't be happier for him.

The woman holds the microphone close to him while the cameraman pans down to get him into frame.

Hammy Bean stands straight as a board, looking dapper in his bow tie. "My name is Hamish Bean Tibby," he says. "I'm a cryptozoological investigator here in Fort Augustus, as well as the editor in chief of the *Nessie Juggernaut,* a quarterly newsletter reporting on all the monster sightings, which will soon be a podcast."

I look over at Mamo Honey and see tears on her cheeks and I wonder if she'd use the same feeling word she told me the other day in *Little Yellow* to describe how she feels watching her albatross soar.

Alive.

Mom and Dad are here too, along with Cornelius Blaise Barrington, Dax and Mr. and Mrs. Cady, the Loch Watchers, Jasper Price, the Kumars from a Wee Spot of Tea and Biscuits, Euna Begbie and Tuna Tetrazzini.

"I believe we have video of your discovery queued up in the studio for our viewers?"

"That's right," Hammy Bean says. "This footage was shot by my amazin' *Nessie Juggernaut* reporter Adelaide Ru Fitzhugh. Ada Ru?" Hammy Bean reaches out his hand.

"I'm here," I say, pushing through the crowd.

"Please introduce yourself." The woman holds the microphone close to me.

"Um, I—I'm Ada Ru Fitzhugh." I stare at the camera, feeling my heart start to pound inside my chest. "I—I recorded the footage."

Mom and Dad give me a *whoop whoop.*

They're *so* embarrassing.

"Roll video back at the studio, Gage," the newswoman calls into the microphone. "Please explain to us what the viewers are watching, Ada Ru." She holds the microphone toward me again.

"Just wait until ye hear this. She sets it up *real* good," Hammy Bean tells the woman.

"Out of the hazy waters," I say, "comes the majestic lair of the fabled Nessie, a monster mystery that has spanned centuries. Is it a plesiosaur? A sirenian? Or just a plain old fish? We are getting closer to learning the true identity of the species."

"Thank you, Ada Ru." The newswoman smiles and turns the microphone back to Hammy Bean.

"One question that has plagued investigators for years is, why can't we find the monster?" he says. "It's long been believed that there may be caves down in the loch an' possibly even a tunnel system that connects it to other lochs—or possibly the sea. And we have just found evidence that this might be true. It's evidence that could bring us closer to learning exactly what Nessie is. Once an' for all."

"My goodness!" the woman exclaims. "That's an amazing discovery indeed, Hamish Bean Tibby, cryptozoological investigator extraordinaire!"

"It wasna just me," Hammy Bean says. "It was my entire team. Team Nessie Quest, please come forward."

Dax, Mamo Honey, Corny and Mac-Talla proudly stand next to Hammy Bean while the man with the camera pans over the six of us.

"My Mamo Honey, the greatest Nessie investigator o' all time. Cornelius Blaise Barrington, who gave up his entire life in London an' has lived lochside for twenty years, an' o' course Dax Cady and Adelaide Ru Fitzhugh, the very first *Nessie Juggernaut* employees an' . . . *my mates.*"

The man with the fast fingers makes a circular gesture to the lady and she gives another wide lipstick smile toward the camera.

"Well, you heard it here first, Gage," she says into the lens. "Team Nessie Quest, led by Hamish Bean Tibby, has just taken the lead in the Nessie Race here in Fort Augustus and most possibly will be providing us very soon with some answers we've had about this mystery for centuries. This is Mysie Maccrum, out at the bonny, bonny banks of the Fort Augustus beach. Back to you, Gage."

To quote the great Dr. Tobin Sky, *"A discovery is meant to be discovered only when the time is right to discover it."*

And boy, is he right about that one.

47

ONE LAST ORANGE POSSIBILITY

The summer has flown by and I can't believe we're leaving at the end of the week.

Today in my feelings journal I write two words in all caps with an exclamation mark at the end.

GOODBYES BITE!

I can't believe we have to leave this place.

The green.

The heavenly steps.

The rolling hills.

The people.

And Hammy Bean.

I've grown to love everything about Fort Augustus and I don't want to leave it.

Me, Hammy Bean and Dax all meet up at the bridge for our last-day picnic lunch at the rickety dock, the new permanent home of the mighty *Little Yellow*. Me with my camera and Dax with Ole Roy.

Scotland has shown us a beautiful last few days with no moody, low-hanging storm clouds raining on us or shaking up drama in the loch. Today the water is flat calm, like black glass.

After eating our cheese sandwiches with potato chips and cans of soda, we lie on the weathered planks in the rare and treasured Scotland sun, listening to the sounds of Loch Ness and watching the clouds change shape above us.

I close my eyes and listen, like Hammy Bean taught me to do.

I hear the water lick the rocks at the shore.

A motorboat sputtering in the distance.

Birds singing their sunny-day ditty.

A truck on the road above us changing gears.

"What are ye thinking about?"

I open my eyes and see Hammy Bean facing me, his head propped up on his elbow.

"Haud yer wheesht," I tell him. "I'm listening to the sounds and trying to memorize them."

"What sounds are ye memorizin'?"

"Every single one," I say. "All the sounds I'm going to miss about being here. I don't want to go home."

"Because o' the sounds?"

"Not just the sounds."

"Because o' me, right? You're goin' to miss me?" he asks.

I smile at the sky and don't say anything.

"It's okay," he says. "Ye doona have to say it. I know you're goin' to miss me."

"Are you going to miss me?" I ask him.

"*Big-time,*" he says.

"I'm definitely going to miss you," I say. "But other things too."

"Like what?"

"Like Mr. Quigley Dunbar the Third, Mamo Honey, Corny, a Wee Spot of Tea and Biscuits and Euna Begbie and the Loch Watchers and . . . just everything. I kind of love it here."

"But you'll miss me the most, right?"

"*Wellllll,*" I say, propping myself on my elbow too until we're face to face. "You're up there, but I'm going to miss the moody and the mysterious and the chock-full-of-story-possibilities Loch Ness too."

"Doona say tatty bye to me," he says.

"What do you mean?"

"Doona say tatty bye to me on the very last day," he says.

"Why not?"

"Because," he tells me, "it's goin' to be a very sad day when that happens and I willna want to hear those words oot loud."

His voice cracks on the last word.

"I won't say it," I tell him.

He lies back flat again. "Do ye—" And then he stops.

"What?" I ask him.

"Haud yer wheesht," he whispers, his body popping off the rickety dock like a rocket-ship blast. I watch him slide his shoes to the very last worn wooden plank, counting them under his breath as he slides.

He stands there listening.

I close my eyes and listen too.

And I realize that he's right, I *am* going to miss him most. But don't tell him I said so; it'll go straight to his head.

"Did ye hear that?" he whispers from the end of the pier.

I sit up. "What?"

"Shhh," he hisses.

"Yeah." Dax gives me an elbow. "Haud yer wheesht."

Me, Dax and Mac-Talla pop up off the boards now too and scramble in behind Hammy Bean, staring out at the smooth, calm waters.

"I don't see anything," I whisper, scanning the loch.

Hammy Bean sighs. "Are ye listenin' wi' yer eyes or yer ears?"

I squeeze my eyelids tight and listen to the orchestra of sounds around me. The breeze blows like the orchestra conductor, guiding the tempo woodsy ballad.

The tree branches sway and crack like a clapper.

The leaves *hisssss* like cymbals sliding.

The birds chime like twinkly flutes whistling.

And somewhere out in the middle of the lake an engine grumbles like a drumstick dragging across a snare drum.

And then . . . *bubbles.*

Hammy Bean grabs my wrist. "That!" he says. "Did ye hear that?"

"Yes," I whisper.

"I hear it too," Dax says.

"Now," Hammy Bean says. "Open your eyes! Do it now!"

My lids pop open and I shade my face from the sun with my forearm, my eyes darting across the flat-calm water until I see white bubbles with a large wake behind them. And then I see something coming up just below the surface. At first it

319

looks like a large overturned boat covered in black rubber, with glistening drops of water sliding off its sides as it rises to the surface.

I stare at it.

Unable to move.

Unable to speak.

"It's her," Hammy Bean whispers. "She's here to say she'll miss ye too."

I cover my mouth with my hand and whisper between my fingers. "It can't be," I say.

"Take a picture! Take a picture!" Hammy Bean exclaims.

I fumble with the camera, my fingers forgetting which button is which, and then, just as I squint through the lens, she slips back into the water as gracefully as she slipped out.

And without a single sound either.

I sigh. "She's gone."

"Yeah, but ye got it, right? Please tell me ye got the picture?"

48

A DEBUT PODCAST

Beep.

"Captain Green Bean to Team Nessie Quest. Do ye read? Come in, Team Nessie Quest," Hammy Bean calls from the radio. "I canna believe this!" he squeals. "I have a major bobble an' ye just have to get over to the *Nessie Juggernaut* office ASAP! Over!"

I sit up in my bed and grab the walkie-talkie.

"I'm going to miss your early-morning wake-ups, believe it or not. Over," I tell him.

"I don't want to talk about it, remember?" he says. "Over."

"I know, I know," I say. "Over."

"Ye have to come over right away. Strings? Do ye read? Over?"

"What time is it? Over," Dax says from the radio.

"Oh, just get oot o' yer scratcher and put yer baffies on," I tell him. "We've got Nessie business to attend to. Over."

Silence.

"Is that some kind of new code? Over?" Dax asks.

"Both o' ye," Hammy Bean tells us. "I need ye immediately. You're going to be gobsmacked when ye hear what's happenin'. Over."

"What is it? Over?" I demand.

"I got the *interview. Over*," he tells us.

"What interview? Over?" Dax asks.

"*The* interview!" Hammy Bean screeches. "The one an' only Tobin Sky! He called last night an' he's Skyping me in two hours an' ye need to get over here and get it recorded. This is the debut podcast that I wanted. It's a dream come true! Over!"

I swing the down comforter to the side and jump out of bed. "I'm on my way. Over," I call into the radio.

"Me too. Over," Dax says.

"I canna believe this is really happenin'," Hammy Bean screeches. "The one an' only Tobin Sky! Captain Green Bean over and out."

∽

Since Dad's done with school for the summer, Mamo Honey invites both Mom and Dad over for tea after they visit the *Nessie Juggernaut* office to make sure we have everything set up just right.

When we're all set, I pace the *Juggernaut* floor, Dax squints out the telescope and Hammy Bean bites on his pinky nail as we anxiously await the Skype to ring.

When it finally does, me and Dax scramble in behind Hammy Bean in his leather desk chair.

"Ready?" Hammy Bean asks.

"Answer it!" I exclaim.

Hammy Bean pushes the button and the one and only Tobin Sky appears before us.

I've Googled him before, and he looks just the same. A skinny man with a mound of red curls, just like Mamo Honey. In every picture I've seen he's wearing a red T-shirt and today is no different. Right this minute, he's sitting at a desk in what looks like an office with posters of Bigfoot scattered all over the walls behind him. Plus, one coatrack with a single safari hat hanging on a hook that has BIGFOOT DETECTIVES INC. written in shaky black letters.

"Good morning, Hammy Bean," Tobin Sky calls from the screen.

"G-good mornin', sir," Hammy Bean stutters. "It—it's an honor to speak wi' you. I'm a very big fan o' yours."

"And I'm a fan of yours, as well," Dr. Tobin Sky tells him. "I've seen the papers and the interview on the news. You have really discovered something important there in the Highlands. It's a step forward for the entire study of cryptozoology. Well done to you and your team."

"Th-thank ye, sir," Hammy Bean says. "It means so much to me to hear ye say those words because I want to be just like you when I'm grown."

"Well, you're already causing quite a buzz here in America with your find," Tobin Sky says.

"*I am?*"

"Absolutely."

Hammy Bean grabs my arm and squeezes it.

"I didna do it alone, sir," he says. "I couldna have done it without my team. These are my *Nessie Juggernaut* employees, Ada Ru Fitzhugh an' Dax Cady. They're my mates too."

I wave. "Hi, Dr. Sky," I say. "Me and Dax are from America. We're just here for the summer."

Tobin Sky nods.

"I just did the intro for the podcast," Dax says.

"They're modest," Hammy Bean says. "If ye want to know the truth of it . . . they're *everythin'*."

"I understand. I wouldn't be where I am today without my partner, Lemonade Liberty Witt," Tobin Sky says. "Partners are an important part of the field. I'm glad you've found them. I can't wait to listen to your future podcasts. In my day we didn't have technology like we do today. Lem and I just had a film camera when we first started." He chuckles.

"Dr. Sky," Hammy Bean says, "I have some questions here that I would like to ask ye, if ye wouldna mind."

"Of course," Tobin Sky says, taking a sip from a mug that has BIGFOOT DOESN'T BELIEVE IN YOU EITHER scrawled across the top.

I can see why Hammy Bean is fanning out on this guy. Tobin Sky is right up his alley when it comes to creatures.

Hammy Bean runs his pointer finger across large index cards lined with Braille letters.

"Can ye give any advice to those o' us who want to be serious cryptozoologists when we grow up?"

"Absolutely," Tobin Sky says. "First, never, ever give up. Never let naysayers negate your drive to find definitive evidence, because it's out there. The only people who don't believe it's true just haven't learned the truth yet."

"Yes, sir," Hammy Bean says.

"And one more thing." Tobin Sky holds up a finger and leans closer to the screen.

"What's that, sir?" Hammy Bean asks.

"It's the most important piece of advice I have," Tobin Sky says.

I can feel Hammy Bean suck air and hold it in, waiting.

"Always remember . . . picture first," Tobin Sky says. "Always picture first."

Hammy Bean turns to me and scoffs. "Did ye hear that, Denver?"

49

~~~~~~~~~~~~~~~

A KIT KAT BAR AND A DOUBLE-LIPPER

The morning I wake up to leave for home is the hardest day yet.

Hammy Bean beeps in around five fifteen and doesn't say one word. I beep back and we leave it like that.

He's letting both me and Dax keep our walkie-talkies even though they won't work that far away. I think he's hoping we'll both be back next summer.

I am too.

Today, for my very last feelings journal entry, I just draw a big sad face.

We already said our goodbyes yesterday.

With the exception of Hammy Bean.

Mom and Dad threw a great big Goodbye to Fort Augustus picnic on the lawn of St. Benedict's Abbey for everyone: Uncle Clive and Aunt Isla and Briony and Euna Begbie and Mr. and Mrs. Cady and Dax, and Mr. Farquhar and Quigley Dunbar III and the Kumars from a Wee Spot of Tea and Biscuits and

Tuna Tetrazzini. Even the Loch Watchers took a break from their Nessie-watching shifts. Dad grilled hot dogs and hamburgers and Mom filled everyone's paper cup to the brim with iced tea. It was around nine-thirty in the evening when I noticed they were gone.

Hammy Bean and Mamo Honey.

He didn't want to say goodbye.

But it was okay by me, because neither did I.

That early-morning beep says everything that needs to be said.

~∽~

Euna Begbie is on the third-floor landing as I'm bringing out bags to help Dad load the car.

"Ada Ru." She smiles down at me. "I hope to see ye again."

I drop the duffel bag that's hanging off my shoulder and wrap my arms around her skinny waist. I feel her arms wrap around mine.

"Me too, Ms. Begbie," I tell her. "I'm going to keep looking for my orange possibilities even back in Denver. But it won't be the same. And every single time I see something orange, I'm going to think of you."

"Thank ye, lass. Here, I made this for ye." She hands me an orange knitted cap.

"I love it," I tell her, slipping it onto my head. "This will come in handy for Denver winters."

"That's what I thought as well," she says. "Ye know, you've taught me some things too."

"I have? Like what?"

"I've started writing a story myself," she says.

"You have?" I exclaim.

"Aye," she says. "I'm looking for my supporting characters now, an' ye want to ken what?"

"What?"

"You're one o' them." She taps me on my nose.

"Me?"

"That's right."

"I can't wait to read it, Ms. Begbie."

"I canna wait to read yours, Ada Ru."

"Can we keep in touch on email?" I ask her.

"Absolutely," she says. "Yer mom has all my contact information."

"Maybe we can have a distant writers' group, just us?"

"I would love that, lass."

❧

On the third trip down the heavenly staircase, I find Dax playing right above the second-floor landing, the exact same place I found him on the very first day we came to St. Benedict's.

I stop and sit down on the step below his, Dad's camera around my neck for some last-minute souls to catch before we go.

"I'm going to miss you playing on Ole Roy," I tell him.

He keeps strumming without looking up and says, "I finished your intro."

I sit up straight. "Yeah?"

"Yeah," he says, still strumming.

I listen for a few more seconds, until I'm about to burst.

"Well?" I say. "Are you going to sing it for me or do I have to figure it out through osmosis?"

"You know I'm not very good at singing in front of people," he says, without looking at me.

"That's fine," I say. "Just pretend I'm not here."

"How can I do that when you're staring at me?"

"I'll turn around, then, okay? Here, look." I turn my body on the step.

"Okay," he says.

I wait while he strums, searching for his tidbits.

Words with Ru is pure dope,
click below to subscribe.
With interviews, tips and words of hope,
her voice and heart exemplified.
Dialogue, setting, theme and plot,
it's all there for you to learn.
If you're a writer you found the spot,
there's no better place to turn.
Come join us today
with your friend, Ada Ru.
You'll be happy to stay,
and that's no goose poo.

I turn back around to face him.

"Come *on!*" I grin.

"I'm kidding, I'm kidding," he says. "There's one more verse."

He clears his throat.

I wait.

Then he looks at me.

"Aren't you going to turn around?" he asks.

I roll my eyes.

"Fine," I say. I turn my back.

He clears his throat again and his fingers start to strum.

Ada Ru is a special soul,
I hope to get to know her better.
I will miss her wit, her sass and grit,
maybe she'll send me a letter?

I turn back around to face him, grinning wider than I mean to. "You're going to miss me?"

He shrugs without meeting my eyes. "Maybe a little," he says. "You think you'll come back next summer?"

"You want me to?"

"Hammy Bean sure would like that."

"I would too," I say.

"Maybe . . . we could email . . . or text or whatever."

"Totally," I say. "I would like that."

He pulls an iPhone out of his jean jacket pocket. "What's your number?" he asks.

I give him my phone number and he types it into his contact list.

"Let me take your picture too," he says. "You know, to attach to your contact."

"Sure," I say. "Can I have yours too?"

"Yeah," he says, aiming his phone in my direction and snapping a shot.

I do the same, and then we just sit there. Him strumming and me watching until Mom shows up.

"Hi, kids," Mom says, stepping past us with a suitcase in each hand and a duffel over her shoulder.

"Hey, Mrs. F," Dax says. "Can I help you with those?"

"Oh, I'm fine to do it," she tells him. "I'll let you two say your goodbyes."

"Thanks," he says, and then turns back to me. "Oh, by the way, Denver, I think this is yours." He hands me a Kit Kat bar. "You left this in my pocket that day I let you use my jacket."

Mom stops in her tracks and sneaks a peek at me over her shoulder.

"*Mom*," I warn.

She just grins real big at me, a grin that's far too wide to be normal without saying one word, and then bounces down the steps.

She's so embarrassing.

"So I guess I'd better go," I say, standing up.

"Cool," Dax says, going back to his strumming. "I guess I'll see you around."

"Yeah . . . I guess," I say.

I start down the steps, stop, and then turn back to face him again. "I'm going to miss some things about you, besides your playing on Ole Roy," I say. "You know, not everything . . . but some things."

He slaps a palm against the strings. "Like what?"

"*Liiiiike* . . . your music and your 'groovy's and your 'right on's and . . . your smile."

He one-lips me and keeps on strumming on Ole Roy.

Just the way I found him on my way up the heavenly staircase on that very first day.

I raise my camera and gaze at him through my lens.

Click.

I know I got the soul of that shot for sure.

50

BRINGING SCOTLAND HOME TO DENVER

I stare out the backseat window as Dad drives to Glasgow in the backward car so we can catch our flight home. The clouds came down from the mountain to make our last day as gray and rainy as our first, which actually seems like the perfect ending to our Fort Augustus story. I watch the scene whizzing by us on the A82 and try to remember every single thing my eyes see.

The gray, drizzly day.

Velvet hills and mountains.

Shaggy cattle in the countryside that need a trim from Supercuts.

I think about all the people I've met and all the words we've shared and I swallow down a large lump.

PAGE ONE

It all started with a boy named Hammy Bean Tibby. A boy who could see what the rest of us couldn't, until he taught me to close my eyes.

Mom leans over the front seat and faces me, putting her chin on her hand. "You're quiet," she says.

"Just thinking," I tell her.

"About?"

"All the things I'm going to miss about Fort Augustus."

"Mmm. Like what?"

I sigh and watch the raindrops race each other to the bottom of the window. "The green," I tell her.

"Anything else?"

"Everything else," I say.

"Like Kit Kat bars?" Dad eyes me in the mirror.

"Mom!" I exclaim. "I can't believe you told him."

She laughs.

"You're *so* embarrassing," I tell her.

"Oh, honey." She waves a hand at me. "Don't you think I tried the same thing on your dad?"

I put a hand on the back of his seat. "She did the pocket thing to you too?" I ask him.

He nods. "Except it was her keys."

"Keys?" I say. "Didn't you need those to get home?"

Mom shrugs. "Desperate times call for desperate measures."

I laugh and sit back again as we drive in silence, except for a low tune playing on the radio.

And then Mom says, "Well, I'm going to miss the scones at a Wee Spot of Tea and Biscuits." She starts her list on her fingers. "Clive, Isla and Briony, Ms. Begbie, Honey, Corny . . . oh, just everything and everybody."

"We should still have our same English Breakfast tea in Denver in the mornings," I say. "And scones too, maybe?"

"Ooh, and we could pick up some scones and other treats from House of Commons on Fifteenth."

"What is that?"

"A British tearoom."

"That sounds pure barry," I say. "We could bring a little Scotland culture home with us to Denver. That's a brilliant plan, Mum. Pure tidy. Oh, but make sure they don't slip in any haggis or any bloody puddings with meat in them."

"Oh, my little Ruby Ring, you *are* a can of corn," Dad says, meeting my eyes in the rearview mirror. "Any more final thoughts as we head home?"

I think hard about his question and stare out at the green whizzing by me in a blur, begging to be its very own one-word dynamic character in a very important story. In Jelly Belly terms . . . actually to be honest, Jelly Belly doesn't have enough green to even come close to capturing it.

They'd have to add a million more shades for that to happen.

Then I turn and meet Dad's eyes in the mirror again. "Aye," I say. "Number one, I'm definitely going to branch out on my Jelly Belly flavors. You know, throw some oranges and greens in there along with the Buttered Popcorn ones."

Even though I can't see his lips, I can tell he's smiling in the mirror at me because of the getting-old wrinkles around his eyes.

"Number two," I say. "I'm going to invite that new girl, Remy Prudant, to eat lunch with me and Britney B in the school cafeteria so she doesn't have to eat lunch alone anymore."

"And is there a number three?" he asks.

"Definitely," I say. "As it turns out, Scotland *was* way better than Disney World."

AUTHOR'S NOTE

I'm often asked, *What inspires you to write the stories you do?* Inspiration comes to me in many forms. But in *Nessie Quest*, one character was inspired by someone very special—my mom. Hammy Bean Tibby is a character who possesses many amazing qualities. He is full of life; he is a steadfast friend; he keeps going in the face of adversity; he is proud to share his Gaelic heritage; he is a Nessie Hunter extraordinaire—and he is blind.

My mom was diagnosed with retinitis pigmentosa when my brother and I were young, and although I don't personally know what it is like to live without sight, I know what it means to be inspired by someone close to me who does.

Growing up, we did things differently from our friends' families—but to us it was just our daily reality. My mom didn't drive, but we got to ride downtown in fancy taxis. She didn't read words on a page, but she got books on tape, a treasured service only available for the blind. She was invited as a speaker for our classes and taught the students how she reads Braille, walks with a cane, and uses her talking wristwatch, among all the other helpful tools and tips that enabled her to adapt. My mom went to a specialized school to learn these new skills and more, including how to reorganize the kitchen to allow her to continue cooking for us.

I have been asked so many questions throughout my life about my mom, from how she matched her socks to how she completed a master's degree in educational psychology. But mostly, I have been asked whether raising children while losing her sight was a struggle. And although the obvious answer is yes, through my young eyes I witnessed something very different. I witnessed her ability to cope, overcome, and thrive despite this adversity. To my brother and me, she was Mom 2.0, a supercharged version of our mom.

Although she has shaped me in so many ways, there was one moment in particular that made me excited to incorporate her experiences into one of my stories. One day I overheard her telling someone about the unique way she navigated the world, which included *hearing the walls*. When I asked her more about that, she described how the air shifts with changes in the environment. She could sense these changes through echoes that bounce off buildings and objects, revealing what is around her. She was describing something called *echolocation*—or seeing through sound. I was so intrigued by this process, I wanted to research it more. As I did, I learned just how similar echolocation is to sonar, which bounces sound off objects to detect size and movement. And sonar is used in the search for the Loch Ness Monster, due to the low visibility in the loch.

I then began to interview others within the blind and visually impaired community and those who support them. They shared the many ways in which they live and navigate without sight, and how our society views them. One common wish voiced again and again was the desire for a real flesh and blood character and not a superhero version of a child who is blind.

In many ways, my mom was no different from anyone else's mom. She taught us the importance of things like knowing the difference between right and wrong, being a responsible and productive member of society, having a good work ethic, choosing your friends instead of allowing them to choose you, and always, *always* checking the date on the Miracle Whip before you use it. But leading by example can ultimately be the most powerful parenting technique there is. And her example of strength and resilience has allowed us to cope with difficulties in our own lives.

My mom isn't a superhero, and neither is Hammy Bean Tibby. Neither leaps large buildings in a single bound or bends solid steel with their bare hands. Neither wears a red spandex cape or letters on their chest. But both possess superpowers nonetheless. To me, they are examples of triumphing over challenges, and in my opinion, overcoming the adversity of losing their sight makes them forces to be reckoned with. I hope Hammy Bean inspires readers to listen even when they can see.

I wish to express my gratitude to all those who helped me build this very special character, especially my mom, who remains my first-string editor, my biggest fan, and my real-life hero.

ACKNOWLEDGMENTS

Thank you to all who have worked with me to make this book the best it can be. I look at each book as a team effort, and I have an amazing team to call my own. As always, I wish to express my gratitude to my agent, Laurie McLean, and my amazing editor, Emily Easton—you have no idea how fortunate I feel to have you both in my corner. And for the *Nessie Quest* team at Penguin Random House, thank you for all you have done to make this book happen. Thank you to Lydia Nichols for continuing to tell my stories with your beautiful artwork—I'm so thrilled to have you on this journey with me.

I would also like to thank all the wonderful people who provided input for this story. To Tracy, Lu, and Bean with Lu & Bean Read (@luandbeanread, luandbeanread.com) for all your help on how to get a podcast up and running, as well as for your support. You do an amazing job sharing wonderful stories with your subscribers—keep doing what you're doing! I'd also like to thank all those from the blind and visually impaired community whose input helped me create a character who lives with blindness. Thank you to all the mobility specialists, teachers, and supporters for your expertise. And I would like to express my utmost gratitude to the experts on this subject. Thank you for sharing your insights, your experiences, your feelings, and your truths about what it is like to live in the world without sight. It was a true honor to listen to your voices and hear your stories. I can only hope this character speaks to your hearts the way you have spoken to mine.

A special thank-you to all the dedicated teachers, media specialists, and librarians who give all that you are to your students. Thank you for sharing my stories with your kids and welcoming me into your classrooms.

Finally, a special thank-you to my mom, who is always my biggest champion and has provided so much insight for one very special character. Hammy Bean Tibby wouldn't be who he is without her. Mom, you are a true force to be reckoned with.

And as always, for Tobin, you are *my* wings in everything I do and you always will be.

OUTLOOK SPOOKY

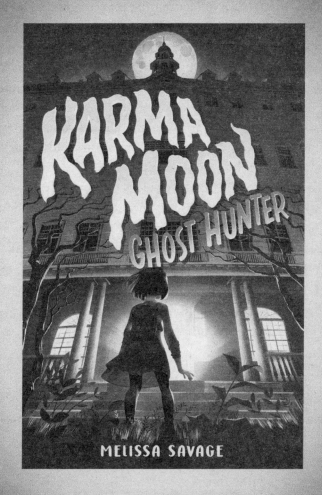

TURN THE PAGE FOR A SNEAK PEEK!

The King of All Noodles

The Netflix people call on a Tuesday after school, and I know it's all because of the moo goo gai pan.

Every Monday night we get takeout from Noodle King of New York in the West Village. It's exactly ten blocks from apartment 4B. That's home for me and Dad, a two-bedroom fourth-floor walk-up on Charles Street.

Not to brag or anything, but it *is* my fortune cookie that predicts it. And everyone who's anyone knows that the almighty fortune cookie is *never* wrong.

FORTUNE COOKIE

A heavy burden will be lifted with a single phone call.

And that cookie is dead-on, too.

The call comes in the very next day, and I'm the one who answers it.

Me and Dad are just sitting there, eating Monday night's cold moo goo leftovers in front of the television like it's any other Tuesday afternoon.

It's my job to answer the phone after school and on weekends at the headquarters office for Dad's documentary film company, Totally Rad Productions.

But let me decode.

By company I mean me, Dad and his two best friends from high school—Big John and The Faz. And by headquarters, I mean apartment 4B's living room on Charles Street, which is littered with empty Noodle King cartons and film editing equipment. At least that's the way it looks since Mom packed five suitcases last summer on a quest to follow the signs to her new life.

A life without us.

And one thing I know is that when someone packs five suitcases . . . it's not a good sign they're coming back. The fortune cookie totally missed that one, but that's a whole other story.

So, this is how the Netflix call goes.

"Totally Rad Productions, where rad is our name and film is our game. How may I direct your call?" I say in my very best grown-up voice.

I've been practicing in the mirror.

Dad gives me a wink while he leans over the coffee

table, taking another giant bite from his wooden chop-sticks and giving me an approving nod with a mouth full of moo goo.

He always says answering the phone like that makes it seem like we're bigger than just me, him, Big John and The Faz. After that, I'm supposed to cover the receiver with my hand. Dad says that makes it seem like I put them on hold—as if we have this very official, multiple-line phone instead of the ancient yellow wall phone with the old-fashioned dial on the front.

I finally had to draw the line when he asked me to hum hold music into the mouthpiece while the caller waited.

That's just weird. Plus, I don't even know who Barry Manilow is.

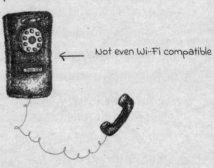

← Not even Wi-Fi compatible

"Please hold and I will see if Mr. Vallenari is available to take your call," I tell the woman on the other end of the line.

That's when I shove the receiver in my armpit and eye-ball Dad hard.

"Dad," I whisper. "It's . . . *Netflix*."

First he stops chewing his moo goo.

Then his eyes go wide.

He points a single chopstick in my direction.

"Karma," he warns me. "If this is some kind of joke . . . it's not funny."

"I'm not even joking right now," I tell him. "It's really them. It's Netflix calling *you*."

He eyeballs me for a few more seconds and then jumps up from his seat on the couch while his chopsticks go flying.

Our extra-round pug, Alfred Hitchcock, is already crouched in ready position for such an event. He gobbles a piece of sauced-up bok choy and a few noodles before they even hit the shag carpet.

When it comes to flying food, he's a rocket. But ask him to do his business out front on the sidewalk in below-zero cold, the kind of freezing cold where your nose hairs fuse together, and he takes his sweet old time.

"Hitchy," I tell him, giving his low belly a scratch. "Dr. Portokalos says you're too big as it is."

Hitchy stretches his fat neck up to sniff at my plate on the coffee table before waddling back down under the glass to await the next flying morsel.

I keep eating, watching Dad pace the kitchen floor while he listens on the yellow phone. He's talking and waving his hands in that upbeat way he does when he's doing business. Up until now, business has consisted mostly of booking weddings and bat mitzvahs, with only the occasional documentary in between.

"Yes, of course," he says, stopping to scribble a note on the back of an unopened bill he's pulled from the messy pile on the folding table in the kitchen.

Dad's so psyched after he hangs up the phone, I'm almost positive I see his feet come off the ground.

"We did it, Karma!" he's shouting. "This is it. This is the call I've been waiting for my whole life. A contract with a major content provider for a docuseries! A *docuseries,* Snooks! And Netflix? Oh, man, they want an entire season, and this could be the beginning of even more. Do you know what that means?"

"That we can finally add egg rolls to our Noodle King order?" I ask.

Grumpy Mr. Drago, the building manager, bangs a broom handle on the ceiling of 3B right below us to say we're making too much noise. Four o'clock to four-thirty is an especially important time for grumpy Mr. Drago.

Judge Judy is on.

I asked the Grump if he has a crush on Judge Judy when I saw him out on the front stoop one morning in his bathrobe, sitting on a ratty lawn chair while he drank his morning coffee. But he just shook his head, waved a hand at me and said, *"Poof."*

But if you ask me, I think it's true love.

"Yeah, yeah, I mean sure, egg rolls . . . but it also means a *house,*" Dad tells me. "Finally. A house, Snooks. Somewhere across the river in Jersey or Staten Island or maybe even Connecticut. Someplace where we'll have an actual strip of grass. A yard for you and for Alfred Hitchcock. It's what Mom always wanted. We can even have a barbecue. A *barbecue,* of all things! Mom loves them."

"I've never heard her say anything about a barbecue," I tell him. "Or grass, either."

He's already dialing the yellow phone.

"Well, she's always wanted that," he says, slipping his finger in the dial and pushing it around.

I wonder if Mom would actually bring her suitcases back if he got her a house with a barbecue and a strip of grass. Obviously, he thinks so, but I'm not so sure.

"Wouldn't you like to barbecue out in a backyard?" he goes on.

I shrug. "Can you barbecue moo goo leftovers?"

"You can barbecue anything," he tells me, pushing the dial around again.

"Are you sure Connecticut has moo goo?"

"Everyone has moo goo," he tells me.

"But I bet Connecticut doesn't have a Toby's," I say.

Me and Dad go to Toby's Estate Coffee every single morning before school. It's our favorite place in the Village. A couple of years ago they changed the name to Partners, but we still call it Toby's because it will always be Toby's to us. It has old brick walls and brightly colored stools, and Ajit, who still wears his Toby's T-shirt and works the morning shift, knows our order by heart. Dad's order is Avocado Toast with a

Decaf Ghost Town Coffee and mine is Egg on a Roll with a hot Apple Betty.

Ajit's name means "unbeatable."

He told me so.

And it fits him too, just like Karma fits me. Ajit is going to college to be a lawyer. He wants to put criminals in jail to keep our streets safer. And I know he will, too.

His very name announces his future success, guaranteed.

Nothing beats unbeatable.

I'm a firm believer that names are very important in the universe.

My mom named me Karma Moon because she believed the theory of karma wholeheartedly. The theory basically states that if you do bad things, bad things come back to you. And if you do good things, good things come back to you.

Dad calls that kind of stuff woo-woo, which is his word for "cuckoo." But the story goes that he agreed to the name Karma only after Mom agreed he could brand the next kid, which they never had. Lucky for that kid, because I think it's really wrong to actually name a child C-3PO.

That's seriously questionable adulting.

"I'm sure there'll be a place we like just as much as Toby's, wherever we land," Dad says.

But I'm not so sure.

I'm used to Egg on a Roll. I love Egg on a Roll. Why would I want to eat anything but Egg on a Roll?

Dad is *still* dialing.

Because that's how it goes with an old-fashioned phone.

"Man, the guys are going to flip when I tell them we've got an actual documentary with Netflix," Dad goes on while he calls the guys. "Do you understand how big this is, Snooks? I think you need to come over here and pinch me. Just so I know this isn't a dream."

I can't help but smile. It's nice to see Dad so happy. To be honest, it's been a while.

"What's the show about?" I ask him.

He doesn't answer me this time.

"Dad," I say louder. "What is the documentary about?"

"Oh, some haunted-hotel mystery up in the mountains of Colorado."

I choke on my moo goo.

"Dude! We got it!" he shouts into the mouthpiece.

"I hate to be the one to tell you this," I call to him, pushing my horn-rimmed glasses up at the bridge. "The last I checked, you weren't a ghost hunter."

But he just waves my words away like that tiny fact doesn't matter.

Even though it seems like a pretty big fact to me.

"Big John! We got a docuseries!" he's shouting into the receiver.

I watch and chew as he listens and paces the floor.

"You'd better sit down for this one," Dad tells Big John. "An entire season with *Netflix*! *Netflix,* dude! Yeah, it's some ghost-hunting thing . . . they want a paranormal *series*!"

He listens.

I chew moo goo.

Alfred Hitchcock waits for flying shrapnel.

"Yeah, they said ten episodes to start and the possibility of extending to a season two. But they said we will definitely have to get an actual ghost on film for that to happen. Netflix is going to put Totally Rad on the map, man! After all these years! It's finally our turn."

I would never actually tell Dad that it was my cookie that predicted it. Because of his whole aversion-to-woo-woo thing. But he only thinks it's crazy because he doesn't really understand it. I knew something would come his way even if *he* isn't open to his woo-woo, because that's how it works with woo-woo and whatnot.

The truth is, the universe has a plan for us all. You just have to be open to reading the signs around you. I'm all about living by the rules of woo-woo.

Karma for sure because it's my namesake, but also the reading of any and all signs, keeping it real with my spirit guide, Crystal Mystic, tarot cards, past-life memories, the power of crystals, any and every Snapple lid fact and of course the almighty fortune cookie.

My personal mantra is and will always be: *Woo-woo isn't cuckoo and without it you'll have bad juju.*

And everyone who's anyone knows you don't want bad juju.

It's the *worst.*

A Bad Case of the What-Ifs

That whole night after Dad's Netflix call, he's far too busy walking around being happy to notice one very important thing.

I am *not*.

Far from it.

After Googling the Stanley Hotel, I learned that the place is so haunted, not one single, solitary guest will even stay there anymore.

Not one.

By bedtime, it's all I can do not to throw up my Noodle King order.

"Lights out, Snooks," Dad tells me from the doorway of my bedroom that night. "School tomorrow."

"Um . . . ," I say. "So, I—I've made a decision."

"Uh-huh," he says, coming in and sitting on the edge of my bed. "About what?" he asks, giving Alfred Hitchcock a pat on the head.

"Yeah, *soooo* . . . I think, I mean . . . I don't think . . . I mean, I c-can't go to Colorado with you guys," I tell him, staring down at my fingers while I fold and unfold them and then fold them again.

"Hmmm" is all he says while he takes in my words.

"What if we never come home?" I ask him.

Still nodding.

"It happens, you know."

"Uh-huh," he says.

"People go missing all the time, and if you want to know what I think about it," I say, "there's a definite possibility of paranormal disturbances behind some of those cases. I mean, unless it's an alien abduction, which is also a legit possibility. But you know, extraterrestrial doesn't really apply to *this* situation. But you never know."

"Hmmm," he says.

"So yeah, I guess I'm just saying, I—I can't go with you."

Here's the thing. Even though Dr. Finkelman, MD, PhD, LP, is supposed to be some kind of expert at getting rid of my bad case of the *what-ifs,* all we really do is talk about my feelings and play Uno during our Wednesday appointments. We meet every week for one hour while Dad waits in the lobby. And even though Dr. Finkelman has more letters behind his name than anyone I've ever met, playing Uno hasn't changed a single thing about my what-ifs.

They're always with me.

Always.

What-ifs may or may not be the technical term written in Dr. Finkelman's chart, but it explains it way better than anything else.

Simply said . . . I worry.

But not about weird things, like belly buttons.

That's an actual thing. The fear of belly buttons. It's called omphalophobia. I suppose I get it, in a way. Like all the lint and everything. But it's still a weird thing to worry about, if you ask me. Math, too; that's called arithmophobia. I totally get that one more than the belly button one, especially if you've ever had Mrs. Frickman for algebra.

There's arachnophobia, too. The fear of spiders. And I mean, that one just makes good sense.

My worries are way more normal than extra lint buildup or algebra.

To put it straight, I'm afraid of what *might* happen. And New York keeps me real busy.

WHAT IF
a nuclear bomb hits New York?

WHAT IF
the next lockdown drill
at school isn't a drill at all?

WHAT IF
Mom never comes home?

My worries run on a continuous loop.

And I don't know about the belly button kind, but mine invade my brain and my body, too. Every second of every day, but especially at night when the lights are out and it's quiet. On the inside of me, it sort of feels like jumping beans are jammed into every vein in my body and never let me be still.

And I know one thing is for sure, a ghost hotel isn't going to be good for my what-ifs.

Dad sighs and covers my fingers with his giant hand.

It's warm and heavy.

The special band is still there no matter how long Mom's been gone or how many suitcases she packed.

Mom taught me all about the woo-woo.

But I bet she doesn't know that my what-ifs went into overdrive after she left us alone here without her.

When I asked the greatest, almighty woo-woo source, aka Crystal Mystic, if what she did was totally messed up, it gave it to me straight.

CRYSTAL MYSTIC
YOU CAN THANK YOUR
LUCKY STARS!

Of all the woo-woo in this world and beyond, Crystal Mystic is my woo-woo surefire system.

Its awesomeness announces itself in its name.

Mystic.

With one solid shake, all your spiritual questions can be answered in one solitary second. The crystal globe awakens with a mystical flashing light, and through the magic of woo-woo and four double-A batteries (not included), it speaks its truth from beyond the stars, transmitting through the small speaker at the bottom.

The one and only problem with Crystal Mystic is it doesn't predict what *might* happen. Which can be a big problem when you have a bad case of the what-ifs.

Huge, actually.

If only I could find the perfect woo-woo that could help me predict the future, I wouldn't have to worry so much. Then the jumping beans would finally sleep.

And so would I.

Dad takes my hand in his.

"How can I possibly go a whole ten days without seeing this face?" he finally says with a grin. "I'm sorry, I can't do it."

"But, Dad," I say. "I feel like I'm having a heart attack even thinking about it."

"You're not having a heart attack," he assures me.

"You're right," I agree. "It might be a stroke."

He stares at me.

"Let's take a deep breath together," he says.

His voice is calm and his smile is that special one he gives me when I need it the most. A smile that says a lot without any words at all. It says I'm okay and he's okay and so is everything else in the world right this minute. And for a few seconds, while that smile is shining its light, a bright ray bursting through a worry storm, it actually feels true.

"Breathe in," he says.

We both take a deep breath, in through our noses and then out through our mouths the way Dr. Finkelman taught me to do.

"How's your heart?" Dad asks me.

I shrug.

"I think you'll live," he says.

"You don't know that," I tell him. "Kids have heart attacks, you know. It's a thing."

"Where did you get that?" he asks.

"Google," I tell him. "But Crystal Mystic confirmed it."

"Snooks, here's the thing," Dad says, inching closer to me and meeting my eyes. "We're a team. You and me. I can't do this without my partner."

"You have Big John and The Faz, though," I remind him.

He nods. "But they're not my Snooks. This is my big break," he tells me. "*Our* big break. This is going to change our life, and you're a part of that. You have to be there."

"But what if—"

"You're Research." He points to me. "We all have a different role. Who's going to do it if you're not there?"

I think about that.

"Big John?" I ask.

He shakes his head. "He's Video Editing and Sound—holding the boom."

"The Faz?" I try again.

"Directing."

That's when I point to Dad in one last-ditch effort.

He shakes his head. "I'm Cinematography. I'll be too busy shooting footage. We all have our role, Snooks. You can't let us down now."

"Fine," I mumble. "I'll go. But you better have a doctor on speed dial. I still may have a heart attack."

"I promise you'll be fine." He kisses me on the forehead and stands up to leave.

"Dad?" I say.

He turns around to face me again in the doorway.

"Yeah?"

"Tell me again why you call me Snooks."

He laughs. "Don't you ever get tired of that story?"

"Never," I say.

"When you were born and I saw you for the very first time," he says, "I knew you were the sweetest thing I'd ever seen. I couldn't decide if you were as sweet as a frosty snow cone on the hottest July day or as sweet as a home-baked cookie fresh out of the oven. So I called you Snookie. A combination of both."

He flips the light switch by the door. "See you in the morning. You know what? I think tomorrow I'm going to try something new at Toby's."

I laugh at that one. "No you won't," I tell him.

"No I won't," he agrees. "We're the same that way, aren't we? Creatures of habit."

DON'T MISS OUT ON ANY OF MELISSA'S ADVENTURES!